S U G A R

JENNA JAMESON

and HOPE TARR

SUGAR

Skyhorse Publishing

Skyhorse Publishing books may be purchased in bulk at special discounts for sales promotion, corporate gifts, fund-raising, or educational purposes. Special editions can also be created to specifications. For details, contact the Special Sales Department, Skyhorse Publishing, 307 West 36th Street, 11th Floor, New York, NY 10018 or info@skyhorsepublishing.com.

Skyhorse® and Skyhorse Publishing® are registered trademarks of Skyhorse Publishing, Inc.®, a Delaware corporation.

Visit our website at www.skyhorsepublishing.com.

10 9 8 7 6 5 4 3 2 1

Library of Congress Cataloging-in-Publication Data is available on file.

Cover design by Brian Peterson
Cover photo credit: Thinkstock

ISBN: 978-1-62914-771-0
Ebook ISBN: 978-1-63220-140-9

Printed in the United States of America

Prologue

*L*os Angeles, California, Present Day

"Give me some Sugar."

"Sugar, who ya meeting?"

"Yeah, who's the lucky guy?"

"Do you keep him . . . whipped and creamed?"

Legendary adult film star Sugar, born Sarah Halliday, breezed into Beso, the closing door barricading her from the quartet of camera-wielding paparazzi. On stakeout in the restaurant's parking lot, they'd descended as soon as her Jimmy Choos touched down on the black-top, dogging her from her black Ferrari to the entrance. Safely inside, she dragged a manicured hand through her waist-length blond waves, reminding herself that dealing with jerk reporters was all part of the job, and yet . . .

I am so over LA.

She scanned the low-lit bar and adjoining dining room with a practiced eye. Tucked into a table near the baby grand, Kim and Khloe Kardashian perched upon overstuffed chairs, noshing on the ceviche sampler. At the far side of the lounge, actress Eva Mendes and her escort made short work of the restaurant's signature tacos. Owned by

Desperate Housewife Eva Longoria, the trendy nightspot served Latin fusion fare to LA's A-listers, as well as those hoping to spot them. An out-of-the-way burger dive would have suited Sarah far better, but Martin, her manager, had cautioned that, with her one hundredth film about to release, she needed to show herself around town. That wouldn't be an issue, not after tonight, but given the gravity of her news, she'd decided to indulge him.

A twenty-something hostess teetered toward her in shiny, cheap heels, her overly made-up eyes huge in her heart-shaped face. "Mr. Levine is already seated. If you'd care to follow—"

"Thanks, but I see him." Remembering all the shit part-time jobs she'd taken to support herself when she'd first come out to California, Sarah pulled a fifty from her purse and handed it to the girl before walking away.

Entering the main bar area, she nodded to Kim in passing, and made her way over to the table occupied by her manager.

A smile splitting his round face, Martin slid out of the wrap-around booth and stood. "I was starting to worry, and then I saw your text." His dark eyes slid over her, an infinitesimal nod signaling his approval of her strapless, candy-apple-red Stella McCartney jersey dress.

Aware of the high whispers and open stares directed her way, she slipped into the curved cushion across from him, glad he'd gone ahead and ordered their drinks, a Laphroaig scotch for himself and a white wine for her. "Sorry I'm late. I got . . . caught up." Thinking of the reason for her delay, presently tucked inside her Prada purse, she reached for her wineglass and took a sip for courage.

He resumed his seat, his smile slipping. "Tell me you didn't get another letter."

Even after ten years together, his ability to read her struck her as uncanny. "I wish I could." She cast a covert glance around the room, relieved that the pianist had resumed playing. Satisfied that any gawkers had returned to their conversations, she opened her bag, took out the folded letter, and slid it across the table. "This makes number five."

When the first anonymous note had arrived more than a month ago, she'd chalked it up to a secret crush, someone she'd maybe met in passing or worked with during the making of one of her films—a cameraman, prop person, or gopher who'd gotten access to her personal information. But then more messages began arriving, one per week, each one referencing one of her film roles, and she was forced to face the terrifying truth. She had a new stalker, and this one was a lot more intense than the random nutcases who shadowed her on social media sites hoping to uncover her whereabouts. Those she could handle. When you had more than 500,000 Twitter followers, you had to expect there'd be a few who tried crossing the line. But this situation transcended cyberspace. The freak knew where she lived. He knew how and where to find her. He *had* found her.

Whoever he was, he was definitely old school: cream-colored vellum stationery, calligraphy penmanship—the strokes bold but methodical, always in classic black ink with a broad nibbed pen. Quaint—and creepy.

Martin unfolded the paper and gave it a glance before refolding it and slipping it inside his jacket's breast pocket. "I'll take care of it."

Sarah set down her glass. "You said that before. Shouldn't we . . . *I* call the police at this point?"

He answered with a ferocious shake of his head, sending salt-and-pepper bangs flying. Despite repping her as well as several other notable adult actors, his hairstyle was circa 1960s Beatles. "You report this to the LAPD and every crackpot in the city is sure to come slithering out of his shit hole to take credit or worse, copycat. Is that what you want?" He paused, sucking at his top teeth. "Besides, what if it's Danny?"

Danny, the B-list TV actor with whom she'd spent four years, the last year devoted almost exclusively to waging a losing war to get him sober. Only Danny hadn't been interested in giving up the booze or the drugs, hadn't acknowledged he had any problem beyond her bitching. She'd put up with it all—the mood swings, the lies, the theft even—until one night eight months ago when their "difference of opinion" had exploded in a backhanded blow across her face. After throwing him out, this time for good, she'd picked up the phone and called Martin. He'd taken one look at her puffy face and pulled out his iPhone. Standing by while he made one call after the other, canceling her following day's shoot and rescheduling a week's worth of appointments, she'd acknowledged there was only one person she could possibly save: herself.

The next day she'd had all the locks changed.

Even if the culprit was an ex, standing by and doing nothing didn't sit well with Sarah. It took her back to that terrible time as a teenager when she'd sat by her mom's bed in hospice and watched, helpless, as day by day the cancer won. The grief had fueled her determination to live life on her own terms and to the fullest, which had meant pursuing her dream of stardom on the big screen. Leaving her native New York and driving cross country to LA in a beat-up Volkswagen with a single suitcase and a couple hundred bucks to her name had been one ballsy big risk. The move had paid off, albeit not in the way she'd intended. At casting calls, she'd been told she was too striking for commercials and too all-American for film work, where a more multicultural look was sought. Unlike her competition, she'd had no college degree and no acting credentials. Without money or experience, getting a SAG card was about as easy as hitching a ride to the moon. Unable to make rent despite working numerous part-time jobs, sick of using pilfered ketchup packets and mugs of hot water to make "soup," she'd accepted a walk-on role in a porn film. At the wrap party, she'd met her future manager, Martin Levine. Under Martin's guidance, her walk-on part had led to a callback for a feature role in another adult film, and then another . . . Before long Sarah was reborn as the adult film sensation, Sugar, with more fans and more money than she'd ever dreamed possible.

Ten years later, she liked to think that gutsy, take-no-prisoners girl lived on inside her, but lately she wasn't so sure. Had success made her soft? Having a manager and a posse of publicity professionals was standard for someone who'd attained her level of stardom, but had all the support blunted her instincts and made her less than self-reliant?

Determined not to back down this time, she demanded, "Then what do I do? And Martin, whether or not it's Danny, at this point I have to do something."

He blew out a breath. "Relax, I have a guy on it."

"You hired a private detective!"

"Security professional," he amended, expression sheepish. "Former FBI, been working the private sector since he retired from the agency. Has an extensive background in executive escort. You couldn't be in better hands."

That was a relief. For an instant, she wondered why he hadn't told her before but then brushed the niggling annoyance aside. What mattered was that the situation was being handled. Besides, her stalker's latest lovelorn missive was only part of the reason she'd called this meeting.

She braced herself to deliver the news that would likely prompt Martin to order a second scotch—this time a double. "Thanks, but I won't need him after next week."

He straightened from the lounging position he favored. "Why is that?"

Sarah steeled herself. She owed Martin a hell of a lot. A leggy twenty-something with big dreams and average-sized breasts, she'd been easy to dismiss as just another wannabe. Martin had seen something in her that the other talent scouts and managers and casting agents hadn't—and he'd pushed hard to make sure producers and investors had seen it too. But no matter how amazing the money, she'd never seen porn as her end game.

"I've decided to leave LA. I'm going home, Martin, home to New York." There, she'd said it. Mouth dry, she retrieved her glass and took a sip. Predictably his eyes bugged.

"Are we talking a break or—"

"Retirement. We . . . I'm . . . talking about retiring." Dreading this conversation as she had, it was a relief to finally get the word out.

"If this is about not wanting to work with Bo Tucker, I'll pull strings and get him replaced. If the studio won't play ball, I'll get you out of the contract. I'll—"

"Thanks, but this isn't about Bo or the film." Given the shit Tucker had pulled on their last film, thrusting into her after the director had called "Cut," he was her least favorite male lead; still, she was enough of a professional to push past her personal dislike for the sake of the project. "It's a decision I've been coming to for a long time."

That was the truth. With the release of her latest, *Camera Sutra*, she had one hundred films to her credit, the final twenty produced under her Wing Star label. The previous year she'd been inducted into the *Adult Video News* Hall of Fame. The AVN recognition had led to cameo appearances on several popular mainstream TV shows, as well as a role in a major motion picture. Her roster of product endorsement contracts ranged from high-end lingerie to exotically flavored lube. Even for those who'd never viewed an adult film, her name was a household word synonymous with sex.

Unlike some in the industry whose money had gone to fund drug, gambling, or spending habits, she'd lived clean, saved smart, and invested wisely. She had an ocean-front bungalow in Venice Beach, a pied-à-terre on Paris's Left Bank, and more money than she could ever spend. What was left to strive for? She thought of several once-well-known adult film stars reduced to scraping for work, some resorting to comic walk-on roles where drooping breasts and wobbly thighs were made a mock of, and suppressed a shudder. Better to give up the game while she was still winning—while she was still a star.

And there was another reason, one she wasn't ready to share with anyone, not even Martin. Her former roommate and best friend, Liz, had breast cancer. Even after Liz got pregnant and left the industry to go back to New York, they'd kept in close touch—until six months ago when the regular contact had fallen off. When her first few messages went unreturned, Sarah had told herself it was the inevitable result of distance and differing life styles. Liz's son, Jonathan, was in first grade now, and as a single mom supporting them with her graphic design business, Liz more than had her hands full. But then Sarah had happened to see Liz's status update on Facebook—she had breast cancer, stage two. Fuck email and fuck Facebook. Sarah had picked up the phone. The fragility of the voice answering on the other end had shocked her. With remarkable calm, Liz had explained that the double mastectomy had gone as well as could be expected, but unfortunately the cancer had spread to several axillary lymph nodes. A rigorous course of dose-dense chemo was her best hope of beating the disease. Hanging up two hours later, Sarah was decided. Whether Liz admitted it or not, she needed hands-on help, and Sarah was determined to give it.

"I need you to make the announcement, send out a press release or call a press conference, whatever you think is best. I've already drafted a statement for my website, a short letter thanking my fans and fellow actors, and of course you, for all the years of loyalty and support." She paused, holding his gaze. "I really appreciate everything you've done for me. I hope you know that."

He let out another long breath. "Look, Sarah, sooner or later every adult film star hits the wall. Take my advice, and don't burn any bridges. Take some time off, a couple of months, and think things over."

"But—"

"Where's the fire?" he broke in with a shrug of beefy shoulders. "Retiring is a lot like dying—once you've done it, there's not much hope of coming back. C'mon, baby, have I ever steered you wrong?"

She swallowed hard, thinking again of all his support while she'd picked up the pieces of her life post-Danny. "No, you haven't."

"Good, then we're agreed. As far as the press is concerned, we're pulling out because this picture isn't the right vehicle for you—period. We're reviewing scripts for your next project, and in the meantime you're taking time off, an extended vacation."

In LA speak "extended vacation" was code for rehab. Martin probably figured the fumes from any such rumors would fuel her career long enough for her to change her mind about coming back. There really was almost no such thing as bad press, even if most of the "breaking news" and Twitter buzz was bullshit. As much as she planned to prove Martin wrong about the finality of her decision, beyond her inner urge for closure, she couldn't come up with a good argument against waiting. Besides, it would be a lot easier to press her point from across the country than a restaurant table.

Sarah reached for her menu, although whatever appetite she'd walked in with was lost. "Okay, we'll do it your way—for now. I'm on vacation. Sorry, 'extended vacation.'"

Extended vacation—but in her heart, she knew what this move back to New York really meant.

Chapter One

*M*anhattan, New York City, One Month Later

"Sorry about tonight." Iraq war veteran and now executive director of his family's charitable foundation, Cole A. Canning bent to the taxi's rolled-down rear window. "Feel better. I'll call you," he added, knowing full well he wouldn't, at least not any time soon.

Candace lifted her chalky face and nodded, the minor movement sending an apparent ripple of pain over her pristinely made-up features. "O-kay, th-thanks?"

His date duties discharged, Cole stepped back to the curb, and the cab sped off. Watching it go, he released a relieved breath. The Canning Foundation Gala at the Soho Grand had been a bust as far as fund-raising—the response to the silent auction had seriously sucked—but at least Candace's martini-induced migraine had given him an early out to the evening.

It was Friday night, or the early hours of Saturday morning, depending on your perspective. Lower Manhattan was party central or close to it for everyone from beer-guzzling NYU students to stressed-out finance guys swilling single malt. The possibilities were, if not infinite, certainly numerous. Another drink at a nearby watering hole? A strip show at one of the many Chelsea gentlemen's clubs? Breakfast at a greasy spoon? Or he could head home to his Upper West Side pre-war and *not* sleep there. He'd moved in just six months ago, and already the hand-woven carpets were showing wear from his pacing. Even though he was a New Yorker born and bred, since returning stateside two years ago, he often felt as if the avalanche of choices was burying him.

Out of habit, he reached inside his tuxedo jacket's pocket for his cigarettes. Pulling out the empty pack, he cursed. Had he really gone through the whole thing in the last three hours? Good thing smoking was prohibited in the city's public places. If he could smoke openly, rather than having to sneak outside, his lungs would be seriously fucked.

But now he wanted a cigarette, and he wanted it too badly to care about the long-term health effects. If two back-to-back tours in Iraq heading an elite bomb disposal unit had taught him anything, it was that life was short and invariably uncertain. What was the point of denying yourself pleasure in the present when "someday" might never arrive?

Fortunately the corner bodega across the street still had its lights on. Pulling up the collar of his tuxedo jacket against the early spring chill, he wove his way through the oncoming cars. Reaching the mini market, he swung open the glass door, setting off the bell's jangle.

The blonde bent over the frozen desserts freezer caught his eye the moment he walked in—or rather her ass did. Considering it was firm and round and worthy of Jennifer Lopez, not to mention all but shoved in his face, how could he not notice? His gaze slid downward to her legs—long and slim and beautifully shaped, with just the right amount of muscle beneath her form-fitting yoga pants. Her hair was shiny blond and pinned up with one of those hinged-clip contrivances that women seemed to reach for when they were in a hurry.

A plastic shopping basket looped over one slender forearm, she inventoried the ice cream selection as if lives hung in the balance. So far her back was to him. Curious to see if she had a pretty face to match the smoking hot body, he circumvented a snack display and deliberately navigated his way nearer. The maneuver gained him a glimpse of a sun-kissed profile and the contents of her basket—a half dozen individual ice cream cups and, so far, nothing else. Single and living alone, he surmised, no longer in any rush to be on his way.

Backtracking to the counter, he nodded to the Indian dude standing behind it. "Pack of Marlboro Black."

The clerk turned away to the shelving behind the counter, grabbed the pack, and pivoted back around. "Fourteen fifty."

Highway robbery but, like any addict, Cole was prepared to pay the price. He reached for his wallet and pulled out a twenty.

Waiting for his change, he cast a look back over his shoulder to the blonde. Should he maybe offer her a cigarette as an ice breaker? Dressed as though she'd come from an exercise class, she didn't strike him as a smoker. Then again, he didn't let his habit hold him back from pounding out his morning five in Central Park or from working out like a maniac at the gym. Some might call it exercise, but for Cole it was therapy, the only kind a Canning allowed himself—that and sex.

"Do you wish for a bag?"

What Cole wished for was an excuse to strike up a conversation with the blonde. Turning back to the counter, he shook his head. "No, thanks."

He slipped the cigarettes into his coat pocket and turned around. The blonde had straightened. She stood, her body ever so slightly turned away from the freezer—and toward him. Holding out a carton of strawberry, she appeared to pore over the product packaging.

Cole grabbed a *Sports Illustrated* from the magazine rack and sidled over. Flipping pages, he cleared his throat. "Big decision, huh?"

She started, her heart-shaped face lifting to his, her full lips parting. Gazing into her emerald-colored eyes, it hit him. *I know her!* He wasn't always the greatest with names, but faces he never forgot, especially beautiful ones. Cole racked his brain. Had he slept with her? No, her he would definitely remember.

"Excuse me?" She looked back at him as though annoyed by the interruption—definitely not the reaction he was used to.

He gestured to the ice cream thawing in her ringless left hand. "Those single servings are kid-sized portions. Why not just buy a half-gallon?" Ditching the magazine, he moved closer.

Her deep-green gaze narrowed. "Not that it's any of your business, but I like variety."

Cole could feel the corners of his mouth kicking up. "What a coincidence, so do I."

He didn't miss how her slender shoulders stiffened. The way she raked him with her gaze had him wishing he'd waited before stripping off the bowtie and opening his shirt collar.

"Heavy night?" she asked, her tone giving the freezer stiff competition.

He shrugged. "Nothing I can't handle."

Her gaze honed in on his coat pocket. "Smoker, huh?" She said the word as though it was synonymous with syphilis.

"Only on weekends," he lied. "Besides, all the recent studies say processed food is the real killer." He'd only read one such study. Okay, so he hadn't read the actual study but had seen it referenced in a *New York Times* article—practically the same thing.

She let out a derisive laugh, her full mouth moistened with the tiniest dab of clear lip gloss. "Research sponsored by what, Phillip-Morris?"

At least he had her talking and smiling—well, sort of. Pressing his advantage, he added, "Why don't we grab a drink somewhere and compare research notes?" Once he set her down with a drink, he'd have plenty of time to figure out how he knew her.

Perfect half-moon brows lifted. "It's almost one o'clock in the morning."

Cole shrugged. "Yeah and it's also New York, so what do you say?"

She pulled a tight smile. "Thanks, but I don't think so."

It had been a long time since a woman had made him work for it, and the blonde was putting him through his paces. Her hard-to-get act was making him hard for real.

"Why not?" he asked.

She dropped the strawberry ice cream into her basket along with the others. "Not that I need to justify myself but judging from the smell of you, I'd say you've already had quite a few cocktails."

The smell of him—ouch! That was harsh. Memo to self: buy breath mints on the way out.

"And my ice cream would melt."

That settled it. Cole meant to make her melt—and cream. "I have ice cream at my place," he said, flashing a smile. To his best recollection, his freezer held only a half-empty bottle of Absolut, but that would work too.

Her pretty lips firmed into a frown. Clearly his jaunty reference to taking her home had been premature, a major miscalculation. "You have a good evening." She pushed past him to the counter.

Shit! She wasn't playing hard to get or playing at all. She was blowing him off for real—and that really sucked. For the first time in . . . forever, Cole seriously considered dropping his surname. Canning wasn't quite Kennedy, but so far as the fishpond of New York City society, it came close.

Ignoring the clerk's smirk, he followed her over. "Suit yourself, but you're missing out. I'd show you a really good time."

Reaching inside her purse to pay, she let out a laugh. "It's all my loss, I'm sure." Her mocking smile sealed the sarcasm.

Cole held up his hands in the universal gesture of surrender. "You win. Have a nice life. Enjoy your ice cream."

She grabbed the plastic bag off the counter and turned to go. "Thanks, I plan to."

He exchanged looks with the clerk, who remained sagely silent. Waiting until she'd cleared the threshold, he pointed again to the behind the counter shelving. "Make it a carton."

A scream sent him spinning. Outside the glass storefront, a young guy in a navy blue hoodie body slammed the blonde. A vicious downward tug snapped the strap of her shoulder bag and sent her folding to the sidewalk. Shit! Cole tore toward the glass door, yanked it open, and raced out. He reached her just as the attacker sped off with her purse.

Cole spared a swift look down, his soldier's eye assessing her for injury. She'd have bruised knees tomorrow, and her shoulder would be sore from where the bag strap had broken, but otherwise she'd be fine, at least physically. From experience he knew that the worst wounds were often on the inside. Once the adrenalin spike subsided, she'd be pretty shaken up.

"You okay?" he asked, holding out his hand.

She grabbed hold and got to her feet. Sparing a swift glance at the ice cream scattered along the garbage-stacked curb, she said, "Yeah but he got my—"

"I saw. Call 911." He reached inside his jacket pocket and tossed her his iPhone.

Heedless of his tuxedo and wing tips, Cole gave chase down West Broadway, his runner's legs pulverizing the pavement, his sprinting strides cutting the thief's lead from more than a block to steps. Coming up on Canal, the scumbag tried losing him in the pedestrian traffic and late night food carts, but Cole kept his gaze locked on his quarry.

Closing in, he lunged. He grabbed hold hard, bringing them both to the ground. The mugger landed in a face plant, the stolen handbag flying free. Pinning him to the pavement, Cole kicked the purse out of reach but not so far that someone might snatch it. Despite two years of disuse, his combat training kicked in, a dizzying, primal rush. He started in, raining punishing punches to the guy's adrenals and kidneys. Groans and gasps, pleadings and promises punctured the collective quiet of bystanders' bated breaths. To a man, the spectators stood sidelined. But then this was New York Fucking City. It wasn't like anyone was going to grow the balls to step up and stop him. He could count on blind eyes and collective amnesia the moment the police arrived. He only hoped no one was Tweeting his picture or worse, taking video to post later. Given his standing in the philanthropic community, being made out as a brute on social media would seriously fuck with his fundraising. But he'd already gone too far to worry about that. Grabbing a fistful of the scumbag's hair, he was poised to grind the guy's face into the subway grill when he caught footfalls running toward them. New York's Finest finally? It was about fucking time.

Out of the corner of his eye, he saw a slender hand swoop down and fasten onto his striking arm. "Stop! You'll kill him!"

It was her, the blonde. Chest heaving, Cole shook her off. "You . . . say that like . . . like it's a bad thing." Holding the mugger down, he risked a look up.

"Please . . . stop." She stared down at him imploringly.

Succumbing to the moment's distraction proved to be a monumental mistake. Beneath him, the bastard bucked, rolled, and rebounded to his feet. Cole shot upright and made a grab for him. He got hold of one arm but lost his grip, catching only cloth. Shedding the garment, the mugger jerked free and peeled off. Darting across Canal Street, he just missed being creamed by an oncoming cab—fucking shame—and disappeared down Baxter Street.

Holding the hoodie, Cole wheeled around to the woman. "I *had* him. What the fuck is your problem?"

She stared as though he'd grown a second head. The latter might not be a bad idea. God knew the one he had was pounding.

"My problem? You're the one who went all *Lethal Weapon* just now."

Swiping a sleeve across his sweating forehead, he glanced around as the spectators dissipated. "What did you expect me to do, cradle him in my arms until the cops got here? Where the fuck are they anyway? Did the 911 dispatcher give you an ETA?"

She hesitated, biting her bottom lip.

Disgusted by the slow police response, Cole threw the sweatshirt to the gutter. "You called 911, right?"

She still didn't answer, and this time her silence told him exactly what he didn't want to hear. "You didn't make the call, did you? Why the fuck not?"

"I don't want any pub . . . any *police*."

Sucking on his split knuckles, he shook his head. "Why? Are you in the Witness Protection Program?"

She folded her free arm about herself as if suddenly feeling the chill. "Of course not."

A cigarette would be really great right now. He pulled the crushed packet from his pocket and threw it to the ground. "Fuck!"

She eyed him, her slightly superior attitude doing nothing to buoy his mood. "Maybe you should consider it a sign."

He jerked his head up. "I'll probably regret asking, but a sign of what?"

A shimmy of slender shoulders answered. "A sign you should quit. In case you missed the memo, cigarettes are bad for you." She smiled, but her eyes stayed serious.

Cole snorted, not sure how he felt about being preached to by a pretty but so far nameless woman. "You work for the Surgeon General or something?"

In Iraq, smoking had gotten him and the other guys through the tedium and the homesickness. Being the leader for an elite three-man explosive ordnance disposal team had brought hair-raising moments and split second decisions juxtaposed with long periods of downtime. Unlike most of his fellow soldiers, he'd drunk little. A bomb, any bomb, wasn't something you wanted to face hungover, and the make-shift ones were a lot harder to detect than the military models. These days most IEDs, Improvised Explosive Devices, were made without metal and electronic parts, rendering standard monitoring equipment next to useless—and the clever fuckers who made them were getting better at it all the time.

"Not . . . exactly." Her voice called him back to the present—the United States of America, New York City, April 2014. The thief he'd wrestled to the ground was only that, not an insurgent and not a terrorist.

"Not exactly, huh?" he repeated, taking a moment to regulate his breathing. Pounding the piss out of the punk had felt good, too good. "Tonight my smoking habit turned out to be damned lucky for one of us—*you*."

As if chastened, she nodded. "You're absolutely right. Thank you for smoking."

Another smile, this one bordering on a grin, lit her face, igniting the sexual spark Cole had felt from the moment he'd set eyes on her inside the store. Where *had* he met her before? The curiosity was damn near killing him.

Wiping his palms on the tops of his pants, he said, "Look, as we've established, I'm kind of drunk. I need to eat something. You wanna grab—"

"Thanks, but no."

Another refusal, seriously! Cole couldn't recall the last time a woman had turned him down, let alone twice in twenty minutes.

His damsel in distress was turning into something even more irresistible—a challenge.

He folded his arms across his chest. "I haven't even asked you yet."

"Sorry, it's just that I don't . . . " Her voice trailed off. For the first time since being knocked to her knees, she seemed less than one hundred percent together.

Seeking out chinks in armor, sniffing out weaknesses, was Cole's specialty, or at least it had been. Pressing his advantage, he said, "Did you or did you not come out tonight for ice cream?"

"Yes, but—"

"No buts. Washington Square Diner makes a hell of a walnut sundae. Their banana splits don't suck either."

She hesitated. "It's late. I should get home."

He stared pointedly at the purse she held by its severed strap. "I just saved your life—or at least your credit history—and ruined my penguin suit in the process. The least you can do is to buy me a greasy breakfast in thanks."

"B-but—"

"No buts," he broke in, unfolding his arms. "It's your karma on the line. We'll negotiate the dry cleaning bill once I've fed the machine." He patted his gut, which was seriously empty of anything but booze, and gave her a deliberately huge grin.

"You're—"

"Persistent, yes I know. It's one of my few good points." Angling away, he faced out onto the street and lifted a hand to hail an oncoming cab, the on-duty light fortuitously shining. The driver skidded toward them, rolling up to the curb.

Cole turned back to the blonde. Nibbling her bottom lip, she still seemed undecided. The last time he'd been so completely enthralled, his obsession had been his first C4 explosive. The high he'd gotten from dismantling it had been unlike anything he'd felt before or since. For a flicker of an instant, it occurred to him to wonder why continuing their . . . encounter had become so goddamned important. Challenge, he reminded himself, the fleeting yet heady thrill of victory, a distraction from another otherwise endless-seeming night, nothing more.

He reached out and opened the bright yellow door. "So what's it going to be?" Heart drumming, he waited, knowing that despite everything she might well walk away.

She hesitated and then took a step toward him. "I hate bananas, and my name is Sarah." Brushing against him, she ducked and climbed inside.

✳✳✳ ✳✳✳

Cole, her rescuer, surveyed her metal ice cream dish with definite disapproval. "Single scoop, plain vanilla, huh? I wouldn't have figured you for a vanilla girl."

The gleam in his eye told her the double entendre was entirely intended. Determined to give as good as she got, Sarah smiled back. "Every flavor has its charm. Sometimes plain vanilla is exactly what I'm in the mood for."

He cocked his head to the side, his deep blue eyes fixing on hers. "And other times?"

"I like all the flavors." Deliberately, she ran her tongue along her lower lip, savoring the last trace of sticky sweetness. It was what Martin liked to call her "money shot," and it always worked, only this time there were no cameras honing in for a close-up—only one pair of ocean-blue eyes.

He swallowed hard, the corded muscles of his throat working. The table hid their lower bodies, but she'd bet her AVN trophy he was hard. "All, huh?"

"Pretty much, yes."

"Me too."

His comment snapped her back to sanity. God, she was flirting! It had been so long, she'd almost forgotten what it felt like. For the past decade, sex had been her job, a very public, very commercial act performed before a director, production crew, and rolling cameras. Private courtship rituals, the subtle interplay of sensual advance and retreat, seemed a relic from a kinder, gentler, bygone time—or maybe not so bygone after all.

Pull it together, Halliday. This isn't courtship. It's breakfast—bad for you breakfast—with a semi-drunk dude.

Drunk, semi-drunk, or stone-cold sober, Cole was altogether too sexy to dismiss as anything other than one hundred percent primal male. Tall, broad-shouldered, and built, dark-haired and blue-eyed, he was hot enough to be a porn star, better looking than many of the name actors with whom she'd worked. Other than offering his hand in exiting the taxi, he hadn't made a move to touch her and yet she felt every stroke of his gaze like a physical caress. Sitting across from him at the Formica-top table, the neon lights overhead searing in their brightness, she was intensely aware of her nipples hardening and her sex moistening. Watching him butter another piece of dry, white-bread toast, the tops of his big, broad-backed hands dusted with black hair, she couldn't stop thinking how those hands might feel palming her breasts and playing in her panties. The fantasy landed a delicious staccato beating between her thighs.

And then he had to go and ruin it all by asking, "Have we met before?"

Fuck! She shook her head. "No, at least I don't think so."

She added the qualifier to throw him off. She couldn't yet put her finger on it, but he had . . . not a cop vibe but something similar, maybe some other area of law enforcement, even though he wore a designer tuxedo and collar-length hair. If she had any willpower remaining, she'd get up, go home and settle for the simple, safe release of her vibrator. But this man, Cole, seemed to melt her resistance, much like the ice cream turning into a puddle on her plate.

He ran his gaze over her, his darkened irises unpeeling her layered clothing, until she felt as though she were naked. "You're not from here."

Despite her desire for subterfuge, his faulty assumption had the native New Yorker in her bristling. "I'll have you know I'm a Brooklyn girl, born and bred. Di Fara's on Avenue J, best slice in the city."

Her reference to the iconic Midwood pizzeria got his attention— and seemingly his respect. "I stand corrected." He eased back in his seat, dunking a triangle of toast in the broken yolk of one over-easy egg. "So, Brooklyn, what brings you back to Gotham?"

Sarah hesitated. Other than her identity, she had nothing worthy of detecting. Starring in porn films wasn't illegal. Neither was being superlatively successful at it. Her taxes were paid, her driving record spotless, her personal life a squeaky-clean solo act—flat lined, boring. Jaywalking was her only infraction, and that just since moving back to New York.

He popped a piece of bacon into his mouth. Chewing, he slid his gaze over her, taking his time. Sarah stiffened, suddenly carried back to her first casting call, those terrible tense moments waiting to take off her robe in a roomful of strangers for the very first time.

Swallowing, he finally said, "You all but radiate sunshine and fresh air, you still smell like the beach, and you're wearing pastels. You don't see all that many New York women in orange and green."

The woman he described sounded mainstream, utterly wholesome, more like a soccer mom than her carefully crafted porn persona. As Sugar, she could make men pop with a single sultry look, but as Sarah she was considerably less confident. Unsure of whether she was being complimented or criticized, she glanced down at her patterned Ann Taylor knit-wool sweater. The v-necked, slim-fitting cardigan was one of her go-to pieces. Until now, it hadn't occurred to her that it might not be right for New York. Then again, other than a weekly coffee meet-up with Liz's friends and a few solo restaurant dinners, she hadn't gone out since she'd gotten here.

"That would be coral and mint," she corrected.

He rolled his eyes in the way of a man who couldn't care less about clothes, despite being dressed in custom-tailored, designer evening wear. The sapphire studs sparkling from his French cuffs would cover the rent on her Soho sublet for several months. "I'm figuring you for West Coast."

Surrendering, she admitted, "LA, I just moved back."

"Job relocation? Family?"

"Spanish Inquisition?"

He dropped the toast point and held up both hands. The movement caused his sleeves to ride up. The sudden fantasy image of strapping cuffs around those thick, masculine wrists took her breath away. "Mea culpa, just making conversation, Brooklyn. Forget I asked."

His sarcasm made her feel silly. Was she taking this incognito crap too far? "Sorry, it's just that I'm . . . a very private person." A very kinky private person who, it seemed, badly needed to get herself laid.

"Duly noted."

"I moved back in part to help out a friend who's . . . going through a hard time." Even to a stranger, okay an almost stranger, who'd never met and would never meet Liz, the Big C seemed too big of a deal to confide.

He nodded. "That's very altruistic."

"Jesus, are you mocking me?"

He looked genuinely surprised. "No, but you might want to offload that chip on your shoulder. It must be getting pretty heavy."

Feeling like a jerk, she subsided back against the vinyl-covered booth. What was it about this guy that made it so easy for her to lose control? "Sorry, it's just . . . weird being back."

"Tell me about it." He rolled his eyes, only this time she sensed empathy, not sarcasm.

"So where are you back from?" she asked, as much from genuine curiosity as wanting to shift the subject away from her.

"Hell." His sudden sobering told her he wasn't joking—and that he was a lot more complicated than just another entitled rich guy out for a thrill.

Whatever his deal—mood disorder, recent divorce, or something much darker—she was done with being a fixer. Her trusty vibrator waited. Thanks to her sexy rescuer, she'd have an inventory of fresh fantasies to play out in her head while pleasuring herself.

"Well, thanks again for coming to my rescue." She shoved a hand inside her broken bag, brought out some loose bills, and threw two twenties down on the table—more than enough to cover their check, along with a healthy tip for their server. Eye on the exit, she scooted out and stood.

Cole rose with her. "This is how you say thank you? You're not the only one who likes dessert. I was just about to order pie. Stick around." He didn't exactly body block her, but his stance meant she'd have to go around him to leave.

She planted a fist on one hip as her grandma used to do, the universal posture of strong women. "Look, I really appreciate what you did for me earlier, and for the record I'm happy to pay for your dry cleaning or buy you a new tux—and yes, I realize it's Ralph Lauren. But if you think I owe you something more—"

"You don't owe me shit." He wisely kept his arms at his sides. Had he attempted to touch her, let alone hold her back, he would have found his groin greeting her knee.

"Great, then we're done here."

"Not quite. I'd like to see you again."

He stood so close she could feel his exhaled breath touching her cheek. The alcohol she'd smelled on him earlier was gone now, obliterated by weak coffee and greasy food and, she suspected, the fistful of candy mints he'd grabbed from the dish on their way inside. Beneath the rumpled tux, his skin exuded expensive cologne, sweat, and the unmistakable musk of male arousal. If she licked him, he would taste briny like the Blue Point Oysters she'd missed while in California. Without looking down, she knew his erection was a hairsbreadth away from brushing the bottom of her belly. Suddenly his hardness and strength were everything she wanted to feel. The thought of all that male muscle and liquid heat grinding against her made her want to scoot back onto the table's edge, slip down her pants, and spread her legs—*wide*.

Instead she shook her head. "Thanks, that's very flattering, but I'm not interested."

That was a lie. Sarah couldn't remember the last time she'd been so interested. Even in his better days, Danny had never made her feel anything close to this. In the last few minutes, her panties' crotch had gone from moist to milking. If she stuck around much longer, she'd be leading him into the bathroom for a quickie.

"It's not meant to be flattering. It's meant to be honest."

"How's this for honest? I don't date."

"Great neither do I. So now that we've settled that, your place or mine?"

His was alpha male on steroids. She should be pissed off; she *was* pissed off, but she was also reluctantly, irredeemably hot for him. "You don't take no for an answer do you?"

His squared jaw jutted ever so slightly. "Never."

"I don't hook up with strangers."

Just because she was a porn star didn't mean any guy who felt like it could walk up and fuck her. For many men, that was news. As much as the public equated pornography with promiscuity, she'd always been picky about her lovers. Her sexual health was too important to her not to be. Given that performers were screened for STDs every fourteen to twenty-eight days, she was a pretty safe bet.

He nodded. "Good plan. Fortunately we're not strangers. I saved your ass, and you just bought me breakfast." Looking beyond her, he flagged down the harried server for the check. "I'm guessing that you live close by, probably just a few blocks from that bodega—unless you have a thing about trekking across town to buy single-serving ice cream cups, which would be a time suck as well as really weird."

Even while turning her on, he could floor her by saying something funny. Fighting a smile, she dragged a hand through her loosened hair, the clip lost somewhere along the way. "I live a few blocks away . . . on Elizabeth Street," she admitted. Jesus, why had she told him that! A man like Cole would see that as an invitation to fuck her. Then again, wasn't it?

His smile broadened. "Great, it's your place then. I just hope you're not a slob or something. Panties on the floor and dishes in the sink are big libido busters for me."

He really was . . . impossible. She shook her head. "Jesus, you don't quit do you? How do I know you're not a serial killer?"

He appeared to consider that. "You said you came back to the city to help out a friend, right?"

Wondering what he was getting at, she said, "Yeah, what about it?"

"So send her a text message. Let her know who you're with." He jammed a hand into his back pocket and brought out a wallet, worn but obviously expensive. "Here's my driver's license. Tell her you're with me, give her my name and license number, and that way in the extremely unlikely event they find you floating in the Hudson,

25

she'll know who to send the cops after." He flipped the driver's license toward her.

Colvin A. Canning. His surname screamed Hamptons set. The photograph, more than five years old, showed a younger, brighter-eyed him. Birth year of 1984, which made him just thirty, four years younger than she, not that it mattered—much. The last name sounded familiar, but then maybe it was because it was so fucking waspy—more fodder for her trust-fund-brat theory.

She looked from the license to him. "You're serious, aren't you?"

He slanted a smart-assed smile. "I guess it's a little late in the game to mention I'm a virgin."

She gave up and laughed. "You're funny." When was the last time a man had made her laugh? Like making her wet, it had been a while.

"Yeah, I know, Letterman had better watch out. Seriously, though, I have one condition."

"You . . . *you* have conditions. You're the one who propositioned me, buddy." Sarah didn't know what she wanted to do more—fuck him or slap him. Actually she wanted to do both—preferably at the same time.

Grinning, he said, "Just remember, what happens in Soho stays in Soho."

Chapter Two

Sarah closed the apartment door behind Cole. Throwing her bag and keys down on the counter, she announced, "So this is it."

Despite all the sexual teasing that had gone down at the diner, he hadn't laid a finger on her in the cab, hadn't made a move to kiss her, either. Now that they were alone, sans leering cabbies or weary waitresses, she felt strangely . . . shy. A shy porn actress, talk about your oxymoron! But then things had gotten seriously messed up in LA. Being stalked certainly wasn't how she would have chosen to close out that decade-long chapter of her history. Once the notes had begun, bringing a man back to her place had been out of the question. But she was in New York now, a whole other coast and a country's breadth between her and whatever menace might remain. So long as she flew under the radar, she was safe here.

This man, Cole, didn't know about any of that. So far, he didn't even know who she was, although from his suggestion that they might have met before, she'd begun to suspect he'd seen some of her films. If her luck held, by the time he placed her, if he did so at all, their hookup would be a distant, hot memory for them both.

"Do you uh . . . want something to drink?" she asked, and then remembered that other than Evian and the vegetable juice she'd made from produce purchased from the Union Square green market, she had nothing to offer him.

God, I really suck at this.

Danny had been her single serious relationship. Before him, she hadn't dated all that much. Without a script, director, and production squad calling the shots, she wasn't sure what to say or do.

Holding back at the door, Cole shook his head. "Thanks, but apparently I've had too much already."

His reference to her earlier rebuff brought out a reluctant smile. "Right, sorry about that. I'm not always so . . . preachy. It's just that my last relationship was with an alcoholic, and I'm trying to . . . turn over a new leaf, I guess."

Danny's boozing and blame shifting and occasional brutishness had reminded her entirely too much of dealing with her dad. The slap wasn't the only reason she'd broken it off with him, but it had shocked her into admitting the truth.

Whether he got clean and sober or stayed wasted and high, she wasn't ever going to love him.

Cole's gaze, unsettlingly serious, fixed on hers. "I want to be upfront with you, Sarah. I'm not a relationship guy. Whatever happens between us, it's just for fun."

The dreaded relationship word had slipped out without her thinking. Worse still, she'd brought up her ex. Clearly she should go back and reread *The Rules*! Her double gaffe had heat flooding her face. A blush? It had been so long, she'd forgotten what one felt like.

Seeking to do damage control, she gave a quick nod. "Got it, thanks, but you can relax. I'm not looking for a relationship either. I'm . . . taking a break from all that." She was, in fact, looking for commitment with all the trimmings, but she'd save that speech for someone who was open to hearing it.

That someone was definitely not Cole. He might have come to her rescue outside the bodega, but he was no Prince Charming. He was exactly what she'd first figured him for, an uber-hot, trust-fund brat who liked to party and play. Still, she had to give him props for doing his full disclosure *before* they'd fucked instead of after. The old-school code of honor wasn't anything close to common.

Like a fish let off the hook, he eased his expression. He pushed away from the wall and took a step toward her. "Good, I'm glad we're on the same page. Now, about that good time I promised you . . . "

She held out an arm, warding him off. "First things first, give me your cell."

He halted. "You're fucking with me, right?"

"No, I'm totally serious—no photos, no videos."

His blue eyes bugged. "I wasn't planning on taking any."

"Great, then you won't have a problem handing over your phone." Palm turned up, she waited.

His tightening jaw told her he was seriously ticked, maybe even enough to turn and walk out. Given her circumstances, it was a chance she had to take.

"I just gave you my word. Doesn't that count for something?"

Sarah felt a bitter laugh bubbling up. If she'd had a buck for every man who'd given her his *word* and broken or bent it, she could have quit after ten films rather than a hundred. "Your promise will mean a lot more if you back it up with action."

Tension throbbed between them. His blue eyes bore into hers. Despite a night of drinking followed by the chase and street fight, despite the obvious hard-on pressing against his pants, he stood with his shoulders back and his head high, his bearing almost military.

Clearly he was used to being the one who gave the orders. Having the tables turned didn't sit well with him, she could see.

The temptation to back down and let him hold onto the phone was strong—but this once Sarah's will was stronger. "So, are you in or are you out?"

He reached out and smacked the phone into her hand. "You really don't trust men, do you?"

"Trust has to be earned." She crossed to the open kitchen. Reaching over the counter, she pulled out a drawer and dropped the phone inside. Turning back to him, she said, "Where were we?"

Fierce eyes raked over her. "We were just about to fuck."

His coarseness would offend some women, okay, most women, especially on a first "date," but Sarah wasn't them. Turned on as hell, she met his unblinking stare head on. "You're a cocky son-of-a-bitch, aren't you?"

He didn't deny it. "Maybe I have something to be cocky about. There's only one way to find out." Shucking off his coat, he let it fall to the floor and beckoned her over.

Sarah stayed put. "It's my place. Why don't you come here?"

Cole closed the gap between them in a single stride, catching her about the waist. "You like being in charge, don't you?" he asked, lifting her off her feet and crushing her against him.

Slammed against his hardness and heat, Sarah swallowed. "Sometimes." At others, nothing got her off quite like being "forced" down onto her knees. But that kind of play required a level of trust built over time, not a single madcap night.

"Yeah, me too."

He swept the purse aside and set her down on the counter, the chipped Coriander cool beneath her bum. Stepping between her legs, he lifted her chin on the knuckles of his bloodied hand.

She glanced down. "You should probably put something on the hand. You want Neosporin? Ice?"

"Right now what I want . . . *all* I want is you."

His hand fell away. Arms like whipcords banded about her. He angled his face to hers. Seen up close, his lips looked luscious, moist and soft. In her experience, a man's kiss said a lot about how he fucked. If he knew what to do with his tongue, odds were he would wield his cock with similar expertise. Unfortunately the opposite also held true.

Cole matched his mouth to hers. From the moment their lips touched, she knew it was going to be amazing—the kissing, the fucking, all of it. His wasn't so much a kiss as it was a claiming. Firm lips took possession of hers. A knowing tongue plundered, punished, and pleased. Strong teeth nipped at her lower lip, the line of her jaw, the pulse point at the side of her neck. Gentled lips soothed her, sipping at her sweetness. A stubble-blanketed jaw scraped across her cheek, scoring her skin, the grazing caress making her shudder.

He drew back, resting his forehead on hers. "Too much?"

Breathless, she shook her head. "I like it."

A low laugh rumbled from his chest. "Right, all the flavors."

He reached between them, his big hand covering her right breast. Capturing her nipple between his thumb and forefinger, he rolled it. The pinching wasn't hard enough to hurt, but it got her attention. Her squeal segued to moaning. Caught, she squirmed on her bottom, seeking to bring him closer, his cock especially. Danny's drinking and drugging had made for a soft dick, and it had been more than a year since she'd been with a man other than on set. Since she never came on camera, those choreographed encounters hardly seemed to count.

Buttons sprayed as he wrenched open her sweater, then pulled it over her arms and off. The bodega run was to have been a quick back-and-forth trip. She wore only a sports bra beneath. He lifted her arms and peeled it off too, bringing it over her head.

Sarah's breasts swung free, the nipples pink from his plucking. Unlike most porn actresses, she'd never gotten implants, despite numerous attempts to persuade her.

Cole sucked down a heavy breath. "Jesus."

Squeezing her together, he bent his head and suckled. Sarah arched against him. She might only be a B cup, but the rich sensations roused by his teeth and tongue, fingers, and palms had her congratulating herself for holding out against the surgery.

But as amazing as his mouth felt on her breasts, Sarah craved his kisses lower, much lower. She couldn't remember the last time a man had eaten her out. As good as her vibrator could make her feel, she'd yet to meet the toy that could simulate cunnilingus close to realistically.

Cole must have read her mind. Taking a step back, he snagged the waistband of her yoga pants and slid them down, taking her thong with them. Gooseflesh pricked her bared thighs.

He squeezed her Brazilian-waxed pubis with his palm, and then slid his thumb along the bisecting cleft. "I'm betting you taste amazing."

A sob caught in Sarah's throat. No director shouting "show me more pink!" No contorting her body into positions that looked sexy on camera but felt like hell. No lurking suitcase pimps looking to get their rocks off by watching their porn-actress girlfriends make out on the set. To be given all this pleasure without having to do anything other than receive seemed such delicious decadence! Giddy with the freedom, she covered her hand over Cole's.

He glided a finger inside her. A second and finally a third digit followed. Flexing brought her bucking hard against his hand. He could have stopped there and coaxed her to coming, only he didn't. Instead, he dropped to his knees. The top of his dark head brushed her lower belly. Feathery hair tickled her inner thighs. Spreading her wider, he blew on her clit. A hot shiver raced through her. Her toes curled. Her pussy pulsed. Deft fingers sank inside her again, all three at once. This time a tongue's point probed her channel, touched the hood of her clit, and swirled lavish circles around the kernel. Sarah braced herself on her palms, seeking to hold off on coming and prolong the pleasure for as long as she could.

But all the flirting and sensual teasing, first at the diner and now here, had taken their toll. Powerless against the pull, her clit fluttered. Her skin tingled. Against the counter, her butthole twitched. Cole sucked her more fully into his mouth, and Sarah split apart. Her buttocks clenched; her inner muscles contracted. Waves of dizzying release rolled over her. She buzzed then spasmed, squirting her milk into his mouth.

Resting back on his heels, Cole licked damp lips. "You're my new favorite flavor."

Pulling herself upright on her palms, she stared down. Perspiration molded his white shirt to broad shoulders and a beautifully muscled back. Looking forward to taking off his shirt and everything else, she said, "Okay, so maybe you get to be a little cocky."

He stood. "Just a little, huh?"

Sarah let a smile stand as her answer. That he'd held himself back from fucking her spoke volumes for his cock control.

"Where's your bedroom?"

Still foggy, she shook her head. "What?"

"Your bedroom, where is it? Or do you sleep standing in the shower? Don't laugh, I know several Manhattan realtors who'll swear some people do."

"No, I have a bed." She jerked her chin across the room to the four curved steps leading to the loft.

"Great, then let's get you horizontal." Cole swept her off the counter and into his arms. Rag doll-limp, she let him carry her to the bed.

✳✳✳ ✳✳✳

Sarah didn't stay limp for long. The moment they hit the mattress, she came alive, taking total charge, stripping off his shirt, unzipping his pants. Her hands were everywhere, so was her mouth—nipping at his neck, trailing biting kisses down the queue of dark hair blanketing his belly, and finally, gloriously, cinching around his cock.

She rolled off the bed and stood. "Hey, where are you going?" Cole demanded, reaching for her. If she was one of those women who got off on being a tease, so help him, he was going to shake her.

But instead of pleading a sudden headache or calling time out for a pee break, she grabbed hold of his wrists, urging him up. Curious to see what she had in mind, Cole followed. Sitting on the side of the bed in only his briefs, he waited.

Holding his gaze, Sarah sank to the carpet. On her knees. At his feet.

More than anything, it was her eyes that were killing him. Large and luminous, they left his and slowly stroked over his body. He felt each brush between blinks like a physical caress. His neck. His shoulders. His nipples. His belly. The tops of his legs, she took him all in. Focusing on his cock, she licked her lips. The sight of that pink tongue was almost his undoing, almost. Cole dug his fingers into the mattress, resisting the urge to grab hold of her hair and force her face down to him, not because they'd only just met, but because he suspected she'd like it a little too much. Instead he waited, interspersing sexy thoughts of how good her mouth was going to feel with random libido-busting musings—baseball scores and budget figures and the entire cast of *The Golden Girls* naked—anything to keep himself from coming.

She settled herself inside his legs. Naked and kneeling, it didn't get any better than that. Her slender hand fitted around his cock. Her eyes found his once more as she slid slowly up and down, stopping just below the tip. Impatient, he pushed against her palm. She punished him by stopping immediately. So she wasn't only a tease but a torturer, the very best kind.

He stilled—everything but his heart, which bolted like one of his family's thoroughbred racers.

"Better," she murmured, rewarding him by resuming.

With her thumb, she massaged his base, and Cole almost jumped off the bed.

Steady Canning!

Bracing himself on his palms, he leaned back, forcing himself to stare up at the ceiling. There was a crack in the plasterwork over the bed and what looked like a water stain bubbling around it. Good thing it wasn't raining tonight, he thought, then started as her thumb stroked over the cleft bisecting his head. Cole glanced down. Jesus, he was leaking!

If Sarah was offended, she hid it well. "Hmm," she said. Still holding him, she glided her glistening thumb into her mouth.

Oh, God!

Moonstruck hair tickled his inner thighs as she lowered herself to his groin, guiding him to her. Moist lips slid over him. A wicked tongue tested his slit, finishing what her digit had begun. Clever hands cupped his balls, gently squeezing. Nails raked the fuzz covering the firmed sacks. The tongue returned, wiggling against the underside of his shaft. Cole caught his breath as her light licking segued to sucking, liquid and rhythmic. Like the tide, it seemed to tow him toward some unseen destination, a place where any kind of self-control was a memory and from which there would be no coming back.

I will not come, I will not come, I will not come . . .

His heart was drumming, his cock poised to detonate. Whatever else he did, he was not leaving that bed until he'd climaxed inside her, her pussy not her mouth.

He reached out, his fingers sinking into the thick gold of her hair. Sarah moaned, the vibration buzzing around him. She sucked him deeper and deeper still. Suddenly it wasn't only her tongue and mouth and hands working him. It was her throat!

Cole squeezed his eyes closed. He allowed himself another few seconds of extreme pleasure before he eased himself free and stood. Sarah still knelt. She looked up at him as if in an altered state, her eyes heavy lidded, her incredible mouth slightly swollen and glistening. Her nipples stood out like miniature cherries, luscious and firm. He couldn't see her pussy beyond the honey brown landing strip, but he'd bet his discharge papers she was dripping. He'd find out soon enough.

"Get up."

When she didn't immediately obey, he reached down and hauled her to her feet. Turning around, he pushed her down onto the edge of the bed. "My turn."

He wheeled away. Retrieving his pants from the floor, he took out a condom, tore open the foil square, and quickly sheathed himself. He turned back to find Sarah watching him. She hadn't moved. Lying on her back, her legs spread, her feet touching the floor, she waited.

He pulled her legs apart and stepped between her thighs. She might like "all the flavors," but when it came to the actual fucking, he was betting she liked it deep and hard. Hooking his hands beneath her knees, he lifted her legs to his chest. She went with it, anchoring her ankles to the tops of his shoulders and lifting her ass against him. Her inner lips were pink and glistening, as wet as her mouth. Reaching down, he pulled the petals apart and positioned himself.

Cole sank into her, burying himself to the base. Despite his size, there was no resistance. She was gloriously wet and surprisingly tight, and when he pulled out and plunged into her again, her whole body shook. Biting at her bottom lip, she moaned and stretched her arms high over her head, as though imagining herself tied. Cole couldn't help imagining it too. Her perfect, pale skin was made for black silk and bondage wear. But the kinky images carried Cole to the cusp of coming, and fucking Sarah felt far too good to go there just yet. Mentally pulling back, he slowed his stroking. Meeting him, she contracted her inner muscles, working him as her mouth and throat had done. He'd had some talented bedmates before, but this woman, Sarah, was in a league of her own—amazing.

"Please," she said, bucking hard against him.

Remembering how she'd tortured him, he pulled slowly out of her. "Please what?"

"Please . . . let me come."

The ease with which she could switch between being dominant and submissive dazzled him. Most women were either one or the other, making it all too easy for him to lose interest. But Sarah . . . All the flavors, indeed!

But right now, her asking his permission was the big turn on. He held her fevered gaze and answered, "You have to earn it, Sarah." He played his penis along her quivering clit, and she nearly came off the bed. "My cock, you have to earn it. Do you want to earn it, Sarah?"

"Y-yes." The word trembled across her lips. Jesus, there were actual tears in her eyes.

He shrugged her legs off and stepped back, his pole sticking straight out. "Then turn over and crawl up to the foot of the bed."

She rolled onto her side and did as he'd told her. He'd imagined her like this since he'd first seen her bent over in the bodega. As lovely as her slender shoulders and elegantly arched back were, it was her ass that held him. He wanted to cover those firm, lush lobes with bruises and bites, lashes and licks. For now . . .

Cole dove onto the bed. He followed her up to the head, covering her slender body with his. Without his asking, she reached out and took hold of the headboard. Seeing those slender fingers wrapping around the metal rungs, he anchored his hands to her hips and slid back inside her. Sarah moaned and ground back against him. The sound and body posture assured him the angle was good for her—*really* good.

It worked for Cole, too, but what was really getting him off was the view. That and fixating on how good she'd tasted when he'd eaten her out in the kitchen. He'd made plenty of women cream before, but the way she'd given it up and squirted had taken the experience to a new level.

"Are you ready to come, Sarah?"

"Y-yes."

"Just y-yes?" he asked, not yet ready to give up the game.

"Yes, *please.*"

He pulled out, smiling. "Good girl," he soothed. Holding himself, he chafed the side of his shaft over her pulsing pussy, rubbing it over her clit.

Sarah stiffened and then bucked. Her hands fell away from the rail, her clit buzzing against his meat. Cole pulled out and then slammed into her—hard, deep. Even gloved by the condom, he felt her heat as searing. He wouldn't be surprised to find later that the fucking thing had melted, but he was too far gone to care about that now, too far gone to think beyond the thrusting, beyond claiming all that wet, quivering, fragrant flesh as his. He wasn't alone. Sarah's orgasm was reaching its crescendo. Violent trembling overtook her. A gasp broke free from her throat. Sobbing, she buried her face in the bedding, her cunt clenching around him like a fist.

Cole let himself go. Pumping into Sarah, he threw back his head and roared.

✳✳✳ ✳✳✳

Cole cracked open his eyes. He lay sprawled on his back in the center of a metal four poster, the sheet riding his waist.

Where the hell am I?

Impressions from the previous night paraded through his consciousness. Masses of soft blonde hair spilling over crisp, white, cotton-cased pillows. Kisses that tasted of vanilla ice cream laced with sex. The slapping of sweaty, scalding skin against flesh equally fevered, an eternally satisfying sound.

Apparently his hookup had segued into a sleepover. That was a first, for him anyway.

He shoved up on one elbow, vaguely registering that his right hand hurt. Sunlight streamed through a pair of floor-length, sheer curtains. Some sort of white blossoming flower, freesias maybe, overflowed a cobalt-colored vase set atop a shabby chic dresser. Out of habit, he reached over to the nightstand for his phone and cigarettes, neither of which was there. Right, the crushed pack had never been replaced. As for his phone . . .

The blonde, Sarah, entered the room, not wearing his shirt as most women would presume to do but instead in an oversized tee of her own. Her hair was back up in the clip. A pair of granny glasses perched on the bridge of her slightly snubbed nose. From the neck up, she looked like a sexy librarian. Lower she just looked . . . sexy.

The fucking had been effortless, second nature, sublime. Now came the awkward part. Girding himself, he sat all the way up. "Good morning."

"Good morning," she replied, stopping at the foot of the bed, again not launching herself at him as so many women might—had.

He scraped his hand through his hair, wincing when the action reminded him that his knuckles were split and swollen. "I didn't mean to fall asleep."

He hadn't. Spending the night, the morning, or whatever wasn't part of his deal. The last thing he'd wanted was to risk freaking out on some stranger, humiliating himself with his thrashing and screaming. But after making love to Sarah, he'd drifted off naturally, as normal people did. Normal, Christ, until last night when was the last time he'd felt anywhere close to that?

She shrugged. "No problem. That's what beds are for."

"What time is it anyway?" Like most people, he'd stopped wearing watches, relying on his phone for the time.

Still keeping the bed's length between them, she answered, "Almost eight thirty."

Eight thirty! Had he really slept through the night? Okay, so granted they hadn't gone to sleep until sunrise, but still . . . Since Iraq, logging in that many consecutive zzz's stood as a record.

He glanced to the floor where his clothes were strewn. "I should probably get going," he announced, anticipating her push back.

Instead of trying to persuade him to stay, she nodded. "You left your jacket downstairs last night when we . . . Anyway, I hung it up in the coat closet." The way she was directing him, it sounded like she didn't mean to walk him down.

"Thanks. How long have you been up?"

Another shrug answered his question. "Since seven."

"You should have woken me."

Her brows snapped together as though being told what she should or shouldn't do didn't sit well. In bed, however, had been a very different story. Recalling how she'd waited for his permission to come, he felt himself thickening.

Distracted, he almost missed her answer. "I've always been an early riser. You weren't in my way. I went downstairs to work."

In her way—until now he hadn't thought of it like that. He almost asked what her work was but stopped himself, not wanting to pry. Besides, what did it matter?

Naked, he slid out of bed. She turned away, pretending to tidy the top of her dresser. Given that she'd kissed, licked, and sucked nearly every square inch of him, the display of morning-after modesty struck him as a surprise—and seriously cute.

Holding back a chuckle, Cole began compiling his clothes. His pants lay crumpled pile beside the bed. His underwear must be somewhere close by too, but rather than prolong the awkwardness by rooting around the covers for it, he decided to go commando. He found his shirt in a ball at the foot of the bed. He put it on and buttoned it. Socks and shoes followed.

He stood from the side of the bed, clearing his throat to get her attention. "Well, I'll be getting going."

"Right, okay." She turned and led the way down, her t-shirt riding up to give him a peek at pink cotton panties.

Cole followed, enjoying the view on his descent. Seen in daylight, her downstairs was small but pristinely kept. From the loveseat upholstered in light blue linen to the shabby chic dresser retrofitted as a home entertainment cabinet, every piece seemed to have a place and purpose. A laptop sat open on the kitchen counter along with a spiral notebook and coffee mug. She wasn't bullshitting him. She really had been working.

Though so far she seemed cool with his leaving, he braced himself. By now he was used to all kinds of morning-after histrionics from classic crying to one semi-serious suicide threat. Some women started in on waking, others waited until he was reaching for the door handle before letting loose with their inner bunny boiler.

Perfectly poised, she opened a closet, took out his tuxedo jacket, and passed it to him. Shrugging it on, he stood as if rooted to the spot. What the hell was his problem? His exit was right there. No one was blocking him.

Cole took a step toward the door, and then stopped. Edging partway around, he said, "I'm hungry, you hungry?"

Her gaze narrowed. "Sorry, but this isn't a B&B. Feel free to grab a yogurt from the fridge to go."

So much for his concerns that she might cling! God, what would it take to fuck the bitchiness out of her? He'd give a lot to find out, more to do it. Then he remembered he didn't plan on seeing her again. A hookup was supposed to be just the one night. At least that's how he'd always played it. If he was smart, he'd set his course for the door and not stop walking until he cleared her street. Nothing, certainly not her, was holding him here. And yet for whatever reason, having her so misread him really rankled.

"To set the record straight, I wasn't expecting you to make me breakfast. I thought I'd pick something up for us, bagels probably."

She blinked as if startled, as if a guy being decent to her was a foreign thing. "Oh, that's . . . really nice of you, but I can't. I have this . . . thing I have to do."

Cole shrugged, wondering why he felt letdown rather than relieved. "Sure, no big deal. I've got a packed Saturday too. I'll let you get to it."

He turned to go. With every step toward the door, he felt as if an invisible rope tugged him back. This reluctance, it made no sense. He'd gotten what he wanted, hadn't he? The sex had been mostly vanilla and yet mind-blowing. It wasn't like him to hang around making small talk. It wasn't like him to hang around at all. Ordinarily he was out of bed and putting on his pants almost as soon as his partner climaxed. That he'd not only fallen asleep beside Sarah—nightmare free sleep— but then found himself making excuses to stick around set off all kinds of sirens.

Behind him, a drawer scraped open. "Cole, wait."

Seizing on the excuse, he swung around. "Yeah?"

"You forgot this." Leaning over the counter, she held out his phone.

Deflated, he walked over and took it, his fingers grazing hers. "Thanks, you're a lifesaver. I might want to shoot some video later."

She grimaced, but the pained look dissolved into a smile. "Or make some calls."

He managed a laugh. "Right, I guess I could do that too." Pocketing the phone, he hesitated. "I had a really good time last night." Really good didn't begin to describe it.

She didn't look shyly downward as a lot of women would but boldly met his stare. "Thanks, me too."

Cole hesitated, considering kissing her. More than considering it, he wanted to kiss her—badly. But now that they were out of bed with their clothes on, a kiss in the bright light of day might be misinterpreted as more. Besides, she'd already shot him down, rejecting his offer of bringing in breakfast because she had a "thing." He recognized the blow off for what it was. Hadn't he spent the past two years coming up with similar excuses? He should feel relieved rather than pissed. With Sarah, he didn't have to worry about extricating himself. She was as good as pushing him out the door.

He settled for pressing a quick kiss to her forehead. "Great, well, take care."

She stepped back. "You too. Stop smoking." She tapped a finger against his chest.

The playful gesture brought a rare sense of tenderness surging through him. He caught her hand and turned it palm up. "Buy ice cream by the gallon. It's safer," he joked, kissing her fingertips.

She smiled. "Thanks, I'll think about it."

I'll think about you, he thought but of course didn't say. Something told him that despite the sleep he'd gotten, he would be more or less useless for the rest of the day.

Cole turned and opened the door. Out of excuses, there was nothing to do but walk away.

Chapter Three

Sarah's ready excuse to Cole also happened to be the truth. Liz had a noon chemo appointment at Memorial Sloan-Kettering, and Sarah had volunteered to drop off Jonathan at his friend's house and then sit with her during the grueling several hours' treatment session.

They met up at the hospital. Liz sat in one of the half dozen occupied, mint-green, vinyl hospital chairs, her head wrapped in a bright, patterned, purple scarf, her left hand tethered to the IV dispensing the drug. To give her the best possible shot at a permanent remission, her oncology team had agreed on an aggressive protocol of dose-dense chemotherapy, wherein the treatments were delivered every two weeks. Halfway through the chemo course, her hair was history. Even the fuzz had fallen out. Her eyebrows looked as though they'd been erased. Her face was thin, pale to the point of translucence. But her big brown eyes were animated above the shadowed crescents. Sarah focused on the eyes. Seeing the light in them gave her hope that cancer wouldn't win. Liz would.

"Hey, you," Sarah called softly from the open doorway.

Sucking on an orange Popsicle, Liz looked up from the open magazine in her lap. "Hi, yourself."

Five other gowned oncology patients shared the treatment room, all receiving their chemo cocktails through identical IV drips. Most listened to music or meditation tapes, heads leaned back and eyes closed, as if willing themselves to a pleasanter place. One, an elderly nun, worked a beaded rosary, her lips silently moving, her navy blue habit half-hiding a mostly bald head. Beside every chair, a plastic tray held a licked-clean Popsicle stick. The frozen treats helped mitigate the mouth sores that sometimes occurred, yet another side effect of the drugs.

Carrying the magazines she'd purchased, Sarah picked a path over to Liz. "Sorry I'm late," she said, avoiding looking at the pump. Even knowing the chemo drugs were killing any residual cancer cells, seeing Liz so sick made it hard not to think of the medicine as poison.

Liz gestured with the Popsicle to the plastic tubing tethering her left hand. "No problem, pull up a stool. As you can see, I'm not going anywhere, at least not for the next few hours. Jonathan get off okay?"

Sarah hesitated. The seven-year-old's playdate had gotten off to a shaky start, but Liz didn't need to know that. He'd dug in his heels when she'd dropped him off at his friend's. "Why can't I come to the hospital too?" he'd demanded, his dark brown eyes, exact replicas of Liz's, filling with tears.

Fighting tears of her own, Sarah had explained that kids younger than twelve weren't allowed, but that his mom would be back home later that afternoon. Then she'd dropped down on her knees and given him a huge hug that she'd needed as much as he.

Glossing over those details, she focused on the result. "Chandler's mother mentioned something about taking the boys to the Central Park Zoo. Looks like a good day for it. How are you doing?"

Liz glanced down to her hooked-up hand. Because of swelling, the delivery site had been moved from her arm to a vein at the top of her hand. "I can't complain, or actually I can, but it doesn't do any good.

Besides, I'm on my second Popsicle. Apparently there's no limit. Oncology here is like one big, lactose-free Good Humor truck."

Taking in the bruises mapping the cannula, Sarah steadied herself not to cringe. "I brought you some magazines." Careful to avoid the tube, she settled the stack in Liz's lap. "Sorry, there wasn't a *Vogue* to be had."

"That's okay. I'm not feeling especially *en vogue* at the moment." Taking another lick of Popsicle, Liz surveyed the stash. "You got *Glamour*, *In Style*, and *Us*. This is awesome, thanks."

Sarah nodded. "Next time I'll be sure to stop at a newsstand before I get here. The hospital gift shop selection seriously sucked."

"Speaking of sucking, Nurse, can we get a Popsicle for my bestie here?" she called out, holding her dripping one aloft.

Hearing herself so described sent Sarah's heart lurching. They'd met on the set of Sarah's first film, *Cheerleaders in Love*. A buxom brunette with a winning smile and natural double-D sized breasts, Liz was the lead, Sarah a lowly supporting role. Their girl-on-girl scene had called for some serious acting. Neither of them into women, they'd managed the kiss okay, but when it came to cunnilingus, they'd cheated the camera big time. The director had been royally pissed, but Liz had sufficient clout to get away with telling him where to shove it. As the new girl, and thereby totally expendable, Sarah had borne the brunt of his anger.

Afterward, Sarah had retreated to the dressing room, wondering if maybe she hadn't made a huge fucking mistake. Liz had followed her back, handed her a box of Kleenex, and sat her down for a pep talk. It turned out they were both from Brooklyn! They shared a weakness for black-and-white films, vintage evening bags, and loser men. Liz had taken her in, insisting she wasn't to worry about rent until she'd lined up steady work. She'd shown Sarah the ropes, sharing trade secrets— use Visine to shrink razor bumps, shave with Neosporin to not get them in the first place, wear lip gloss beneath lipstick rather than over it to keep your hair from sticking to your mouth. Liz had filled her in on who was a doper, who followed safe-sex practices and who didn't, taking her to the heavy-hitter parties and making sure she met the right people and steered clear of the wrong ones.

They'd been BFFs ever since, at least until Liz had gotten knocked up by another actor, a genuine jerk whom Sarah had disliked on the spot. Predictably he'd split as soon as Liz told him about the pregnancy. Rather than have an abortion or put the baby up for adoption, she'd moved back to New York to bring up Jonathan. Sarah was saddened and embarrassed that it had taken cancer to reunite them.

Gloved, goggled, and sheathed by a plastic apron, the oncology nurse walked over with a tray. "These are supposed to be for patients, but I'll make an exception," she said to Sarah with a wink. "I only have grape and cherry left."

"Grape would be great, thanks." Sarah reached over and took a Popsicle in solidarity. She tore off the wrapper and took a tiny, teeth-freezing bite.

"Welcome aboard." Liz made a show of fellating her orange Popsicle, drawing dirty looks from the nun but grins from everyone else.

"You're so bad. I love it!" Sarah exclaimed, glad to see Liz hadn't lost her spirit in spite of losing so very much else.

Drawing the Popsicle from her lips with deliberate slowness, Liz shrugged thin shoulders. "Someone's got to liven up this morgue." She reached for a tissue and used it to wipe the orange stain from her mouth. "So spill it. How was he?"

Sarah hesitated. "I told you, Jonathan's fine."

Rolling her eyes, Liz leaned forward as far as the tubing would allow. "Don't pretend you don't know who I'm talking about. Cole Canning," she added in a high whisper.

Oh, crap.

She sat back. "I almost shit myself when your text came in. I want the dirt, the dirtier the better."

Darting a look around the room, Sarah resisted the urge to shush her. Thank God she'd worn her glasses! With her blond hair pulled back and next to no makeup, she looked a lot more like an elementary school teacher than an adult film star—or at least she hoped so.

But anonymous or not, she wasn't thrilled with other people, strangers, being in her business. She might be a sex machine on camera, but off it she'd always been reserved, even kind of shy. Around the room, ear buds now lay on laps. Eyes opened. Heads cocked their way. Even the Catholic sister had dropped her rosary and appeared perched on the edge of her seat. Another few inches and she'd be in danger of toppling.

"Well," Liz prompted, tapping her hospital footie.

Still Sarah hesitated. Weird though it was, she was still old-fashioned about a few things, not many but a few. One of them was that in her personal life she didn't fuck and tell. But clearly her friend wasn't going to let this one go.

"Right, sure. It . . . he was . . . good."

Liz rolled her eyes. "Good, that's all I get? C'mon, be a sister and throw me a bone. Is he like hung?"

This time Sarah didn't hold back. "Shush!"

Gaze glinting, Liz nodded. "Okay, you don't have to say a word. Just blink when I'm getting warm. Medium?"

Sarah didn't bat an eye. He was so not medium, not anything close to average.

"Large?"

Again, no blink.

"Extra large?"

This time Sarah blinked—twice.

Liz let out a whoop, drawing a scowl from the battle axe nun. She raised her tube-free hand in a high five. "Extra-extra large! Excellent!"

Sarah smiled. "I had something in my eye."

"The hell you did. Holy fucking cow, I know a lot of women and a few men who'd give an eye tooth for a night with that guy without even knowing the size of his package."

It wasn't an exaggeration. That morning while waiting for Liz to finish getting ready, Sarah had run a Google search on Cole. She'd figured him for rich, but she'd never imagined he came from one of New York's most elite families, his family's global financial services firm on par with the late Lehman Brothers. Apparently the Canning name was but a notch or two below "Cuomo" or "Kennedy." Any thought she had of weakening and calling him up for another "date" had shriveled on the spot. He was old money as well as a prominent personality on the city's social scene, the executive director of his family's charitable foundation, which focused on kids whose parents had cancer—speak of serendipity!

But what had floored her most was his war record. At the diner, his oblique reference to Hell had frightened her, but now it made perfect sense. He'd meant Iraq. Given his pedigree and connections, enlisting as a grunt during the Surge made no overt sense, but he must have had his reasons. His military occupational specialty, explosive ordnance disposal, was another surprise. Considering he still had all ten fingers, he must have been pretty fucking good. When his convoy ran afoul of a makeshift bomb planted by the insurgency, he'd run into the flames, risking his life to carry a crippled soldier to safety.

From war hero to professional schmoozer, talk about a leap! Clicking through a myriad of media clips of him at one black-tie fund-raiser after another, always with a different stunning woman as arm candy, she felt her post-coital high from that morning dip. Even if she was willing to risk the publicity, which she wasn't, a man like Cole Canning wouldn't be caught dead in public with a porn star. Fortunately he wouldn't have to risk it. The information exchange had been one-sided. She hadn't given him her phone number—or her last name.

"By the way, did he say what the 'A' stood for?" Liz's question startled her back to the present. "Don't tell me, let me guess. Awesome?" She grinned.

Guilty at having drifted, Sarah repeated, "The A?"

Liz gave her an exasperated look. "His middle initial."

"Oh, right. I didn't ask." Once they'd gotten past the standoff over the cell phone, they hadn't done much talking beyond random exclamations of pleasure. Regrettably that awesome sexual satisfaction would never see a second act.

As if reading her thoughts, Liz asked, "When are you going to see him again?"

"I'm not," Sarah said and left it at that.

Liz's smile slipped. "Why not?"

Sarah hesitated. "Last night was a onetime shot, a slice-of-life moment, nothing more. Besides, like you said, he has women lining up to fuck him."

Liz lowered her voice. "Excuse me, Miss AVN Hall of Famer, it's not like you're chopped liver." She sank back against the headrest with a sigh. "You gotta grab your bliss while you can. Believe me, if I were in your place, I'd be texting him right now to set up meet-up numero duo." She glanced down at her flattened chest, and her eyes filled. "Sorry." She swung her face away. "Chalk it up to the chemo brain— first foggy thoughts and now poor impulse control."

Heart in her throat, Sarah reached out and caught a fat teardrop on its downward roll. "Liz, honey, it's going to be okay."

"Yeah, I know, it's just . . . " Dropping her Popsicle stick onto the tray, she turned to look at Sarah. "My breasts, I really miss them, you know?"

It was all Sarah could do to swallow over the lump lining her throat. "Sweetie, I can't even imagine."

Liz reached for the box of tissues. "All those years, they were such a big part of who I was. When the script called for a brunette with big tits, I was the go-to girl. And now look at me—no tits, no hair. Shit, I don't even have eyebrows anymore."

"They'll grow back in after you finish the treatment, your hair too."

So far as Sarah knew, that was true. Over the past several weeks, she'd blown through the brochures in the waiting room and then visited every reputable medical web site she could find. By now she had the cycle of treatment, side effects, and recovery memorized. Like an adult film, the process was highly formulaic, even scripted—only cancer's script seriously sucked.

Liz paused to wipe her nose. "Yeah, I know. Too bad my boobs won't grow back, huh?"

Sarah reached out and gently squeezed her friend's shoulder, feeling sharp, knobby bone where once generous flesh had been. "Give reconstruction a shot. Plastics have advanced light years from what was possible just ten years ago. They're doing amazing things." Jesus, could she possibly sound more like an infomercial!

"I will. I mean, assuming I . . . get that far."

What she meant was if she survived. Sarah fought back the panic that came with considering the alternative. She would not cry, not when Liz was going through so much and being so brave about it all.

"You'll get there. You *will*. You're the strongest person I know." The latter wasn't only a pep talk. It was the truth.

"Yeah, I guess you're right. But if something—"

"Don't say it."

Liz reached out, gripping her hand. "Sarah, please, I have to say it, and you have to let me. I'm fighting this shit with all I've got, but we both know that might not be enough. In case it's not, in case I, you know, die, I need to ask you. Will you take Jonathan?"

Struggling against crying, Sarah said, "Oh, Liz, I—"

"Look, I know it's a lot to ask, too much, but you're the closest to a sister I've got. Even if Steve were to step up and finally be a father, he's a stranger to Jonathan. Besides, I wouldn't trust him with a cat, let alone my kid. And since my mom broke her hip last year, she's doing good to take care of herself. My Bible-thumping brother and his wife are still out in Kansas. Trust me, Jonathan would *hate* it there."

"I was going to say I'd be honored. Jonathan's a great kid."

He was. What she didn't add was that she'd always wanted to be a mom. Like so many career-minded women, she'd assumed she had plenty of time—to make her mark, to meet and marry the right guy, to start a family. Only Mr. Right had yet to show. At thirty-four closing in on thirty-five, her window for motherhood felt frighteningly finite.

Tears sparkled in Liz's eyes. "Really?"

Sarah reached out and took her other hand, the one without the IV, and gently squeezed. "Yes, really. Now no more talk about dying. Let's flag down that nurse for another round of popsicles and concentrate on getting you well."

✳✳✳ ✳✳✳

Back at his Upper West Side apartment, Cole stripped off his tuxedo and stepped inside the marble-tiled shower stall, reluctantly lathering away Sarah's scent. If only she were that easy to scour from his thoughts. Scenes from their sexy night together followed him beneath the jets of steamy water. Giving up, he jerked off, shouting Sarah's name as his release overtook him.

Toweling dry, it struck him. Why shouldn't he see her again? Not only was she hot and beautiful, smart and a smart-ass, but she obviously wasn't looking for a regular relationship, either. She was like the female . . . *him*.

Her matter-of-factness should be a relief. Instead he felt frustrated. Until now, he'd always been the one to do the post-coital pushing away. The role reversal didn't sit well with him.

Disgruntled, he pulled on sweats and padded into the large living room. Even on weekends, he was hardly ever here. When he was, he always felt at loose ends. During the two years he'd been deployed, he'd had little time to himself and virtually no privacy. His personal space had been measurable in inches, not square feet, let alone more than two thousand of them. Stripped of the regimented routine and the oddball security of living in such close quarters, he didn't feel so much free as . . . lost. Even after being back for two years, any unscheduled time weighed on him. Planning the simplest solo activities could trigger tremendous anxiety. His executive assistant might not realize it, he hoped she never did, but at times she'd literally been a lifesaver. Humbling as it was to admit, he still had a hard time being on his own. Structure was his friend, free time his enemy. Maybe he should get himself a dog, someone to walk and feed and look after on a regular basis. On second thought, God no!

Looking around, he fought down the agitation by cataloguing his more obvious options. He could go for a run or workout. Sure, he'd just gotten clean, but it's not like a second shower would melt him. He could go into the office and tackle the pile of grant proposals awaiting his approval. He could eat something. He probably should. Most of those diner carbs had been burned having hot, sweaty sex with Sarah. But though he'd been starving at her place, bothering with breakfast suddenly seemed like too big of a hassle.

Stacks of moving boxes crowded the four corners despite him having moved in six months ago. He'd lived with them for so long he scarcely saw them anymore, but out of the blue he found himself wondering what Sarah might say if she were here—a crazy thought since he never brought women home. Her loft must be one-tenth the size of his pre-war classic six, and yet everything had seemed to fit without crowding. His sister, Chloe, the feng shui enthusiast, swore he was blocking all kinds of positive chi with his clutter. He didn't know about that, but suddenly he wanted the boxes gone, done, out of there. Juiced to get going, he grabbed a pair of scissors from a kitchen drawer and started in.

Hacking through cardboard and packing tape, he felt as though he were unearthing the contents of a time capsule. So that was where his blue cashmere cardigan was, good to know. He came across the medal case holding his Silver Star and tossed it back inside. "For Gallantry in Action." Ha! Running through an explosion he should have seen coming to salvage what was left of his team had been a case of too little, too late. The Army might have honored him with a medal, but minus both legs, Sam had spat in his face. Cole hadn't blamed him, not then and certainly not now.

His thoughts circled back to Sarah. Since Iraq whatever allure a woman held for him dissipated once he'd had her, but with her their night together had only whetted his appetite for more—much more. Thinking of all the things he still wanted to do with her, he felt himself firming yet again—and seriously considering seeing her a second time.

Hours flew by. He looked up and realized he'd winnowed the towers down to a final few boxes. The next to last held his old porn DVDs. God, he'd all but forgotten he had this stuff. Like the cigarettes, the adult films had gotten him and his buddies through the tedium and stress of being bunkered. Though he didn't need the movies now, he also wasn't sure what to do with them. It's not like he could drop them off at the Salvation Army or Goodwill. Should he toss them down the trash chute or maybe leave out the box with a note, Free to Good Home? For old time's sake, he shuffled through the box covers, thinking maybe he'd hold onto a few of his favorites as mementos—or a backup plan in case the city saw a mass exodus of cocktail hostesses and bottle girls. Without exception, all his videos starred the actress known as Sugar. Once he'd seen his first film of hers, there was no need to explore further. He'd been hooked. Whether playing the innocent ingénue or the worldly whip-cracking dominatrix, she could sell it like no other porn diva. He took out one of his favorites, *Whipped and Creamed.* The DVD case pictured a whip-wielding Sugar, her gorgeous body flanked in skimpy black-leather bondage wear, her blond hair flowing about her slender shoulders, her gaze intense as she appeared poised to crack the flogger over a pair of bare male buttocks. But as always, it was her face that got him—the curve of her cheek, the lushness of her lips, and the intensity glowing from her emerald-colored eyes, ever so slightly upswept at the corners.

Emerald-colored eyes just like the ones he'd spent most of that morning gazing into!

No wonder Sarah had seemed so familiar. Either she was Sugar, the internationally famous porn star, or her doppelganger. The decade in LA, her paranoia about his cell phone, and, weirdest of all, her freezing up instead of calling 911, all pointed to the former. She hadn't wanted to report the mugging, because involving the police would almost certainly have meant leaking her presence in New York to the press.

Once he got over the shock, he realized he'd just struck the equivalent of sexual pay dirt. Who better to explore his kinky fantasies with than a porn star? Unlike the other women he'd been with since his homecoming, Sarah wasn't going to cling. She wasn't going to pressure him to make promises. She wasn't going to beg and plead, threaten and cajole him into committing to a future, because she didn't want a relationship any more than he did.

Resting back on his heels, Cole decided. He wasn't yet done with Sarah—Sugar—not nearly. Now that he knew the previous night was only a taste of the sexual buffet to be had, he was determined to sample each and every spicy, hot dish.

✳✳✳ ✳✳✳

Drained from her day at the hospital, Sarah also felt guilty about all the times her thoughts had drifted to Cole, her mind ablaze with hot scenes recalled from the previous incredible night. He had amazing cock control, serious stamina. Given how long he'd gone down on her in the kitchen, she hadn't expected him to last beyond the blow job. The deep throating she'd added at the end would have sent more than a few professional actors over the edge but not Cole.

Even once he'd penetrated her, he'd managed to take them to the edge and then pull back again and again. By the time he'd finally let himself pop, the sky outside her window was lightening. She hadn't intended for him to stay, let alone to fall asleep in his arms. Both had just . . . happened. Though she wasn't usually much for cuddling, curling up beside him had felt . . . right, as well as really good.

Above all, Liz being so sick drove home what a mistake it was to live for "someday." The present was all anyone had. If Sarah had doubted that before, seeing her friend hooked up to that chemo pump had convinced her.

Unfortunately given what she'd discovered about Cole's pedigree and position, their one night would have to last her. Mulling over those morose thoughts, she'd got Liz settled back home, grabbed some groceries, and walked back to her apartment on Elizabeth Street. She'd chosen the fifth floor loft in a converted turn-of-the-century brownstone primarily for its proximity to Liz's, about a five minutes' walk, and because she'd been able to sublet it for six months instead of the usual year. Six hundred and fifty square feet was *a lot* less space than she was used to, but high ceilings and period details made it seem roomier. Beyond the practical considerations, she just really liked the funky, artsy vibe of Soho. After a decade in LA, she appreciated how easy it was to walk almost anywhere rather than being in a car stuck in grid-lock. On her block alone, there were numerous art galleries, boutiques, and cafes, most of which she'd yet to explore.

Approaching, she spotted an athletically built, dark-haired man sitting on her top step, head downturned and muscular arms extended forward in a stretch. Sarah tensed. He was too well dressed to be a deliveryman even if he hadn't been empty handed, and she didn't think he was one of her neighbors. Was it possible he was a reporter? Even though she'd held off from calling in the previous evening's mugging, any number of bystanders might have snapped her photo. She hadn't noticed anything unusual on her Twitter traffic, but still. Slowing her stride, she took several seconds before registering that the waiting man was Cole.

Relieved, she drew up at the base of the steps. If possible, her sexy rescuer looked even better in daylight. Today's ensemble was a collar-less T-shirt, Diesel jeans, and sandals. She'd never thought of herself as having a fetish for feet, and yet the sight of his long, slender toes struck her as unbelievably erotic.

Lifting his head, he unfolded his long body and stood. "I'm not stalking you if that's what you're thinking."

The joke struck a chord of genuine alarm. "That's not funny."

"Sorry," he said, walking down to meet her. "I just want to talk to you."

She crossed her arms across her chest, a shield against her heart's wild pumping. "So talk."

Joining her on the sidewalk, he gestured to the building at his back. "Can I come in for a few minutes? I won't stay long—unless you ask me to."

As much as she hated to concede it, his in-your-face confidence was totally justified. The night before, he'd been amazing, a fucking machine. But if she were honest with herself, it was the frequent flashes of tenderness that had really gotten to her, as much or more than the size of his cock and the fact that he really, *really* knew how to use it.

"Ha, dream on!" She might already be moist at the sight of him— she *was* moist, but he didn't need to know that.

"You know, you don't always have to be such a hard ass." Before she registered what he was doing, he'd commandeered the grocery bags and started back up.

Left with no choice, she followed. The elevator was a relic of a bygone era, a European-style lift barely big enough for two, originally installed for an earlier wheelchair-bound owner when the house was still a single family residence and not subdivided into apartments. Fortunately it was working today. They pulled back the caged door, stepped inside, and rode up to the fifth floor in silence.

Inside her place, he set the groceries on her counter. Thinking about what had gone down there last night, Sarah whisked inside the kitchen and began putting away the perishables.

He waited for her to finish before starting in, "About last night—"

Sarah shoved the bag of broccoli into the bin. "We fucked, end of story." She slammed the refrigerator door and straightened.

His blue eyes glinted. Sarah had the disconcerting sense that he wasn't only mentally undressing her but seeing through to her soul. "It doesn't have to be the end. There could be another chapter—or two." One corner of his mouth kicked up.

Thinking about how good it would feel to slap his smile away, she rested her fisted hands on her hips to keep him from seeing their shaking. "Really? And how do you figure that? You see, I know who you are or rather what you are?"

For a few seconds, his handsome face registered shock. Recovering, he asked, "Yeah, what am I?"

Jesus, did they really have to have this conversation? "A blue-blood, old money. Growing up, you probably spent every summer in the Hamptons."

He shrugged. "Most of 'em, why? You got something against the beach?"

She ignored him. "Oh, and a war hero, we can't forget that."

The scoffing comment sent his face freezing. Obviously she'd struck a nerve, a major one. Even though the counter stood between them, instinct sent Sarah backing up.

"You can cut the hero crap," he hissed, his fierceness confirming she hadn't only crossed a line but vaulted over it. "I did my job, I served my country to the best of my ability, and then I came home—in one piece. You want to talk to a real hero, go see my former teammate, Sam, at Walter Reed in DC. He doesn't have legs anymore, but he's learning to get around on prosthetics. Bionic stilts, he calls them. He kinda moves like R2D2, but on the bonus side, I guess he doesn't have to worry about blisters."

The self-loathing lacing his tone took her aback. Yet again it hit her there might be more to Cole Canning than the privileged party boy she'd first met in the bodega. It wasn't only his buddy, Sam, who'd been wounded. Cole's big, beautiful body might be unscathed, but he obviously bore deep emotional scars.

"Sorry, I didn't mean to—"

Sarah never had the chance to finish. "Save it, Sherlock." Cole's eyes burned into hers. "Because I know who—what—you are too. Or do you prefer I use your professional name . . . *Sugar*?"

Chapter Four

He *knew*! Panic seized Sarah. Had he outed her online? Last night she'd taken his phone, but that didn't mean he couldn't have sent a Tweet or posted a status update on Facebook once he'd gotten it back that morning. New York entertainment reporters were pussies compared to LA paparazzi, but if they knew she was in the city, it wouldn't take them long to track down her rental and stake out the building. For all she knew, someone was on it already.

"You son-of-a-bitch."

Cole smiled. Obviously savoring having the upper hand, he picked up an apple from the counter and tore off a big bite. Mouth full, he went on, "I'm your biggest fan, or at least one of them. Last night I knew I'd seen you somewhere before, but I couldn't place where. It was like we'd met, and yet we hadn't. I was going through some stuff in my apartment, and I came across a box of DVDs—your movies. I would have brought a couple so you could autograph the boxes but knowing how prickly you can be, I didn't want to presume."

Sarah rested a fisted hand on either hip. "What are you going to do?"

A lifting of black brows greeted her question. Chewing, he took his sweet time in answering, "Well, I'm not going to TMZ if that's what you're worried about. Given you obviously Googled me, you must know I don't need the money or the media attention."

As a Canning living in New York, he would have an abundance of both. It didn't hurt that he was young and hot and heralded as a hero. Still, sometimes people did crazy, illogical things for no apparent reason, and Sarah's safety was at stake. Tipping off the media meant tipping off her stalker as well. Even a casual comment made in passing could bring heavy consequences. If he'd talked, or worse bragged, about sleeping with her, she needed to know.

Pointedly she demanded, "Have you told *anyone*?"

Biting off more of the fruit, he shrugged. "The only person I've talked to since I last saw you is Carlos . . . my doorman. We exchanged *opinions* on the Yankees versus the Red Sox—he's from Boston—but that's about it." Swallowing, he added, "What makes you so sure I'm going to out you?"

She was the world's highest-paid porn star, as well as the only female actor in her industry to launch her own production company. Did he really imagine she'd gotten to that level by being dim? "I dunno, let me think. Bragging rights?"

Tossing the apple core into the can, he looked at her askance. "Do I seem like a guy who needs to come up with shit to brag about?"

He had her there. "No," she admitted.

Even though she'd met Cole fewer than twenty-four hours ago, he struck her as a lone wolf, not a pack animal. Last night he'd been out by himself. He'd just admitted he'd been on his own again today. More to the point, he couldn't out her without outing himself. Considering his social standing and position in the philanthropic community, sleeping with a porn star would be seriously bad press.

But the problem of Cole Canning remained and not only because he was once again inside her apartment. She couldn't undo meeting him, even if she wanted to—and to be honest she wouldn't want to.

More than just sex, their night together stood as a powerful symbol of reclaiming her sexuality, her body, as hers alone. Maybe there was a way to turn the situation into a win-win. She was a former porn star living incognito and looking for a partner she could trust to pleasure her privately and discreetly. Cole was a rich guy with a sexual appetite to match hers and a similar desire for discretion. Based on the previous night, they were compatible—okay, incredible—together in bed. As long as they stuck to their mutually agreed upon rule of no-strings-attached sex, there was no reason the situation couldn't work brilliantly for them both.

Suddenly ravenous, Sarah tore off a stalk of celery from the bunch and bit in, the briny juice squirting into her mouth. The salty taste reminded her vaguely of Cole. Assuming he stuck around for a while, she looked forward to having him come in her mouth on occasion.

Imagining his spray striking the back of her throat, she swallowed—hard. "I have a proposition for you?"

The glint in his eye was back, as was the boner pressing against his pants. "A proposition, huh? I like the sound of that."

Swallowing, she said, "Hadn't you better wait until you hear it?"

"Okay, let's have it."

"You can walk away now, and we never see each other again, or you can stick around for a sex-only relationship strictly behind-the-scenes."

A black brow lifted. "Are we talking exclusivity?"

Sarah hesitated, mulling that over. "For safety's sake, that would probably be best—but only for the time we're together. Once one or both of us gets bored, we go our separate ways, no drama, no hurt feelings."

"What kind of sex are we talking about? All the flavors?"

She nodded, feeling her panties dampen. "The whole freezer case, provided whatever we do is safe, consensual, and discussed in advance. Oh, and we both need to get tested."

By law Sarah had had to be screened monthly for HIV and other STDs in order to have on-camera sex. That along with the passage of Los Angeles County's Measure B mandating condom use on all porn-film sets made her a much safer bet than the socialites, bottle girls, and barflies a guy like Cole ordinarily hit on. If anyone had taken a risk last night, it was her.

His face registered astonishment. "Let me get this straight, you want *me* to get an HIV test?" He thumped a hand to his chest.

Sarah nodded. Sucking him off sans protection the night before hadn't been her most brilliant move, but there was no point in beating herself up about it—or in continuing to be careless. "Unless you've been living like a monk before last night, which I seriously doubt, then yes. Besides, once you have the results, unless you also start sleeping with someone else, you can deep-six the condoms. I'm on the pill."

As she'd anticipated, the condom-free sex sold it. He nodded. "Fair enough, I'll make an appointment and go first thing on Monday."

Could it really be this easy? All the angst people went through over relationships, the online dating sites, the endless search for that perfect someone that might or might not exist. Had she and Cole just reduced all the heartache and hassle to a straightforward contractual arrangement?

"Great, I will, too," Sarah said. Having polished off the celery, she wiped her hands on a towel.

Cole hesitated. "I'd like to suggest a . . . modification."

Sarah went into instant alert mode. Damn, she'd known it was too good to be true. In her experience, conditions meant caveats, and for the person on the receiving end, they never meant much good.

Bracing herself for a deal buster, she asked, "Really, and what's that?"

"We act out the scripts from your films, one boy-girl scene per film."

Sarah relaxed her shoulders, the rest of her body following. His suggestion held enormous appeal. No one, not even Liz, knew it, but she'd never come on camera. It had all been acting. Having Cole as her friend with benefits would be a golden opportunity to revisit—and reclaim—each filmed scenario, this time purely for pleasure—hers.

"You do realize I've done a hundred films?"

A smart-ass smile broke over his face. "In that case, consider it a career retrospective."

"Even if we met every night, it would take more than three months to go through all the roles."

He shrugged. "I have some time. Any thoughts on where you'd like to start?"

It was Sarah's turn to smile. "We start by having dinner."

✳✳✳ ✳✳✳

"I can't believe you cook," Cole said, following her over to the stove, a stupid statement since she was doing exactly that and with a fair level of expertise from what he could see. The way she took command of her closet-sized kitchen, marshalling her un-matched pots and pans and random cutlery, reminded him of Rachel Ray.

Turned away to puree the tomatoes she'd just finished peeling, Sarah answered with a shimmy of slender shoulders, a subtle movement that wreaked havoc with his reason—and his erection. The latter had throbbed to life more or less the moment he'd crossed her threshold. Her simple white cotton T-shirt, skinny jeans, and flat sandals turned him on far more than the couture his usual "dates" draped themselves in.

"Porn stars have to eat just like everyone else, besides I'm part Italian. This spaghetti sauce is my grandmother's recipe," she added, turning away to stir the pot and inadvertently giving him a full-on view of her sexy, spankable backside—or maybe not so inadvertently. Considering her background, had she maybe planned it?

The prospect pissed him off. Growing up under the rule of a manipulative mother—his made Margaret Thatcher seem like a cuddle bear—that a woman might be playing him made him all kinds of crazy, especially *this* woman.

He resolved to keep his gaze high and his hard-on in check, at least until they'd finished with the formality of the meal. "Right, keep up your strength."

She dropped the wooden spoon. "Son of a bitch!" Whirling, she reached out and punched him in the arm—hard.

"What was that about?"

Pretending to be hurt, he made a show of rubbing the sore spot. What he really wanted to fondle stood squarely in front of him, a petite, bristling blonde whose proud, perfect breasts, he knew from last night, fitted his palms like she'd been fashioned for him.

"Consider it a reminder," she shot back, her beautiful eyes aiming arrows. "Better yet, a warning."

"Of?" he asked, beginning to enjoy their cat-and-mouse game, wondering if tonight's play would lead them to bed before dinner rather than after. As amazing as her grandmother's secret recipe smelled and probably tasted, it wasn't food that would satisfy him.

She didn't back down, not that he'd expected her to. "A warning not to be an asshole," she answered. Her steely gaze and lifted chin reminded him that he wasn't the only one of them invested in keeping their "relationship" as strictly sex only. "Just because we're fucking just for fun doesn't mean you have a Get out of Jail Free card to treat me like shit. So, let's be sure to keep the 'buddy' in fuck buddy, okay?"

She stretched out her hand. Small and slender, the medium-length nails painted with clear polish, it could as easily have belonged to an elementary school teacher as it did to her—a world famous porn star.

He reached out and wrapped his own, much larger hand around her fragile wrist. Feeling her pulse hammering beneath the pad of his thumb, Cole found his smile. She might try playing things all badass and cool, but the truth was she wanted him as much as he did her. Before the night was through, she was going to get him—all of him.

"You've got yourself a deal."

In one clean, swift, calculated movement, Cole jerked her toward him, crushing her body to his.

✳✳✳ ✳✳✳

It was a good thing Grandma Campanelli's sauce called for several hours of simmering. Sarah and Cole's first scripted encounter proved to be even more intense than the previous night. Rested and unrushed, they took their time easing into their first reenacted movie scene.

Straddling him on the sheet-covered couch, Sarah asked, "Coach Runk, must I?"

Loosely based on the seventies classic *Debbie Does Dallas, Cheerleaders in Love* wasn't exactly an epic piece of film making. The dialogue was on the silly side, but the simulated power exchange between the sexy, older football coach and her character, Nicole, the virginal captain of the cheerleading squad, was a favorite with diehard fans. Acting it with Cole sans film crew felt more exciting and . . . real than Sarah would have imagined. Unfortunately she hadn't had any pom-poms lying about. A pullover sweater, pleated white tennis skirt, and side ponytails tied with red ribbon were her improvised cheerleading costume. The loveseat in her living room served as the sofa in the coach's office.

Sitting on its edge, his dampened hair combed back from his forehead, Cole stared up at her. "I'm a busy man, Nicole. I have a football team to coach. Do you want to go to Paris with your class in the fall or don't you?" His tone struck just the right chord of sexy severity.

"Oh, I do," Sarah simpered, slipping more deeply into her role. She'd always gotten off on kneeling, and the couch burn on her already bruised knees only seasoned her excitement. "It's just . . . I'm going steady with Matt. He gave me his varsity jacket to wear, and I don't know if it would be right—"

"Do you want to earn this or not?"

A folded fifty materialized between his index and forefinger. Holding it out, he tempted her with the money—and his smoldering stare.

She nodded solemnly. "I do. I want . . . to see Paris so badly."

He brought the Benjamin higher, just beyond her reach. "Then stop stalling and show me your breasts."

"O-okay." Descending deeper into the fantasy, she felt her mouth trembling as though she really was Nicole, about to relinquish her purity for the possibility of Paris.

Recalling her first time seeing the Eiffel Tower and strolling along the Seine, Sarah couldn't blame her. A stunning, magical city, Paris existed for lovers. She'd bought her first, and so far, only overseas property on its Left Bank, a balconied pied-à-terre in Saint-Germain-des-Prés, with the thought that it would make a great honeymoon hideaway. She'd taken Danny there a time or two, but the short trips had been far from fairytale. She'd promised herself that her next visit would be with a man she truly loved who loved her back.

The wistful thought fueled "Nicole's" heavy sigh. She snagged the hem of her sweater and slowly lifted it, pulling it over her head and off. She wore nothing beneath—that was the point. Dropping the garment to the floor, she looked back at Cole. Though he'd lavished her breasts with plenty of attention last night, this was the first time "Coach Runk" was seeing them. The intensity of his stare brought Sarah budding.

His broad chest rose and fell sharply, as if breathing had become an effort rather than an automatic response. "Very pretty." His hand holding the money hovered between them. The other fisted at his side.

Sarah drew back, allowing him to look his fill. When he was ready, he reached for her. Slowly, very slowly, he dragged the edge of the folded bill across her left nipple. It was new money, the paper crisp and fresh-smelling, as though recently minted. It scraped across her sensitive skin, back and forth, side to side, circles, soft and slow, hard and fast, again and again. It was Sarah's turn to struggle with breath. The small room suddenly felt very warm—burning. Bracketed by her thighs, Cole's jeans-clad hips shifted. A massive erection tented his pants, shoving against his zipper. Another flick, this time over her right nipple, tore a sob from her throat. Moisture dampened her panties. A strumming ache settled low in her loins. How was it possible to be this turned on this soon?

During the filming, the byplay with the bill had done nothing for her, the chafing mostly annoying, even uncomfortable. But with Cole as Coach Runk, suddenly Sarah saw what her younger actor self had missed. After all these years, she got it. Nicole didn't only want to go to Paris. She wanted to go with the knowledge that she'd afforded the trip by prostituting herself to the sexy, worldly coach, first by stripping and then by selling him various favors for which he had to explicitly ask—and pay. Cole's character might hold the money, but Sarah's cheerleader held all the cards. The moment she'd taken off her top, she was the one with the power.

Owning it, she cinched her thighs tighter around him. The short, pleated skirt bunched at her waist, exposing damp thighs and a glimpse of her panties. Locking her gaze on Cole's, she took the folded money—and slipped it inside the front of the thong.

Cole swallowed—hard. He dragged his gaze up to hers, his eyes fevered. "Fuck yourself for me. Fuck yourself *on* me." Despite the command, his voice came out ragged.

Sarah didn't hesitate and not only because it was in the script. Scarcely able to wait, she rose up, shifting position to ride his leg.

Seating herself over his erection, she anchored her hands to the shelf of his shoulders. He shoved the skirt up to her waist and locked his hands on her hips. Heart racing, Sarah looked down. The thong she wore was a whisper of silk, the see-through crotch slit for easy access, the beaded strip bisecting her buttocks, grazing her anus. As if reading her mind, Cole reached behind her, slipping his fingers beneath the beads. A sharp tug sent her bucking, the metal biting into her ass, a thrill thrumming through her.

"Ride me," he hissed. Bringing his face close to hers, he stroked slow rings around the puckered flesh, which like her pussy pulsed and pounded.

Sarah didn't need to be told twice. She began moving against him, back and forth, again and again, faster and harder, scraping her labia and clit across the coarse denim. Trapped within it, Cole groaned. He lifted against her, his swollen mound brick hard beneath her. Sarah ground against him, her stiffness from the previous night's push as good as forgotten.

Perspiration filmed the backs of her knees. A trickle of sweat slid between her breasts. Still, she kept on, going until she swore she would explode. Before that happened, she stilled. The script next called for mutual masturbation, and she didn't plan to cheat the scene—or Cole.

She eased back, just far enough so that he could reach between them and unzip his fly. He did, taking himself out and wrapping a hand around. His cock looked huge and engorged, the tip glistening as though he'd come close to leaking. Maybe he had. His musk filled Sarah's senses. A bead of moisture slid free from his slit, trickling down the side. Remembering his taste and texture from the previous night, Sarah's mouth watered, making it a battle not to bend her head and taste him.

Instead she stuck to the script and covered herself with her hand. Though she masturbated regularly, it had been a while since she'd pleasured herself in front of a partner. The novelty of doing so lent relish to the act. Leaving behind worldly Sugar and embracing neophyte Nicole, Sarah trailed her fingers along the opening, testing the sensitized flesh as if for the first time.

Mirroring her, Cole slid his hand up and down his shaft, the rhythmic stroking reminding Sarah of how expertly he'd worked himself inside her the night before. Her gaze riveted on his, not because the stage direction called for her to do so but because she couldn't bring herself to look away. Cole's ocean-blue irises were like sinkholes, sucking her in, separating her from her mind, allowing her to occupy her body completely.

She entered herself, sliding three hard fingers inside and burying them to the hilt. Her body welcomed the invasion. Though she'd yet to stimulate herself there, her clit hitched. Cream blessed her fingers, leaked onto Cole's jeans' leg. Her scent rose up, a peaty perfume that had him licking his lips. Aroused by him watching and equally focused on him, she moved back and forth and side to side, seeking to strike the perfect angle.

The finger fucking felt like it went on forever, only unlike the actual filming, Sarah didn't tense. She didn't need to call for lube. She didn't hold her breath, silently counting down the minutes until the director called "Cut!" Slippery and scalding, she hovered on the cusp of climax, too caught up in Cole to be in any rush to reach it.

He was close, though, she could tell. Taking in the tensing of his muscles, the feral gleam in his eyes, she girded herself to go over the edge with him. His hand tightened about his cock, spanning its length and breadth, beating it ever harder in his quest for release. Sarah followed, increasing her pace, her pressure, her boldness. She withdrew her fingers and found her clit. Working her wet finger around it, she focused on Cole. Tossing back his head, he flicked his thumb over his cockhead, once, twice, thrice.

He jerked back with a groan, then came, a perfect arc of rich warm cream striking Sarah on the breasts, belly, and thighs. Caught up in his release, she felt herself carried along. The buzzing against her hand was but a beginning. Spasms rocked her. Golden warmth filled her. Tingling took possession not only of her pussy but her whole being. She knocked back her head and cried out, not a scream so much as a prayerful keening.

Cole's hand spanned her waist, pinning her to him. Secured to his safety, Sara submitted, riding out each strike of the storm, her body quaking. The last convulsive contraction ebbed, leaving an exhausted well-being in its wake. Spent, she sagged against him, her arms and legs shaking. Cole hauled her across his lap. Heedless of the mess they'd made, Sarah fell back against him. Resting her head against his chest, she closed her eyes, content for the moment to listen to their commingled breathing.

Cole was the first to recover. "So, Sarah, do you still want to go to Paris?"

Lost in sensation, at first she wasn't sure she hadn't misheard. Unpeeling herself from the stickiness binding them, she lifted her head to look at him. "Nicole," she said, noting the flush climbing his throat.

"Right, sorry—Nicole. Do you uh . . . still want to go to Paris?"

Suddenly in her mind's eye she didn't only see herself walking along the Seine. She saw herself walking the riverbank hand-in-hand with Cole. Determined to dislodge the unbidden image from her mind, she found her voice—and her smile. "Yes, Coach, I do. But before I go anywhere, what I really want is a shower."

❋❋❋ ❋❋❋

CONGRATS TO @SUGAR ON #100. WHERE R U GIRL? PARTY W/ME. #MIA #CAMERASUTRA

@SUGAR, SAW #CAMERASUTRA. CONGRATS ON ANOTHER MOST EXCELLENT ADVENTURE.

LA MISSES YOU @SUGAR. WHEN R U COMING (HE HE) BACK TO US?

STAY STRONG @SUGAR & REMEMBER THE STEPS. YOU *WILL* BEAT THIS! #TWELVESTEPS #RECOVERY #ADDICTION

Monday morning saw Sarah sipping coffee at her kitchen counter and skimming messages from her many fans on Twitter. That she was in rehab for substance abuse was a popular theory, but there was plenty of other misinformation being bandied about. She was pregnant. *If only!* She'd been in a bad car accident and was undergoing extensive plastic surgery. *Soap opera-ish but still scary.* She'd run off to marry her latest costar. *Marc was a nice guy but given his breath, not so much.* The absurdity of the assumptions had her shaking her head—and occasionally laughing out loud. Fortunately, appreciating the well wishers and disregarding the douches was second nature by now. When you were a public figure, it was the only way to keep your perspective—and sanity.

Since leaving LA, she hadn't responded to any of the messages, naughty, nice, or otherwise. She didn't plan to. Even with her location setting turned off, a savvy reporter sniffing around her social media might still track her. There were too many ways to unwittingly disclose your whereabouts. Mentioning a product specific to a certain area, a film or play that had a limited regional run, or a meal in a restaurant that wasn't part of a national chain were all potential giveaways. Why chance it? Besides, she'd slated today for writing—not 140-character snippets but actual pages.

She'd started journaling not long after she moved out west and now the nondescript blue binder was filled with entries spanning the past ten years. Writing down her experiences and, more importantly, her feelings about them had started out as a sort of self therapy. Over the past few months, though, she'd begun to wonder if maybe the material in her journal might have the potential for a book, not a sleazy tell-all but more a chronicle of a woman's very personal journey—hers. With the release of her hundredth film and retirement from the industry, she finally had the time and hopefully the perspective to test if that was true. Transcribing her hand-written entries into an electronic file was a time-consuming task, but it was nothing compared to structuring her sometimes stream-of-consciousness passages. She felt as though she were being introduced to her younger self. Her handwriting wasn't the only thing that had changed. In the process of becoming Sugar, she'd grown up.

She was on her third cup of coffee and deep into editing a particularly tangled paragraph when her cell sounded. It was Liz. She grabbed for it, feeling the now-familiar jolt of anxiety. "Is everything okay?"

From her periodic check-in calls, she knew that unlike hers Liz's weekend had not been awesome. It had involved intermittent throwing up as well as extreme tiredness, all side effects of the chemo.

Liz quickly reassured her. "Totally, in fact I'm feeling so much better I'm going to walk Jonathan to the bus stop myself. I thought I'd save you a trip in case you have, you know . . . company."

She meant Cole of course. Once Sarah had relaxed about him knowing her as Sugar, it had been a pretty amazing weekend. With the terms of their arrangement nailed down, she could chill out and enjoy him for what he was—her personal, in-house fucking machine. By mutual assent, he'd left shortly before midnight. Neither of them wanted to make his sleeping over a habit. Lovers stayed over. Fuck friends went to their own homes.

Her gaze flickered back to the laptop screen. "Okay, if you're sure."

Liz hesitated. "I also wanted to remind you about tonight. You're coming, right?"

Begun by Liz before she'd been diagnosed, Adult FATE—Faith, Acceptance, Trust, and Enlightenment—was an informal meet-up for former adult entertainers who'd left the industry but still sometimes struggled with matriculating into mainstream life. A onetime English

Lit major, Liz had loosely based the title on the Three Fates of Greek mythology, only instead of spinning the destinies of strangers, her idea was for members to empower themselves and each other to break free of the past and "write" their new life stories. The weekly coffee klatch, not a trio but a quartet, met from six to eight PM every Monday at Liz's. Sarah thought back to the previous week's meeting, her first. Even though Liz had introduced her as "my friend, Sarah, from LA," everyone had done an immediate double take.

Peter, by far the most extroverted, gushed, "OMG, am I really standing in the same room with Sugar! *The* Sugar! I will never wash this hand again!"

"Cool!" exclaimed Brian, whom in the course of the night she'd come to think of as One Word Brian because of his propensity for single-worded responses.

A retro-styled brunette, Honey had regarded Sarah with earnest brown eyes. "The way you bypassed the male establishment and set up your own production company is inspiring. All the films produced under Wing Star are so beautifully shot."

"Thank you, that means a lot," Sarah had said sincerely. The FATEs weren't just random fans. They were her people.

But signing up for a support group didn't exactly jive with flying under the radar. If Liz knew about the stalking situation in LA, she wouldn't have pressed her to join, Sarah was certain of it. It was her fault for not speaking up. But she'd figured her friend had enough on her plate without adding another worry. Besides, that issue belonged to the life she'd left behind. At least she hoped so.

"Are you sure you're up for it?" As she'd seen firsthand, Liz often started out strong in the mornings but faded fast.

Liz answered with a brittle laugh. "I'm not sure of much these days but I know this: Right now Jonathan, FATE, and you are holding me together."

That decided her. "Of course I'll come."

✳✳✳ ✳✳✳

"Sarah, you came!" Jonathan abandoned his iPad and launched himself at her, his skinny arms wrapping around her legs.

Sarah squatted down to return the hug. Closing her eyes, she inhaled his little-boy scent. Kids, she wanted them so badly. One of each, a boy and a girl, would be so great, but at this point she wouldn't be picky. Lately she'd begun to ask herself if she'd ever get to be a mother at all.

Tamping down that bleak thought, she answered, "Of course I came. You don't get rid of me that easily."

"Jonathan isn't crazy about being sequestered in his room," Liz explained, walking out from the kitchen. "I've explained these meet-ups are for grownups, which of course only makes him want to hang out with us more."

Might this be her out? "I don't mind hanging out with Jonathan in his room while you have the meeting."

Liz slanted a knowing look in her direction. "Nice try, but I've arranged for Jonathan to go downstairs to Mrs. Ritter. She spoils him more than his actual grandmother, plus she's got cats. You'd think the ten bucks I give her was the Lotto jackpot, so it's win-win for everybody."

So much for easy outs! Straightening, Sarah said, "Okay, I'll walk him down, that is if you'll show me the way, kid?" Jonathan was already barreling toward the door. "C'mon, Sarah!"

"Don't forget to give her this." Liz took a ten out of her purse and handed it over.

Mrs. Ritters' cats, one calico and the other part-Persian, were exceedingly good natured as well as geriatric. The moment the apartment door opened, Jonathan was absorbed in fur and tinkling toys.

Satisfied that he had a happy two hours ahead, Sarah handed over the money and went back upstairs.

Stepping off the elevator into the hallway, she saw that Liz's apartment door was ajar. Judging from the high-volume chatter filtering out into the hallway, FATE was in full force. Entering, she confirmed that everyone had arrived. Congregated in the small living room, gabbing over mugs of coffee and assorted cookies, they looked like any meet-up group might. Liz moved about carrying her coffee pot, topping off cups and pausing to compliment a new scarf or to ask after a boyfriend. Seeing her friend so smiling and at ease, Sarah was glad she'd set aside her reservations and come.

Liz beckoned her over. Addressing the room at large, she said, "Now that Sarah's back, let's get started."

Watching Liz in action as the informal discussion leader, Sarah privately considered that her friend had missed her true calling: counseling. Then again, given the fluid job market, it was never too late for a second or even a third career. She made a mental note to mention that thought once Liz came through her treatments—once not *if.*

"Hey, gorgeous, come join the party," Peter called out, waiving her over with a half eaten Oreo.

A gay, fortyish former prostitute now working as a window dresser for Ralph Lauren, Peter was of medium height and build, with shoulder-length, dark-blond hair, mischievous blue eyes, and a spa tan worthy of Southern California. He and Sarah had hit it off from her first session.

His polar opposite was Brian, a former videographer for a once popular lesbian porn site. Second to watching women fuck, Brian loved cars. These days he worked as a mechanic at one of the West Side garages. Single-word responses—thanks, cool, great, okay, hi, and bye—comprised his social vocabulary. Wiry and dark, he sat quietly with his hands laced around a coffee mug, his lean body tilted forward, as if listening avidly. No one ever pressed him for more. FATE was first and foremost about feeling safe, and for those who'd been involved in AE, feeling safe meant not feeling judged.

"Lovely to see you again, Sarah," said Honey, looking over her shoulder from her perch on Liz's salvaged, orange-striped sofa.

"You too, Honey." She poured herself a coffee and settled into the circa 1950 lounger covered in faded floral fabric. "Great suit," she added, gesturing to the other woman's smart, hot-pink silk ensemble. "Is it vintage?"

"Vintage Chanel," Honey admitted with obvious pride, smoothing a gloved hand over the tight pencil skirt.

The twenty-something brunette bore more than a passing resemblance to the late Audrey Hepburn, an image she cultivated with chic, short bangs and piled-high hair, liquid-black eyeliner, and a carefully modulated accent that bordered on British. Sarah seriously doubted Honey was her real name anymore than Sugar was hers. Then again, in an age where celebrities were known to christen their kids after fruit—Apple, seriously!—she couldn't one hundred percent say. Like her screen idol, Honey was reed slender with big brown eyes, a pert nose, and a pearlescent complexion. Her standout feature was her "upside down" mouth, the top lip extending beyond the bottom. It was a mouth made for cock sucking, to put it crudely, which would have given Honey a definite edge in her former profession as an escort to hedge fund managers and visiting Saudi sheiks. Boat-neck dresses, broad-brimmed hats banded with bows, and elbow-length gloves were her fashion staples. Sarah wasn't buying that she'd left the life, at least not entirely. That Hermes scarf wasn't bought on a stylist's salary.

Settling onto the sofa, Liz called them all to order. "Sarah, you went last the other week, so why don't you get us started tonight. Anything you want to bring up or get input on?"

Sarah hesitated. As nice as she found the FATE folks to be, she wasn't a group person. She might be a former porn actress, but in her off-camera life she'd always been more of an introvert.

"No, I think I'm good," she said quickly, perhaps too quickly.

"Are you sure?" Helping himself to another cookie, Peter asked, "After last week, I feel like you know so much about us, but we still don't know anything about you apart from the screen legend."

Wow, a legend! Hearing herself so described had her feeling really flattered and kind of old. Sarah took a sip of coffee. Above the cup's rim, she sent Liz what they'd used to call their SOS Look.

Catching the signal, Liz said, "Pete, Sarah can share when she's ready—or not. We don't judge here, and we don't push."

Chastened, he nodded. "Sorry, Sarah, I get carried away sometimes."

Feeling like a jerk, Sarah shook her head. "No, that's okay, and you're right. If I'm going to be here, I should participate. So, here goes . . . " Sending her gaze around the small sitting area, she said, "Hi again everyone. You all know me as Sugar, but my real name is Sarah, Sarah Halliday. I grew up in Brooklyn Heights long before it was the trendy hot 'hood it is today. Even though I'm part Italian and Irish, I'm an only child—crazy, I know."

"My boyfriend, Pol's from Dublin," Peter broke in with a grin.

Sarah acknowledged the commonality with a nod. "That's cool. My father's people were from Belfast, my mom's family is from Sicily."

"Do your parents live here?" Honey asked.

Sarah hesitated. "My mom passed away when I was seventeen." Aware of Liz watching her, she avoided mentioning that it had been from breast cancer. "My dad's a retired NYPD detective, but don't let that freak you out. We don't really talk all that much. Actually, we don't talk at all." Feeling like she'd majorly over shared, Sarah sealed her lips and sat back.

Honey's doe eyes filled with sympathy. "I'm so sorry about your mother, Sarah. Your father must be so thrilled to have you back home."

Sarah hesitated. "Well, actually I left him a voice mail before I left Los Angeles, which he never returned. Then again, he has a bad habit of letting his phone bills go unpaid, so it's possible he never got it." Her dad had a lot of bad habits, and his unpaid bills weren't limited to the phone.

"How does he feel about your career in adult films?" Peter asked. "Sorry, I should say *former* career," he amended with an apologetic smile.

Sarah slanted him a look. "He's a NYPD cop from Brooklyn, a devout Catholic, and half Irish. How do you think he feels about it?"

Peter chuckled. "Pol's parents are Catholic too, and so conservative they still see Vatican II as some sort of personal betrayal, so enough said. But still, Sarah, shouldn't you at least make sure he knows you're back?"

No matter how well meant, unsolicited advice from virtual strangers was tough to take. Annoyed, she looked over to Liz, seeking support.

"Maybe he has a point," Liz said, shocking her to speechlessness. "It's something to think about anyway."

More than anyone, as her former roommate Liz knew the hell Sarah's father had put her through. It took effort, but Sarah screwed her jaw shut and forced a shrug. "So are pigs flying, but I'm not checking the sky anytime soon."

Rather than being put off by her sarcasm, Peter pressed forward. "Look, Sarah, I know you're the newbie here, and other than Liz, you don't know any of us from Adam, so here's my deal: I spent more years than I care to count as a closeted drunk, a functional alcoholic, until one day I wasn't even that anymore. A group of friends talked me into joining AA. It turns out drinking served a lot of needs for me, but mostly it was about numbing myself against all the anger I was afraid to let myself feel, especially against my family for not accepting me for who I am—a pretty awesome gay man." He shot her a good-humored wink and Sarah found it impossible not to smile back. "I don't know your dad, maybe he's a real son-of-a-bitch, but it seems to me that you're being back in New York is an opportunity for making amends."

"No promises, but I'll think about it," Sarah said, reaching for a cookie. Hello, stress eating!

Biting into the Oreo, she made a quick mental review of the last three weeks. Committing to turn her journal into a possible book, caretaking for Liz, finding a fuck buddy, and now possibly making peace with her dad—her return to New York was shaping up to be a lot busier of a "retirement" than she'd bargained for.

Chapter Five

Sarah and Cole spent the week working their way through her roster of film roles. Having received their respective lab results, uniformly negative for all STDs, their play began in earnest. They fucked in the back of a hired stretch limo. They fucked in the bodega where they'd first met. They fucked in the bathroom of Balthazar, not very imaginative but fun nonetheless.

So far as the fucking went, there were no rules, only hard and soft limits. Outside of sex, Cole was a consummate gentleman. He opened doors. He held out chairs and remained standing until Sarah was seated. At meals, he always served her before himself. Grudgingly, she began to admit there was a lot more to him than the bored party boy she'd first met at the bodega. Like the props they used to recreate their movie fantasies, his dilettante demeanor seemed to function mostly as a mask for pain.

Whatever had happened in Iraq had messed him up majorly. She wasn't a psychologist, but even for a layperson like herself, his sudden silences, chain-smoking, and admission of insomnia pointed to at least mild PTSD. His stubborn refusal to so much as acknowledge his war hero status was laudable but frustrating.

Standing in her bathroom getting ready for their next "date," she reminded herself that his mental health wasn't her worry. Fucking, not talking, was the objective of their meet ups. Gliding the tube of pink lipstick across her mouth, Sarah could scarcely wait for their afternoon session to start.

※※※ ※※※

The manager at Top of the Rock's Pulse restaurant owed Cole a favor. To ensure that he and Sarah would have the privacy to play out their next film-related fantasy, Cole had secured the banquet room as if for a private midday function—*very* private. Sweetening the deal with a few hundred bucks had guaranteed him that none of the lunch staff would bother them. He had the rest of his life to eat lunch. Today he was much more interested in making a meal of Sarah.

Dressed in an overcoat, despite it being May, an Armani suit, and striped silk tie and carrying an attaché case, he stepped off onto the complex's third floor. Striding through the sleek, maple-paneled hallway, each carefully calculated step carried him that much closer to fully hardening.

Today's reenactment was the opening scene from *Sugar Baby*, Sarah's—Sugar's—breakout role. In it, a suave, domineering businessman embarked on a mutually satisfying master-slave relationship with a secretly submissive restaurant coat-check girl. Increasingly intense punishment and humiliation eventually led the pair to fall in love. The premise wasn't all that original. The mainstream movie, *The Secretary*, was a cult classic by the time Sarah's porno had released. The quirky 2002 romantic comedy had starred James Spader as the dominant boss and Maggie Gyllenhaal as his enthusiastically submissive secretary. Cole was a fan of the film as much for its offbeat humor as for the sexy subject matter.

To prepare for today's Don Draper-esque role, he'd dug *Sugar Baby* out of the box of DVDs and watched it the night before. Knowing Sarah as he now did, he could appreciate how much acting had been involved. Though she sometimes enjoyed being submissive in bed, outside of sex she was the opposite of meek and mild.

By prearrangement, she waited for him inside the deserted coatcheck room. Sidling up, he saw she'd recreated her film appearance to perfection. Despite the movie being seven years old, she looked almost exactly the same. She wore her hair pulled up into a high *I Dream of Jeannie* ponytail and a demure little pastel-print dress he couldn't wait to peel off. So far the gated door kept him from seeing her feet, but he'd bet anything she had on hot pink stilettos.

She greeted him with a tentative smile. "Good evening, sir, can I check your coat for you?"

The shelf in front of her held a tip jar with some change and a few crumpled ones. Behind her were several racked coats, including one impressively authentic floor-length faux fur. Vaguely he wondered how she'd gotten them up.

Reminding himself that wasn't his concern, he focused back on his character. "I don't know, *can* you?" He forced himself to stare at her coldly. Given how completely cute she looked, pulling off the iceman routine was harder than he would have thought.

"Sorry, I should have said *may* I check your coat."

Flushing, she bit her bottom lip, her display of school-girl nervousness pitch perfect though, he suddenly recalled, the anxious habit was drawn from real life. He'd recently begun teasing her that soon she'd have no lower lip left.

"In that case, yes." Sticking to the script, he made a show of looking around before turning back. Leaning toward her, he whispered, "In fact, you *may* perform several services for me."

"Sir?"

She sent him an uncertain smile and peeked up at him through her artificial lashes. The modest mien conveyed the impression of a much younger woman, the girl she'd been almost a decade ago, not the sultry sexpot he knew her to be. The temporary transformation was impressive. She not only looked different. She *smelled* different, doused with some fruity, floral fragrance in place of the minty soap he'd spent the last weekend licking off her.

He reached into his pocket and pulled out a gold money clip. Counting out five one-hundred-dollar bills with deliberate precision, he asked, "Would you like the chance to earn this?"

She widened her eyes like a guileless girl might. "Five hundred dollars! But I'm just a coat-check girl. What could I possibly do for you that would be worth so much money?"

Cock thrumming, Cole forced down his smile. A grinning dom would never do. For their role-playing to really take off, he needed to stick as closely as possible to the arrogant businessman from the film.

"Open that door and let me in, and you'll find out," he dared her, his erect penis pressing against his pants. Neither of them had so much as dropped a button, and yet he felt closer to coming than he usually did after minutes of heavy making out.

She hesitated, her pink smile slipping. "But sir, I'm not allowed to bring customers back here. If the manager finds out, he'll—"

"I'll decide what's allowed," he broke in, perspiration pearling on his forehead and not because it was too warm for a coat. "I'm the only one you need to worry about pleasing—or angering," he added harshly.

She moistened her mouth, pretending to prevaricate. "My mother is sick. She needs surgery. I've been trying to save, but I . . . I don't earn very much stuck back in here." Her sad gaze circuited to the tip jar.

Cole decided for her. "Then it's settled."

She sighed. "Yes, I suppose it is." She stepped back, bringing the hinged half door with her.

Cole whisked inside, his heartbeat quickening as though there were real urgency. The door banged closed behind him. He took hold of her forearms and ferried her to the racked coats at the back of the closet. The previous play with rolled-up money had been intensely exciting for them both. Dropping his hand, he brushed the fold of crisp notes over her lips, her jaw, and lastly the scooped neckline of her dress.

Summoning his most severe voice, he said, "If you want this, you know what you have to do for it."

Sarah's breath hitched. She trembled, not just her mouth but her whole body. "Y-yes."

Jesus, were those actual tears in her eyes? Damn, she was good. Reminding himself that none of it was real, he hoisted a brow. "Yes, what?"

"Yes, *sir*."

He nodded briskly. "Better. Now be a good girl and do exactly as I say, and if you please me, I'll give you this money and even more."

"Y-yes, sir."

"First, take off my coat. I'm paying you good money, so you'd better start doing your job, or I'll have to punish you."

A mute nod signaled her acceptance of his terms. Bending her head to his buttons, she went down the line, releasing him from the heavy wool with nimble fingers. She slid the coat off his shoulders and stepped back, waiting.

Catching his cue, Cole said, "Now hang it up with the others, and be sure to do so neatly and straight, or I'll make you do it again."

"Yes, sir." Turning away, she secured the coat on a hanger, careful to do up all the buttons.

Covering a hand over his cock, Cole watched her. "Now turn around and take off your dress."

Sarah slowly turned back to him. She raised one arm and then dropped it to her side, her eyes pleading. "Please, sir, don't make me do this."

"I'm not making you do anything. I'm giving you a choice. Life is about choices. Do you want to help your mother or do you not?"

"I do . . . sir, but—"

"Then take off your dress."

Breathing hard, he leaned back against the wall, folding his arms. Her dress had a zipper at the back. She reached behind to pull it down, making a show of struggling. On second thought, given the location, it might not be a show at all. Cole could have helped her, but doing so would mean breaking character—and taking them both out of the fantasy.

She finally got the zipper down. A shimmy brought the dress slinking off her shoulders. She threaded her arms through the sleeves, tears spangling her bottom lashes. *So damned good.* The dress rode her waist, exposing her pretty pink bra and the gorgeous full breasts he couldn't wait to worship once more.

A tug took the garment the rest of the way off. Sarah—Sugar— stepped out of the pink pool at her feet. Her bra and panties were confections of matching pink lace. Cole ran his gaze over her, pretending he was seeing her for the first time. Her waist was tiny, her belly flat and supple, her slender hips flaring into long, shapely legs with just the right amount of flesh and muscle. Hot pink stilettos graced her slender feet, tipped in pink-painted toes.

Looking away, she crossed an arm over her breasts and covered a trembling hand over her mons. "Please, sir—"

"Drop your hands and straighten your shoulders," he demanded, his barking voice sending her starting.

Recovering, she obeyed. "Yes, sir," she said, sniffing back tears.

Back still braced against the wall, he nodded. "Good, very good. Now it's time to earn my cock."

She blinked. "Sir?"

"Get down on your hands and knees."

She hesitated and then knelt, stretching her slender arms before her.

"Palms flattened on the floor for now and whatever you do, don't dare look at me unless I give you my permission," he commanded, shoving away from the wall.

An infinitesimal nod signaled her continued obedience.

He silently counted to ten, making her wait. "Head down," he warned when hers started lifting.

Closing the space between them to a few inches, Cole swallowed hard. He lifted his right foot several inches, the wingtip freshly polished and immaculately clean. "You know what I want," he hissed, his every muscle going rigid.

Shoulders shaking and eyes down, she lifted both hands to take him.

"Touch only the shoe, not me," he emphasized. "You haven't yet earned the right," he added, resisting the urge to reach down and stroke her head.

Cradling his arch, Sarah brought her mouth to the shoe's polished toe. Watching her press her lips to the leather, Cole nearly lost it. A bubblegum pink tongue darted out and swiped a slow circle over the dimpled vamp. Cole lifted his leg higher. Angling her face, she started lapping at his sole. Her mouth returned to the wingtip, and she opened wider. On the brink of blowing his load, Cole pulled free.

"You may look up at me now."

Eyes streaming, Sarah looked up.

Bracing a hand against the sidewall to balance himself, he carefully probed her with the point of the shoe—the valley between her breasts, her belly, and finally between her legs.

Pushing against her lightly, he whispered, "I will allow you to come now."

Cole had no doubt that he was the one of them closest to climax. He'd never thought of himself as having a fetish but the boot worship byplay might just prove him wrong. That she was nearly naked while he remained fully and formally dressed, his tie still cinched around his neck, further amped up the head trip. Suddenly he wasn't playing at dominating her. He was doing it, much to their mutual pleasure.

Like an ancient maiden submitting herself as sacrifice, Sarah remained kneeling. Hands resting atop her legs, she waited. Cole gently nudged her pubis. She moaned and rocked against him. Her hands left her legs to cradle his foot once more, this time guiding him to her core. Holding on, she began working the wingtip against herself like a toy, wriggling against the hard point, grinding her hips in greeting, her movements coming faster and surer, harder and more deliberate. Sweating through his suit, Cole couldn't take his eyes off her. He couldn't be completely sure, but he didn't think what he was seeing was all acting. Her breaths became more rapid, the tops of her breasts flushed. Suddenly she jerked, spasmed—screamed.

She collapsed forward. Wrapping her arms around his calf, she pressed her face against his pant leg and sobbed.

Knowing he wore her juices on his foot, Cole was so turned on, he nearly forgot his next line, all of two words. "Get up."

Letting go, Sarah stumbled to stand. Tears tracked her cheeks. Pebbled nipples pushed hard against the bra cups. The dampened front of her panties was a darker pink, a kinky scarlet letter.

Sliding his hand from the wall, Cole sucked in a ragged breath. "Now turn around."

She pretended to misunderstand. "Sir?"

"I said turn around!" The dom character in the film had a thing about not allowing his sub to look into his eyes, at least not without his "permission." Cole had never gotten that part, but suddenly he did, oh how he did.

Sarah turned.

Staring at the elegant arch of her back, her beautifully molded buttocks, and dancer's gorgeous, long legs, Cole hesitated, reaching for his next line. The blood pumping through his penis seemed to have paralyzed his brain.

"That's better," he improvised, losing patience with the play.

How did these BDSM guys keep it going? Rock hard and throbbing, he was half tempted to forget the scripted scenario and just fuck her.

But they had a deal. She'd just come using nothing more than his foot. Regardless of their respective roles, their play was as much about her pleasure as his. Judging from the wetness staining the front of her panties, under the right circumstances submission suited her.

Picking up the thread of paraphrased dialogue, he said, "Lift your arms over your head and grab hold of the bar with both hands."

Once again Sarah—Sugar—obeyed.

"Now bend over and offer me your ass."

Sarah bent. Cole reached around and grabbed her roughly, first her waist and then lower, his hand squeezing her crotch. She moaned and pushed back against him, grinding into his groin. Cole gulped down a breath. He'd never wanted to bareback a woman so badly in his life, but that wasn't part of this scene—or their deal, not yet anyway.

"Take hold of the bar, and don't let go until I tell you."

Sarah hesitated and then reached out, her slender fingers curving around the coat rack, the hooks of the hangers no doubt biting into her palms. In one swift motion, he pulled down her panties, stopping at her knees as though she were a naughty child about to be spanked. He grabbed her front again. With the lace barrier gone, his fingers sank into the strip of drenched curls and wet, willing flesh. If he'd had any doubts as to whether or not she was really into it, the cream coating his hand set them to rest. Like springtime grass still slippery from a storm, the earthy, sweet scent of her rose up to tantalize him.

As in the movie, she struggled against his probing. "Sir, please," she whimpered, not with pain, he knew, but more likely because the friction further stimulated her G-spot.

"Be still or I'll punish you," he warned, chafing his forefinger inside her.

But the threat was an empty one. Cole wasn't going to last much longer. Fortunately he didn't have to. With their sexual health confirmed, there was no need to press pause and put on a condom.

"Please, sir," she whimpered, twisting against his hand.

Easing back, he reached down between them and unzipped his trouser fly. "I'm going to give you my cock now," he said, fitting himself against her. "You've earned it."

He thrust into her, the force knocking her forward and buckling her knees. Fortunately her white-knuckled hold on the metal rod was solid. Like a good submissive, she hadn't presumed to release it without him telling her to.

Thinking how hot she'd looked mouth fucking his foot, how helpless and hot she looked now with her arms, slender yet strong, stretched over her head and her beautiful ass stuck straight out, Cole pulled out and slammed into her again. She moaned and pushed back against him, her back beaded with moisture.

As if suddenly remembering her stage direction and closing line, Sarah twisted to look at him over her shoulder. "Please."

Jaw clenched and sweat pouring, Cole demanded, "Please what?"

"Please come inside me, sir."

Cole didn't need to make her say it a second time. He reared back, re-entered, and thrust, pumping himself into her.

❊❊❊ ❊❊❊

Sarah lifted her head from Cole's shoulder. "Please tell me those shoes were clean."

They were lying on the coatroom floor, the full-length fur spread out as a buffer beneath them. Cole had stripped off his suit jacket, but otherwise he'd stayed dressed. Sarah wore only her bra and panties. The close air was heavy with the scents of fruit and flowers, sweat and sex. The perfume from her pussy was so intense Cole wondered if maybe there wasn't a way to bottle it.

Lying on his back and staring at the ceiling, he chuckled. "You can relax. I put them on inside the elevator."

She turned to look at him, visibly relieved. "Thank you. Playing out fantasies is all well and good, but I wouldn't want to risk trench mouth."

Pushing up one elbow, he shifted onto his side and asked, "What is trench mouth anyway?"

Rolling over to face him, Sarah laughed. "You know, that's a good question. I *think* it's some form of gingivitis. My mother was always threatening me with it when I was little. I know this will be hard for you to believe, but I liked finding things and putting them in my mouth." She followed the admission with a saucy smile.

"Shocking," he concurred with a chuckle, thinking he really ought to get back to work, though so far he hadn't been able to muster the willpower to get up and get going. Now that the fucking was over, he was just really enjoying hanging out with her. "On the other hand, it'll be a great detail for your future biopic, *A Porn Star is Born*."

"Something to look forward to, I guess." Smile slipping, she dropped her gaze, idly plucking at the faux fur.

Had his joke hurt her feelings? Whatever he's said seemed to have struck a nerve. Reaching down, he took her chin and tilted her face up to his. "Hey, what is it?"

She sighed. "Would you believe I went to LA with very different dreams, all more or less involving me dipping my hands in wet cement outside of Grauman's Chinese Theatre?"

"Seriously?" Until now, it hadn't occurred to him to wonder, let alone ask, how she'd gotten into porn. She was Sugar, after all.

She sent him a solemn nod. "I'll have you know I played Juliet to Robbie Sanders' Romeo at Fiorello H. LaGuardia High School."

"You went to La? No shit?"

Cole was impressed. The magnet public high school for the visual and performing arts had stringent admission requirements, including a live audition. Its roster of acting alumnae, a Who's Who of Hollywood notables, included Adrien Brody, Jennifer Aniston, Wesley Snipes, and Robert De Niro.

"Oh, if my Theater Arts teacher could only see me now. On second thought, maybe he has."

"What happened?"

She sighed broadly. "Life happened. Once I got to LA, I found out fast that the streets were in fact not paved with golden-for-me opportunities. I was just another blonde with big dreams and no college degree. Apparently La training doesn't count for all that much on the West Coast, at least not without the advanced degree to back it up. Actually it doesn't count for squat."

"That sucks," he said, careful to keep his tone even. He suspected if she so much as sniffed pity on him, she'd go ballistic.

"Yeah, it did." Threading her fingers through the faux fur—a card-carrying member of the animal rights group, PETA, she apparently really would rather go naked than wear the real stuff—she continued, "Valet parking cars, waitressing, even dog walking—you name it, I did it, and went to auditions in between. But when I couldn't make rent, I had to decide: either let the dream die or figure out a way to . . . modify it."

Fascinated, he finished the story for her. "And overnight Sugar was born?"

Again, that half smile seemed to speak volumes. "Not exactly overnight but close enough. I made friends with another AE actress on set, Liz, who took me under her wing and mentored me. And once I met Martin, things really took off."

"Martin?" he asked, shifting to rest on his other arm, an unpleasant prickle of jealousy disturbing his post-coital peace.

She nodded. "My manager, who I might add is none too pleased about me retiring."

Her manager, whew! Wondering why he'd cared, even for a few seconds, about who she might have fucked in LA, he said, "Adios fifteen percent, huh?"

"That's for sure, but I think he also feels a bit . . . betrayed."

He felt himself frowning. "But it's a business relationship, right?"

"It is, but even so, we've been together for nine and a half years. He's spinning my pulling out of this last film project as a leave of absence, but I've told him it's permanent. Hopefully he's started to accept that decision as final."

Feeling as if he were holding back from breathing, as casually as he could Cole asked, "Is it . . . final?" On camera or off, the thought of her fucking other guys was . . . Well, he just didn't like it.

She didn't hesitate. "Yes, it is. I have other things I want to do with my life, and I'm fortunate to be in a position to be able to take a break while I figure out what's next."

"That's great." The other day, she'd mentioned getting up early to work. Recalling the laptop lying out on her counter, he asked, "What is next? Are you working on a script or something?"

The frown line appearing on her forehead suggested she didn't appreciate his prying. "Right now my main priority is Liz."

That threw him. He'd read that a lot of female porn stars were bisexual in their private lives. Might Sarah and this . . . Liz be lovers? The possibility should have turned him on, but instead it left him feeling lost, empty. Sex with Sarah might revolve around her movie roles, but the overarching fantasy, for him anyway, was that she was all his in every way, at least for the next few months.

Fishing, he asked, "The friend, I thought she was in LA."

"She retired years ago and moved back to New York. She's built a freelance graphic design business, a total do over." He could be wrong, but she didn't sound like someone talking about a lover.

"That's great!" Cole enthused, feeling a measure of relief.

She sat up, her eyes dimming. "Yeah it is, or at least it was."

"I don't follow."

She hesitated as if weighing how much or little to tell him. "She's going through a pretty rough time, coming back from breast cancer. She's midway through her course of chemo, and things are getting . . . pretty rough."

"Jesus!" he said. "I had no idea."

Hugging her tented knees, she said, "Yeah, well, it's not exactly fuck-buddy chat. Besides, my mom died of breast cancer, so I've been having some flashbacks, but they're no big deal."

Flashbacks, Cole definitely copied that, except for the part about them being no big deal. He knew firsthand how vivid and crippling the unintentional recall could be, especially when you couldn't control when or where it happened.

Sitting up beside her, it struck him. "The scenario we just played out. When you said your mother was sick, that's how you made yourself cry, wasn't it, by thinking about your real mom?"

She shrugged. "Crying on command is any actor's toughest challenge. Unlike laughing or yelling, you can't force it. Drawing on a personal experience is the only way I've ever been able to make myself tear up."

Cole felt like a heel. Their-role playing wasn't supposed to really have hurt her, not physically and not emotionally either. Stroking a hand along her spine, he said, "We could have . . . skipped those lines, you know."

She shrugged again. "It was my choice, besides it was kind of cathartic. And it made the scene work better, you have to admit."

Cole didn't deny it, but still . . . "Does Liz have family here, people who can help out?"

She hesitated. "Not really. Her mom broke her hip, so she's more or less housebound, and her sister and family live out-of-state. Jonathan is a really great kid, but I know Liz worries about how all of this may be affecting him."

"She has a kid, too!" As sob stories went, this one was getting sadder by the second.

"She's a single mom and an awesome one, but don't try telling her that. She keeps kicking herself that she didn't take him to Disney World last year when he asked. Now she's afraid she might never get to. If—I mean when—she's finished with her treatment, she may not be able to afford the trip. Even with insurance, she's pretty much blown through her savings."

Cole nodded. Cancer didn't only eat away at bodies. It tended to decimate finances, too. He sent her a sideways glance, wondering if she'd been hinting. "You do realize the foundation I run provides programming for kids in Jonathan's position?"

"I'd read it had something to do with kids whose parents have cancer, sort of like the Make-a-Wish Foundation, only in reverse."

"We operate on a similar model," Cole admitted. "Our kids submit their wishes for the experience they want to share with their ill or recovering parent. A team of reviewers assesses the viability of each application. Once an application is selected for funding, we work with the recipient, the parent, his or her caretaker, and coordinating health care provider to structure the activity in a way that won't put the parent or child at risk."

She looked up at him with shining eyes. "That's wonderful."

Cole hesitated. Until now he'd taken his leadership position for granted. Having an office to go into, fundraisers to preside over, a budget to manage, and a board of directors to deal with provided the structure he needed to keep from slipping away and falling apart. But seeing his role through Sarah's eyes, eyes that were looking at him as though he was Santa Claus and Hercules rolled into one, had him feeling differently.

Without thinking, he heard himself say, "Maybe I could, you know, meet them sometime, not as any kind of formal evaluation, just a casual get to know you over lunch or a snack or something."

She slanted him a skeptical look. "You'd do that?"

She was offering him an out, but Cole couldn't bring himself to take it. "Sure, why not?"

Why not indeed? For starters, she was his fuck buddy, not his girlfriend. And not any fuck buddy but an international porn star. Signing up for a public outing where they might be spotted—and photographed—together wasn't smart. And really, what was the point of him meeting her friends, getting involving in her life? It wasn't like their "relationship" was any kind of a permanent thing. His offer made absolutely no sense, and yet it felt so . . . right.

"Are you sure about this?" she asked, chafing the tops of her arms as if suddenly chilly.

"Does Liz's kid like pizza?"

His question had her letting out a laugh. As sexy a submissive as she'd made, it was seeing her happy and relaxed that really got to him. "Jonathan's seven. He *lives* for pizza."

"Great," he said, standing. The air conditioning wasn't turned that high, but unlike her, he was fully dressed. Reaching down a hand to help her up, he said, "I'll give you a call later to set something up, okay?"

"Okay," she said, taking hold. Gaining her feet, she added, "But if you change your mind, I don't want you to feel like—"

Still holding her hand, Cole pulled her against him, cutting her off with a kiss. Refusing to think about what he'd just signed himself up for, he drew back and smiled down at her. "Fuck changing my mind. I'm a Canning, remember? My word is my bond, so consider it a date. Now get dressed. You're turning blue."

Chapter Six

FATE Monday rolled around before Sarah knew it. After the usual twenty or so minutes of snacking and socializing, they started in. When Peter didn't dive in as usual, Sarah decided to get her "contribution" out of the way. She was still struggling with whether or not to see her dad, she admitted, hating the hitch in her voice. On one hand, it seemed silly not to reach out to him now that they were living in the same city. On the other, she wasn't really buying that he hadn't gotten her voice message. Was it so wrong to expect him to meet her halfway? He'd moved from the Brooklyn brownstone where Sarah had grown up. The last address she had for him was in Astoria, Queens. As Honey and Peter both pointed out, Queens was another borough, not a foreign country. What would be the harm in extending one last olive branch?

She felt as if, over the past decade, she'd extended not a single branch but the equivalent of an entire olive tree. "I'll think about it," she said, signaling to Liz that it was another person's turn to talk. If her father still wanted nothing to do with her, maybe it wasn't in anyone's best interest to push him.

They continued around the room, weighing in on Brian's situation with his bullying shop boss, AKA "fucking ass wipe," and Honey's worries about ending up as an old maid. Apparently her hotshot hedge fund manager had stopped making noises about marrying her now that she'd moved into his Park Avenue apartment. At least her dating a hedgie set to rest Sarah's suspicions about the source of all those vintage, couture clothes.

Fingering the edge of her headscarf, Liz admitted to sometimes waking panicked in the middle of the night. Her fears about whether her cancer was truly beaten or only hiding made everyone else's problems, including Sarah's, seem piddling.

Apart from encouraging her to see her father, Peter had hardly said a word. Watching him pick an uneaten cookie into crumbs, Sarah could tell something was very wrong.

She and Liz exchanged looks. "Pete, you're unusually quiet," Liz prompted. "What's been going on with you this week?"

"Not much . . . everything . . . I don't know, maybe I'm just being stupid."

Sarah reached over and laid her hand on his for a brief moment. "I doubt that. If you think talking about it will make you feel better, then go for it. But it's up to you."

Setting his plate aside, he blew out a heavy breath. "So the other day, I took my boyfriend, Pol, out to a romantic dinner at August. My plan was to wait until dessert and then ask him to move in with me."

"Oh, Peter, that's splendid," Honey cut in. "From everything you've told us, you're positively perfect for one another. And . . . and the most important thing is to enjoy your life, to be happy. It's all that matters."

Sarah was reasonably sure that last bit was a direct quote from Audrey Hepburn. It also happened to be pretty good advice. For now, she held back from commenting. Peter's grimace gave her a heads up that his romantic dinner had gone anything but perfectly.

"Everything was perfect—the food, the ambiance, the service. I wish I could say that the wine was perfect too, but we're alcoholics, we met at an AA meeting, so we can't drink. Still, the Pellegrino definitely had the right amount of fizzle."

He paused to make way for the chuckles that reliably followed. Sarah joined in, though she sensed he was delaying getting to the real issue.

His blue eyes went around the room, brushing briefly over Sarah's. She couldn't shake the feeling that he was silently asking for her support, more so than that of the others, which was crazy since they'd only met a month ago. Then again, that was just one week less than she'd known Cole. Thinking back to all the things she'd confided that day in the cloakroom, she supposed it wasn't the length of an acquaintance that mattered as much as the level of trust. Rightly or wrongly, she trusted Cole not to betray her.

She focused back on Peter, who was saying, "We'd just decided on dessert—the apple crumble for Pol, the poached pear for me—when in walks this tall, distinguished man with his wife on his arm. He made a big deal about this being their anniversary, their thirtieth, and asked for the best table. He looked familiar, more familiar than someone I'd only met in passing. French cuffs, custom-cut suit, a scarlet silk handkerchief folded into the breast pocket. It was the handkerchief that placed him for me."

"He was a former client, wasn't he?" Liz asked, her voice gentle.

Face crumpling, he admitted, "My Friday afternoon four o'clock for nearly four years."

"Jesus!" Brian exclaimed, tilting forward from the sofa seat.

"Actually I knew him as Simon," Peter deadpanned, though his stressed-out expression diluted the humor. "Always punctual, always polite, always paid up front in cash. Every Christmas he'd hand me an envelope with an extra five hundred bucks in it. He was that kind of guy—low maintenance; no muss, no fuss; always a gentleman. Liked for me to go down on my knees and suck him off while he stuck his finger up his ass. Sometimes if he was feeling frisky, he'd have me pull down his pants and whack him a couple of good ones with the flogger, but that was as kinky as he got."

Liz shook her head. "I'm so sorry. I can't imagine how awkward that must have been for you both."

Exhaling heavily, he admitted, "It gets worse."

Honey's doe-like gaze looked suspiciously watery. "Worse?"

He nodded. "Wouldn't you know it, the hostess sat them down at the table next to ours? Every time I reached for my water glass—and my mouth was so dry by then that I reached for it a lot—my arm brushed his. I was mortified. Dessert came. I couldn't touch a bite, could barely breathe. Pol kept asking me what was wrong, which of course made it even worse. I finally told him I thought I might be coming down with something—a migraine, Avian Flu, a heart attack, I honestly can't remember. My pits were perspiring rivers. I couldn't stop my hands from shaking. I called for the check, had our desserts boxed to go, and got the hell out of there."

"Jesus!" Brian repeated.

This time there was no possibility of Peter's turning the exclamation into any kind of joke. "New York can be one big, small town. I've always known it could happen. I just never thought it would."

"Sometimes life throws us curveballs," Liz put in gently. "We don't always see them coming, but once they do, all we can do is pinch hit and try to make it to first. It sounds like you did exactly that. What happened, running into Simon at a restaurant, may never happen again."

Peter raked a manicured hand through his hair, making one side stick out. He looked so stressed Sarah wished she'd sat closer, if only so she could hug him. "I know, I know, I just can't get it out of my head. I haven't slept through the night in a week. The other day on my way home from work I caught myself backtracking to a liquor store. For the

first time in almost two years, I seriously thought about screwing everything and buying a bottle. I guess you could say almost being outed
as a former whore is one of my triggers." A crack of mirthless laughter
punctuated the caustic comment.

"Peter, no!" Honey cried, catching at his arm.

He covered the top of her hand with his tanned one. "Don't worry,
I didn't, but it still scares me that I thought about it. Last week I was
lucky, but what if the next former client I see doesn't have his own deal
to protect? Most of the guys were nice enough, but like in any business, there was the occasional rotten apple. What if one of them outs
me—and what if I'm with Pol when it happens?"

His reference to being outed struck a sensitive nerve with Sarah.
Thinking of her own situation, she asked, "You've never told him about
your past?" If Cole hadn't recognized her as Sugar, might they be dating
now instead of only fucking?

He shook his head. "Pol is the sweetest, biggest hearted guy imag-
inable, but you have to understand he was raised real traditional. He
emigrated from Ireland when he was thirteen. He didn't come out until
he was thirty and only then because the booze was going to kill him
if he didn't get help. His folks didn't disown him exactly, but when he
visits, they never talk about his dating life. I know he loves me, but if
he found out I spent almost five years as a prostitute, I'm not sure he'd
be able to get past it. Should I take a chance and tell him or keep quiet
and hope he never finds out?"

They went around the circle. "I don't know," Honey said, nibbling
her lip. "Either way, there's a risk."

Brian spoke up, not in two words but in a full sentence and a
lengthy one, considering the source. "Tell him. He either loves you or
he doesn't, no ifs, no conditions."

"But I think all love comes with some conditions," Liz said. "In a way, it's an exchange, a transaction, too." She glanced over at Sarah. "What's your opinion?"

Talk about being put on the proverbial hot seat! Feeling like a hypocrite, Sarah set down her cup and saucer. "For me the game changer is the life commitment. You're not just . . . fuck buddies." Weird, saying the phrase had never bothered her before, but thinking of her and Cole, she had to strain to get the two words out. "You're in a relationship, and you don't want to just date him anymore. You're planning to ask him to move in. It seems to me that kind of commitment deserves, maybe even requires, honesty."

"Maybe Sarah's right," Peter said. "One thing's for sure. Confessing to the man I love that I'm a former whore makes admitting to alcoholism seem like a walk in Central Park."

Sarah could sympathize. That first night she and Cole had been together, he'd made love purely to her, not her legend. As hot as their reenactments of her movies were turning out to be, more than once lately she'd found herself wishing "Sugar" had never entered the picture.

Still mulling that over, she caught up with Liz after the session. "Hey, let me do that," she said, frowning at the dirty plates Liz was stacking.

"Now that the others are gone, how are things going with *your* fuck buddy?" Liz asked, stepping away from the sink.

Sarah took her place at the sink. Running the tap and squeezing a green glob of dish soap from the bottle, she said, "Funny you should ask, because we were talking the other night and your name came up."

Every time she'd tried broaching the topic of money, Liz had clammed up. The oncology treatment program at Sloan Kettering enjoyed its worldwide reputation as cutting edge for good reason, but it couldn't come cheap. Even with insurance, there were substantial out-of-pocket costs to cover. Whatever money she'd set aside from her porn days was likely blown through by now.

So far she'd refused any financial help from Sarah, never mind that she wouldn't miss the money. But maybe having the money come from an organization rather than a friend would make accepting it easier? The more Sarah thought about the Canning Foundation, the more it seemed like it might be the answer for Liz and Jonathan—or at least *an* answer. To get through the next tough few months, they needed something fun to focus on, a proverbial light at the end of cancer's tunnel. Instead of settling for a single wimpy light, why not have the elaborate pyrotechnics display at Disney's Cinderella's Castle to look forward to?

Liz's face shuttered. "Talking, huh? That sounds like a waste." She set the cookie tray on the counter.

Sarah shut off the tap and turned around. "We do talk sometimes." She didn't add that most of their conversations were recitations of her X-rated scripts. "Anyway," she went on, picking up the coffeepot for rinsing, "he wants to take you and Jonathan and me out for pizza."

Liz smiled slyly. "He wants to meet your friends, huh? That sounds like more than a fuck buddy to me."

Sarah shrugged. Tempting as it was to get her hopes up, it was wiser not to. Cole wasn't a relationship guy. He'd laid that out before he'd even kissed her. Their time together was "just for fun." She might wish for more, she *did* sometimes wish for more, but she also had to respect his honesty—and his boundaries. She needed to enjoy their time together for what it was—great sex.

"The charity he runs is like a Make-a-Wish Foundation, only for kids whose parents are recovering from cancer."

She'd made certain to emphasize "recovering," but Liz still bristled. "I'm not looking for handouts, not from you and not from any charity. I can take care of my son. Once I get back to work full-time, Jonathan and I'll get to Disney World on our own steam."

Taking in her fierce face, rather than upset her further, Sarah backed down. "No one's saying otherwise. Look, sex aside, Cole's really cool to hang out with. I thought it might be fun for Jonathan. But if you don't think it's a good idea, I'll tell him so, and you can forget I even mentioned it."

Her scowl softening, Liz leaned back against the pantry cabinet. "Jonathan's been cooped up too much lately. We'll do it, but be sure to tell your . . . buddy to keep his checkbook to himself." Eyes flashing, she added, "And I'd better not see Jonathan or me in any brochure!"

✳✳✳ ✳✳✳

"So I spoke to my friend, Liz, and she's cool with us meeting up for pizza this week with her and her son," Sarah said to Cole later that night, her tone the carefully modulated one she used for feeling him out. Moving about the kitchen wearing only his costume white shirt, she added, "Will Saturday at lunchtime work for you?"

"Absolutely. Lombardi's or John's on Bleecker?" Seated on one of the high-backed counter stools, he reflected he really should get off his lazy butt and help her, but the view was too goddamned good to give up.

Her relieved look confirmed his suspicion that she hadn't expected him to follow through. Not for the first time, he wondered how many people—men—had let her down. The few times the subject of fathers had come up, she'd evaded all but his most casually framed questions. Apparently hers was a retired NYPD detective living in one of the city's outer boroughs, Brooklyn he thought. That was all he knew.

"John's is closer to her place, and she tires fast."

"Great, John's it is. Noon, okay?"

Standing on tiptoe to take down salad plates from the cabinet, she answered, "Noon would be perfect." Big as his shirt was on her, the stretching posture brought the shirt tail riding up, revealing the sweet curve of her perfect and perfectly bare ass. "Only don't say too much about the foundation," she warned. Retrieving the dishes, she closed the cabinet door. "She's pretty sensitive about what she sees as 'handouts.'"

Distracted, it took him a few seconds to find his way back into their conversation. "Right, no problem, I'll just talk about myself."

"Well, it is your favorite subject." Setting down the plates, she shot him a dimpled grin.

"Sometimes," he admitted, "but not always." The night they'd met, she'd made it pretty clear she viewed him as a spoiled one per-center, but did she really still see him that way? Gaze snagging on her computer, lying open at the opposite end of the counter, he added, "Right now I'm pretty curious about what you've got going on your laptop?"

His earlier swooping in and carrying her upstairs to bed hadn't exactly allowed time for tidying. That day's reenactment had been of her only period piece, loosely based on *The Four Musketeers*. In the X-rated film adaptation, four male actors, the musketeers, had taken turns plea-suring and penetrating the delectably deceitful Milady de Winter— Sugar. Only in Cole's version, there was only one Musketeer—him. A white pirate's shirt repurposed from last Halloween, fitted riding pants, and boots he kept for his rare rides in Central Park, had brought him close enough to character. As for the plumed hat . . . well, there was no way that was happening.

Sarah had met him at the door. As always, she hadn't disappointed. Corseted and dressed in tight-fitting, camel-colored pants, thigh-high boots, and boasting a black-velvet beauty patch on one cheek, she'd looked much as she had in the film.

A dungeon room would have been difficult to improvise on the fly, but Sarah's stripped bare bed had made a decent enough "rack."

The props were prosaic but effective. Silk scarves, in this case his ties, had seemed to suit "Milady's" pleasure for restraint. Dragging a rubber "play" knife, also repurposed from his pirate costume, along her creamy, quivering body had been more arousing than Cole would have thought. By the time he'd penetrated her with his "sword," they were both breathless and perspiring.

And now they were hungry. The frenzied fucking and the shared shower afterward had worked up an appetite. The leftover lasagna in Sarah's refrigerator promised to be a satisfying early supper. Other than Sarah herself, Cole couldn't think of anything he'd rather be eating.

Using a spatula to lift a wedge of lasagna into a microwavable dish, she said, "It's just some . . . stuff I'm writing." The pasta slid off the spatula and landed splat on the counter. "Shit," she cursed, grabbing a handful of paper towels.

"What kind of stuff?" Cole prompted, wondering why she suddenly seemed so jumpy.

Maneuvering the mangled lasagna back into the dish, she answered without looking up. "It's nothing."

"Does nothing have a name?" Sliding off the stool, he reached for the laptop.

He was fast, but Sarah was faster. She dove, grabbing the Netbook and snapping it closed. Holding it behind her back, she said, "N-not . . . yet."

Cole rounded the breakfast bar and joined her in the kitchen. Based on the blush climbing her cheeks, whatever was on that laptop screen must be pretty personal. If she were anyone else, he'd assume she was hiding porn—only Sarah didn't hide porn. She starred in it, or at least she had until recently.

Blocking him with her body, she looked up at him with blazing eyes. "Since when are you interested in my mind?"

"I'm interested in all of you." *Oh, shit*, he thought, mentally kicking himself, not because it was a glib lie, but because Jesus, God, it was true.

"Okay, yes, it's sort of a . . . book."

Was she keeping some kind of diary or . . . worse, writing some sort of tell-all? From Condoleezza Rice to Justin Bieber, celebrity memoirs seemed to appear on every bookstore and book club reading list. He thought back to their first night together and her paranoia about his phone. Was he the one who should have been worried?

The Cannings weren't celebrities per se, but they were prominent players on the city's social scene. Across the generations, any private misbehaving had stayed strictly behind-the-scenes. Cole might not give a shit about his last name, but he cared about the foundation. A charity that worked with kids couldn't afford any sort of sexual scandal.

He forced a shrug. "What's it about? Is it fiction or nonfiction?" *Let it be fiction!*

She looked away. "You'll laugh."

"Why not try me?" Reaching out to cup her chin, he turned her face gently toward him. "Better yet, why not *trust* me?"

Green eyes bore into his. She let out a sigh. "Okay, you win. It's a memoir . . . of my decade in LA."

LA, as in *pre*-him. Dropping his hand, Cole let out a whoop. What a relief! "Sarah, that's great!" Smart and funny, well-read and well-traveled, she didn't fit any of his stereotyped expectations of a porn star, except, of course, in bed—definitely in bed.

"We'll see. Right now I'm still mainly transcribing. I started a journal on the drive out ten years ago, and I kept it up over the years."

He felt another inconvenient stab of male jealousy. Any memoir of hers would surely include her previous lovers, on camera and off. Not for the first time, he found himself obsessing over her number.

How many men, and perhaps women too, had worshipped the beautiful body he was coming to think of as his?

"I'm not even sure it's really a book," she admitted.

Putting his pettiness aside, he shifted to cheerleader mode. "It's a book. I'm sure of it. And I bet it's going to be great. I have some publishing contacts. When you're ready, I can put you in touch with a reputable agent to shop it for you."

Most aspiring writers he'd met would jump on that offer, but Sarah hesitated, gnawing away at her lip. "Thanks, but I'm not anywhere close to showing it to anyone. I haven't said anything to Liz even. You're the only one I've told so far."

The admission had Cole feeling ten feet tall. Still, he had to remember that Sarah was his fuck buddy. Beyond sticking to the boundaries they'd set, the so-called soft and hard limits, he shouldn't care about her feelings. No one, including Sarah, expected him to log in a lot of time wondering what went on inside her head.

Only he did wonder. He did . . . care. The extent he wondered and cared and obsessed about her not only in bed but out of it set off a bevy of alarm bells. Retired or not, she would always be Sugar, her face and body recognizable around the globe. He couldn't afford to forget that.

Still, she looked pretty damned adorable in only his shirt, most of her makeup scoured off by his kisses. He reached out and traced her bottom lip with the pad of his thumb. "Hey, ease up and leave some for me."

She sighed. "Shit, I'm biting my lip again, aren't I?"

Cole nodded, thinking of all the places he'd like to bite her—her neck, her breasts, and the firm lobes of her ass were all top candidates. "Yep, you are."

"Sorry, it's a nervous habit. I thought I'd kicked it. I hadn't done it in years, and then some stuff happened in LA and I started . . . Well, never mind. Thanks for telling me."

"You're welcome." Cole sensed there was a story there, but he was too distracted to pull it out of her. Imagining slipping his member between her pretty, pink lips, he added, "Your mouth is way too talented to waste."

The gleam in her eyes transformed her. "You want to fuck my mouth don't you?" Suddenly she was Sugar, the screen siren who could make men like him shoot their wad with a single, sultry look.

He nodded, feeling himself thicken. "Yeah I do."

Sliding back and forth between her lips, having her lap him like an ice cream cone, watching her long, elegant throat working to drink him in—the images carried him close to squirting.

Reaching between them, she covered him with her hand. "And then what?"

Hunger for food forgotten, Cole skimmed a hand up her thigh, his knuckles brushing the strip of crisp curls. "Our deal is I get to have you every way you've done it on screen. I want your ass." Claiming her that way was the final frontier.

She stiffened. "I only did anal in one film."

"*Kink Ass.*" He'd watched it so many times he was surprised the DVD hadn't disintegrated.

"I didn't like it. It hurt me. We were running over budget, the director had us under pressure to shoot the scene fast, and we rushed it."

Slipping a hand behind her, he stroked his index finger along the curved cleft. "You'll like it with me. I won't hurt you. We won't rush. The moment something hurts, we'll stop. *I'll* stop. You have my word."

"You say that now." She rolled her eyes as if a man's promise meant next to nothing. Was it her . . . career choice that had soured her on men or something less obvious, deeper?

He speared her gaze with his, willing her not to look away. "Have I ever lied to you, Sarah?"

She looked at him askance. "I don't know, have you?"

"I think you know the answer to that as well as I do, but for the record, the answer is no." He found the ring of puckered flesh with his finger and slowly circled. "Does that hurt?" he asked, already knowing her answer. Their play with the beaded thong had proved she really liked being touched there.

Sarah shivered. "No, of course not but that's foreplay, not penetration."

He resumed stroking. This time when he circled, his digit slid inside up to the first joint. Applying gentle pressure, he leaned in, bringing their mouths close to meeting.

She caught her breath. "We'll have to start slowly with toys first, butt plugs. If those go okay, we can . . . negotiate penetration."

"Fair enough," he said, knowing he'd as good as won.

Their butt hole games would be far better than "okay." By the time he finished with her, Sarah would be begging him to enter her ass. But they had to start somewhere. Withdrawing, he mentally mapped the layout of her loft. So far she hadn't broken out her "goody drawer," but it must be up there somewhere. The prospect of using toys bought and broken in by other men prompted another pang of pure jealousy, but he guessed he'd have to get over it. Considering their casual status, coming off as needy would be way uncool.

She let out a laugh. "Sorry to disappoint, Canning, but I left my toy chest back in LA. Other than a very boring, standard-model vibrator, the kink cupboard is bare."

Feeling as though he'd just been handed a clean slate, a grin broke over his face. "In that case, put on some pants, Halliday. We're going shopping."

The West Village had no shortage of sexual aid and BDSM costume shops, most open late. They hadn't had to go farther than Sixth Avenue to fulfill Cole's wish list. Along with an array of butt plugs, they'd picked up an ass master, a flogger, and a package of clit teasers. Cole had insisted on covering everything—in cash of course. Paying with plastic would be the equivalent of Tweeting their location to *TMZ*. Baseball caps, Sarah's glasses, and casual clothing had them blending in with their fellow Manhattanites—or so Sarah hoped. Even with all the precautions, the outing was risky. Nearly everyone had a camera phone. All it would take was one keen-eyed store clerk or fellow shopper to take their photo and post it online, and they'd be outed. By the time they got back to Sarah's, she was relieved to be in for the night.

Standing in the living room, Cole reached for the remote. "I almost forgot, tonight is a *Doctor Who* marathon. Would you mind if we watched?" he asked, calling out to her in the kitchen.

That he was into the BBC Sci-Fi series was yet another happy surprise. Poking her head over the counter, she looked into the living room. "*Doctor Who* is only the most awesome time-travel series ever. I've geeked out to it for years."

Cole seemed surprised, too. "No shit?"

"No shit," Sarah said, turning to punch the button on the microwave. "So which actor is your penultimate Doctor Who?" Eleven actors had played the lead role.

"Who's yours?"

"David Tennant!" they called out together.

Sarah quickly finished reheating the meal. They carried their plates of lasagna, salad, and garlic bread out into the living room and settled onto the loveseat. Later during a commercial break, she got up to make popcorn.

Cole followed her into the kitchen. "Wow, you do it the old fashioned way in a pan with oil," he said with an approving nod. "Other than my grandma, who does that anymore?"

She looked up to find him standing just behind her, his solid warmth blanketing her back. "Microwave popcorn always tastes like Styrofoam to me. And there are some things that are still worth being old-fashioned about."

He laid a hand on her shoulder. "Yeah, like what?"

Sarah started to answer seriously when she realized he was leaning over to leer at her breasts. So much for his supposed interest in *all* of her.

"Pervert!" Reaching around, she swatted him, which of course he loved.

Drawing back, he said, "I thought you liked that about me."

Sarah hesitated. "I do, it's just . . . " More and more lately, she'd caught herself fantasizing about being more than his fuck buddy.

He sobered, his blue eyes boring into hers. "Just what?" he asked, reaching out toward her.

Telling herself she was stressed out about Liz as well as lonely, she shook off both his question and the hand that accompanied it. "The show's back on. Go in and watch. I need to finish this," she added, overriding his protests. "You can fill me in when the commercials come on."

She'd seen the episode if not a hundred times, certainly a lot. She'd bet he had too.

"Sure you got this?" he asked, gesturing to the stovetop.

"Abso-fucking-lutely." She forced a grin, but her heart felt suddenly inexplicably heavy. Did he have to be so fucking perfect? So perfect and so unavailable?

Doctor Who segued to *Buck Rogers in the 25th Century*. Eyelids heavy and stomachs full, they sacked out on the sofa.

Waking up in the middle of the night to a lit room and the TV still on, Sarah lifted her head from Cole's chest and slid her arm from his torso. So much for a ban on sleepovers! Soft snoring confirmed he was out like the proverbial light. She thought about waking him, but he looked so peaceful and, well, cute with cushion creases on his cheek and his normally neat hair mussed that she didn't have the heart. Besides, he'd admitted he wasn't the best of sleepers. She eased off the cushion and stood, thinking to go upstairs and bring down an extra blanket.

Apparently he sensed her shifting. He woke, eyelids fluttering open. "What . . . time is it?"

Resigned, Sarah answered, "Bedtime. Are you coming or not?"

She stretched down a hand. Taking it, he staggered to standing, still half asleep.

Sarah looped an arm about his waist. "Hold tight, we're taking this TARDIS upstairs to bed."

Chapter Seven

Sarah stole a look at Cole as he leaned across the restaurant table to Jonathan. "So, Jonathan, I'm figuring you for a pepperoni man. Am I right?"

"I *love* pepperoni!" Jonathan swiveled to his mom. "Can I?"

Head wrapped in a purple-print scarf, Liz smiled faintly. "You know our deal. You get to order whatever you want when we're out."

Looking back at Cole, Jonathan explained, "My mom's a veggie." He punctuated the explanation by pulling a face.

"Vegetarian," Liz corrected with a laugh. Despite the eye makeup, blush and lipstick she'd gone to the effort to put on so as not to seem sick, she looked hollow-eyed and wan.

Casting his gaze to Jonathan, Cole took care to look suitably horrified. "Pepperoni it is." Looking between Liz and Sarah, he asked, "Ladies, what's your pick? Sarah, I know you're a green pepper girl. What about you, Liz?"

"Not feeling the peppers today," Sarah lied.

The stuffed peppers she'd cooked and carried over to Liz's earlier in the week hadn't stayed down. Liz's periodic nausea and vomiting were worsening as the treatments went on. The weight she'd shed over the last week alone was worrisome.

Still, that Cole had remembered her topping preference had her heart feeling fluttery and warm. "Why don't we do half pepperoni and half mushroom?" she suggested. Mushroom was ordinarily her friend's favorite, and of all of them, Liz badly needed to eat. "Or is that too spicy?" she asked on afterthought, turning to Liz.

Liz cast a hesitant look toward Cole, and Sarah mentally kicked herself for drawing further attention to her illness. The outing was meant to be a break from the cancer. Instead she'd just reminded everyone of it.

"I'm sure it's fine, Sarah, but I'll probably have the house salad," she added, setting aside her menu.

Packing carbs would have served her better, but catching Cole's warning look, Sarah swallowed the suggestion. The wordless ease with which they communicated lately sometimes made it hard to remember they weren't really a couple.

The waiter returned, and Cole placed their orders. While they waited for their food, he kept the conversation lively and flowing. Sarah took part, but mostly she held back, awed by the ease with which he managed to win over Liz and Jonathan in turn. Perhaps his trick, if there was one, was that he treated them with total normalcy. And of course dealing with the public, kids, and their parents with cancer, was his job. Within thirty minutes, he'd hit sports, technology, and current TV and film, all topics certain to appeal to a small boy. *Iron Man* was awesome, he agreed though the first film in the trilogy was definitely the best. Jonathan hadn't yet seen the inside of the no-longer-so-new Yankee Stadium? Well, they would have to fix that ASAP. Privately Sarah wondered if he meant to stick around to make good on all the promises. For Jonathan's sake, she hoped so.

By the time the pie arrived, Cole and Jonathan were fast friends. Glancing over at Liz, Sarah saw the telltale sheen in her friend's sunken eyes. They exchanged silent smiles and looks, and Sarah felt herself tearing up, too. Barring an ironclad guarantee of a permanent remission, Jonathan's laughter was the best gift anyone could give her.

Cole thwacked the serving spatula against the side of the metal pizza pan, calling the table to attention. "Okay, so we have here sixteen inches of coal-fired, thin-crust pizza." He gestured to the bubbles blistering the golden brown crust. "Who's ready to tackle it?"

"W-o-w," Jonathan exclaimed. Eyes popping, he reached toward the pan.

"Whoa, ladies first," Cole intervened, catching his hand before he could burn himself. "Liz, you sure you're okay over there with just the salad?"

Liz nodded toward her heaping platter. "Me and Bugs Bunny are like this," she said, crossing her index and forefingers.

"Okay, then Sarah, here you go." He cut the spatula along the perimeters of a slice, and then slipped it off the pan and onto an empty plate. "Mangia, baby," he added with a goofy grin, passing it over.

Taking it from him, she felt her heart further melting. He was just so . . . *great*, including being a big kid, a side of him she hadn't seen before but very much liked. "Thanks, this looks great."

"Jonathan, ready my man? Think you can handle this big slice here in the center?"

"Oh, boy, can I ever!"

"That's the spirit," Cole said, dishing up a second slice.

After they'd finished, including boxing up the leftovers for Jonathan to take home, Cole suggested a stopover at nearby Bleecker Playground. Sarah was surprised he'd even heard of it, doubly surprised that he was willing to risk being seen with her in such a prominent public spot. She started to make their excuses, but Liz cut her off. Shooting a look in Jonathan's direction, she insisted she was totally up for it, that a walk in the warm air would do her good, and that she'd been at risk of climbing the four walls all week. But coming up onto the gated playground, Liz seemed to flag.

"You okay?" Sarah asked, though she obviously wasn't.

Liz managed a smile. "Just running a little low on steam. Mind if we sit?"

"Of course not," Sarah said, her gaze going to Cole.

Backtracking toward them, Jonathan hanging at his side, he offered Liz his arm rather than grabbing hold of hers, which Sarah happened to know she hated.

Liz sent him a look of gratitude and laid her thin hand over his forearm. "I was just telling Sarah I need to take five."

"Take as long as you need," he said, ferrying them toward the sitting area.

Taking note of the smart phones in nearly every adult's hand, including those using them to take pictures of their kids, Sarah slipped on her sunglasses before following them over. Wishing she'd thought to bring a hat as well, she joined Liz on one of the few open benches. Looking out onto the sea of strollers, pushed by happy parents and the occasional nanny, Sarah felt envy momentarily eclipse her anxiety about being recognized. Would that ever be her life?

Seeing them settled, Cole reached for Jonathan's hand. "I'll take Jonathan to work off some steam." He gestured to the sanded play area, trafficked with children awaiting their turn on the crayon-colored equipment. Tots on tricycles circuited the periphery or ran screaming through the sprinklers. "If you need me, holler."

Jonathan hesitated, shooting a worried look at his mother. "Are you okay, Mom?"

Liz reached out and touched his face. "I'm fine, honey. Go have fun."

He and Cole headed off toward the play area. Watching them walk away, Jonathan swinging off Cole's arm as though it was a rope, Sarah felt her eyes misting for the second time that afternoon. She'd assumed

Cole liked kids—his foundation worked on their behalf—but it hadn't occurred to her to consider how much he liked them. If today was any indication, he was a natural parent. Her fuck buddy had more facets than the Hope Diamond, and the true grit to back up all the glitter.

Liz barely waited for them to move out of earshot before breaking forth with, "Jesus, I could tell he was hot from the photos, but he's even better looking in person!"

"Yeah, I know," Sarah said around a sigh.

Bone structure like Cole's should be limited to statues of Greek gods and rare works of art. Ditto for eyes that deep oceanic-blue. Seeing him pushing Jonathan on the swings, most people would assume they were father and son.

Liz sighed. "Hot, hung, loaded, and he's obviously crazy about kids. I don't use 'awesome' all that much, but in Cole's case it fits."

It was just what Sarah *didn't* need to hear. "He does have some . . . flaws, you know."

The insomnia he sometimes mentioned, the restlessness that invariably led to a massive fuck fest or bingeing on cigarettes—she was pretty sure he not only had PTSD but that his case wasn't necessarily mild. She wished he'd come around to getting himself some help. The one time she'd suggested he join a veterans' support group, he'd all but bitten her head off.

But a stiff upper lip taken this far was bullshit. And he was so fucking hard on himself. In Iraq, he'd raced into the flames and carried out his teammate, making him a hero in everyone's eyes but his. The bare-bones account she'd found online had sounded harrowing. She couldn't imagine what it must have been like to have lived it.

Liz looked skeptical. "Don't tell me he picks his nose?"

"Ugh, of course not! Now that would be a deal buster."

"So what exactly is your and Cole's deal?"

"I told you, we have an arrangement. With rules," Sara added for emphasis.

Liz snorted. "You know what they say, rules are made to be broken, especially the ones that aren't working anymore."

Feeling defensive, Sarah folded her arms. "Who says it's not working?"

Liz sent her a sage smile. "You can't fool me, Sarah. We were roomies, remember? I saw the way you looked at him at lunch when you didn't think anyone was watching."

God, was she that transparent? "So maybe he's gotten under my skin a little, so what?"

Liz tipped her head, the scarf slightly slipping. "A little? Try a lot."

"Okay, but if I press for more, I'll scare him off. At least this way I'll have incredible sex for the next few months with someone I can trust not to run to the media or make a secret sex video or . . . whatever."

Reaching up to straighten her scarf, Liz asked, "Wanna trade problems?"

The question left Sarah feeling like a pretty terrible person. Unfolding her arms, she said, "I'm so sorry. What was I thinking?"

Liz covered her hand over Sarah's. "Do yourself a favor and stop thinking so much. You talked yourself into Danny. Don't talk yourself out of Cole. Really great guys like him don't grow on trees, you know."

Pinned beneath her friend's knowing gaze, Sarah couldn't deny any of it. Doing so would be pointless anyway. Liz had known her too long and too well. "Yeah, you're right, only once he figured out I was Sugar, he was never going to see me as anything but a fuck buddy."

"Never is a long time," Liz answered with a faraway look. "And think of how far you've come in the last ten years. Sure, you didn't set out to star in AE films, but once you did, you weren't just any porn star. You were *the* porn star. Be honest, would you really want to undo all that and go back to being Sarah from Brooklyn?"

"When you put it like that, I guess not," Sarah admitted.

Had she never ventured out to LA, she'd be doing . . . what now? Working a dead-end day job? Dating some loser or maybe married to a hard-drinking cop like her dad? Instead she'd had ten years of stardom. Because of it, she had the resources to reinvent herself, to do and be anything she wanted. She would always be "Sugar" in many peoples' eyes, but she could be a lot more, too.

She thought of her diary-turned-memoir, which she still hadn't brought up to Liz or the other FATEs. Cole was still the only person who knew. Once he'd realized what she was working on, he'd been so supportive and encouraging, even offering to open his publishing network to her once she was ready. Her fuck buddy had turned out to be not just a great lay but also a first-rate friend.

Jonathan bounded over, his knees encrusted with dirt, his smile bright enough to light a Times Square billboard. "Cole wants to take me, I mean us, for ice cream," he announced, eyes sparkling as he looked back at his new hero.

Pizza, playground, and now ice cream, talk about your kid-pleasing trifecta! Cole walked up to them, his beaming smile equal to Jonathan's. Other than in the immediate aftermath of sex, she'd never seen him so relaxed.

Liz smiled. "Remember your manners, honey." She reached out and swiped at a smudge on his chin. "Mr. Canning can speak for himself." She glanced over at Cole.

"I'd love to—"

A friendly-faced brown Labrador gamboled up to them, cutting him off. Cole's smile froze. His gaze darkened.

"Jonathan, get back!" He swooped, scooped up the boy, and began backing away. "Get, I said *get!*" he hollered, kicking dirt up at the dog.

Sarah leapt up from the bench. "Stop it!" Stepping between Cole and the dog, she hissed, "What the hell's wrong with you? This is obviously someone's pet that's gotten loose. He's got a collar, and look how well-kept he is."

She turned back to the dog. Ears pinned back and tail dragging, he backed away. "It's okay, sweetie," she soothed. Slowly she extended her hand and let him sniff. Once she'd established trust, she reached for his collar.

Cole set a squirming Jonathan back on his feet. "Pets aren't allowed in New York City playgrounds," he answered coldly. Despite the ice in his voice, his forehead and upper lip were pearled with perspiration. "Check out the signs. They're posted everywhere."

"I guess he can't read," Sarah shot back.

Out of the corner of her eye, she saw Liz watching them intently. Like her, Liz was a dog lover, and yet when Cole went ballistic she hadn't spoken up.

Holding on to the collar to keep the dog from wandering further, possibly into the busy street beyond the gates, she scratched behind one silky ear. The animal began to relax. She moved on to the other ear. How could Cole be so cruel? It seemed completely out of character.

A young brunette hurried up the quartzite pavement, leash in hand. Reaching them, she expelled a ragged breath as if she'd been running. "Sorry about that. Some idiot left the dog park's gate open, and Colby ran out before I could reach him." She dropped down on one knee and pulled her pet to her. "Thank God you're okay. You had mommy so worried," she said, planting a smacking kiss atop his head.

"It's okay, we're all animal lovers," Sarah said, cutting Cole a look. His expression remained wary.

Jonathan walked up to the dog. "Can I pet him?" he asked, dividing his eager gaze between the owner and his mother.

The brunette took a moment to hook on the lead before answering, "Sure, Colby's really friendly. I adopted him from the ASPCA a year ago. He's never bitten anyone to my knowledge, and he's current on all of his shots," she added, lifting one of the tags from the lab's collar.

"Okay, but pet him gently, Jonathan," Liz advised. "Let him get a whiff of your hand first, and don't put your face down to him."

They stood in silence as Colby, tail beating the bushes, basked in the full measure of a little boy's rapt adoration. Venturing a look up to Cole's stony face, Sarah wondered again what his problem was.

Rising, Colby's person pulled gently back on the retractable lead. "Colby and I have to be getting on home. Again, sorry for any scare," she added, giving Cole a broad berth as she led the dog away.

Liz got up from the bench. "I think ice cream will have to wait. Sorry, Jonathan, but I'm going to have to head home and take a nap."

Jonathan's narrow shoulders slumped, but good kid that he was, he nodded without protest. "That's okay, mom, we have ice cream in the fridge." He looked up to Cole. "Do you want to come back with us and have some? It's mint chocolate chip," he added as an inducement.

Cole reached down, laying a hand on either of the child's shoulders. "Thanks buddy, but I'm about ready for a nap myself. You were a maniac on those monkey bars."

Jonathan brightened. "I was, wasn't I?"

"Thanks for a lovely afternoon," Liz put in.

"I had a great time," Cole insisted. Lowering his gaze back to Jonathan, he added, "I'll take a rain check on that ice cream."

Jonathan's big brown eyes met his. "Promise?"

Cole nodded solemnly. "How's next Saturday sound?"

Jonathan beamed up at him. "That'd be *awesome!*" He edged his gaze over to his mom's. "If it's okay with my mom?"

Liz hesitated. "Actually, your taking Jonathan that day would be a huge help. I have a . . . doctor's appointment at noon that will take a couple of hours." She looked over at Sarah.

The appointment was another chemo treatment, and Liz was guaranteed to be wiped out afterward, as well as possibly puking. "I'm going with Liz that day, so if you're free—"

"Sarah can message me your address," Cole broke in, stepping back from Jonathan and swiveling to Sarah. "Or better yet, we'll come over together," he added.

Offering to keep her friend's kid, making plans a week out, plans that involved her, he certainly acted like they were a . . . couple. Or was he just working double time to make up for his freak-out?

Rather than risk reading too much into the gesture, Sarah settled for a nod. "Sure, that'd work."

Liz looked overwhelmed. "Wow, okay, great, we'll look forward to seeing you both then." Despite Cole's and Sarah's pleas to let them put her into a cab, she insisted on walking Jonathan the last few blocks home alone. Dividing her tired smile between them, she wrapped an arm about her son's shoulders. "I don't need a babysitter, not yet anyway. Besides, it's still a beautiful day. You two should enjoy it," she added, shooting Sarah a meaningful look.

Sarah relented. "Okay, but text me when you guys get home, otherwise I'll worry."

Liz nodded. "Okay . . . Mom."

Ignoring the sarcasm, Sarah persisted. "Promise?"

Liz lifted a hand to the left side of her chest. "Cross my heart and hope to die . . . Actually, let's leave it at 'cross my heart,'" she added with a wink.

Sarah didn't find the gallows humor at all funny, but if it helped Liz get through the next few months that was all that mattered. Hugs and handshakes made the rounds and then Liz and Jonathan were off.

She waited for them to clear the park before turning back to Cole. "What's your deal with dogs anyway?"

Fair or not, she'd always thought of people who disliked animals as sort of soulless. Lately she'd been giving serious thought to adopting a rescue dog, not a rambunctious puppy—that would require too much work up front—but an older animal in need of a good home and a second chance. Doing so would be a big additional responsibility, as well as a powerful symbol that she was ready to put down roots again. Whether she stayed on in New York after Liz's treatment ended or moved elsewhere remained to be seen.

His gaze shuttered. "They're okay," he said, and left it at that.

For once Sarah knew better than to push him. Pushing boundaries in bed was one thing, but what had just gone down here was something different entirely, something sex couldn't begin to touch, let alone solve.

Chapter Eight

Clancy's in Astoria was a cop bar where the Guinness was poured with a perfect head, the Jameson shots came as a double, and the city's ban on smoking in public places was seen as more of a misguided suggestion. Sarah found her father at the brass-railed bar, a stein of half drunk dark beer and an empty shot glass set in front of him.

Picking her way through the plumes of smoke mushrooming from the closely packed tables, Sarah walked up. "Hi, Pop."

Her dad didn't stir. "Look what the west wind blew in," he said, taking a sip of his beer.

She settled onto the empty stool beside him. "I stopped by the house, but your neighbor said you'd gone out. I figured I'd try you here." She'd called first, but it seemed his land line was disconnected once again.

Keeping his gaze straight ahead, he asked, "To what do I owe this honor?"

"I left you a message that I was back in town."

He snorted, stabbing his cigarette into the ash tray. "You've been back how many weeks is it?"

Despite the booze he regularly knocked back, he had a mind like a steel trap, as well as cop connections just about everywhere. Whether or not he'd gotten her message, he likely knew down to the hour when she'd set foot in the city.

"I've been . . . settling in."

She deliberately avoided bringing up Liz. Mentioning her, any friend, would only trigger an interrogation, starting with how they knew one another. Once she admitted they'd met on a film shoot, his ears would close to everything else.

He gestured to behind the bar, the liquor shelves filled with dusty bottles and backed by mirrored glass. "You want something?"

Sarah hesitated. *I want your love.* "A Guinness, I guess." She wasn't much of a beer drinker, at least not anymore, but the wine at Clancy's would come from a box, and she'd never had much of a head for liquor.

He beckoned to the bartender, the low light catching on his retirement watch. Thirty years on the force from patrol cop to detective first-grade. Unfortunately playing the ponies had blown through his pension, along with her mother's small savings. "One Guinness, no shot, and put it on my tab."

"So, you back for good?"

Sarah shrugged. "I'm not sure, maybe."

He let out a sharp laugh. "A definite maybe, huh? That's good, Sarah, real good. I can see you haven't changed."

Sarah stiffened. "Neither have you."

Except that he'd grown older, a lot older. The last time she'd seen him was Christmas five years ago. His thick thatch of hair was all gray now, and his slope-shouldered posture spoke of too many days spent like this one, hunched over a bar. Seeing him again, she didn't feel any of the anger she'd expected and only a little of the hurt. What she mostly felt was sad. He might feel she'd pissed away her life, but she felt the same about him.

The bartender set down her beer. "Thanks," she said, dodging his goggle-eyed stare. He obviously recognized her as Sugar.

Her father's hand tightened to a white-knuckled fist about his glass. "Don't you got some glasses to wash or somethin'?"

"Sure thing, Marty, sorry." He made a beeline for the other end of the bar. Her dad turned back to her, lip curled. "Occupational hazard, huh?"

"You could say that." She took a sip of beer, and then set the glass down. "It's good to see you, Pop." Five years ago he'd thrown her out of the house—literally. Sitting down to a beer together showed they could be civil at least. "I thought maybe I could come by the house this weekend, make Sunday roast like mom used to."

Bringing up her mother was a mistake. Man's man though he was, his eyes filled with water. "You look just like her, God rest her soul." He made the sign of the cross.

Reflexively Sarah joined him, a lump settling into the back of her throat. Raised Catholic, she wasn't sure what she was now. Apart from attending the rare wedding, she hadn't been to church in years, let alone taken mass. She liked to think of herself as spiritual, not religious. Practically, though, what did that mean?

"You still know how to cook?" Drying his eyes on his sleeve, he sent her a skeptical look.

Cole had expressed similar surprise the first night she'd made him dinner. What was it with men that they assumed you couldn't act in porn and be in any way domestic? As if she and the other AE actors must be so busy doing body shots off one another that no one could pause to put on water for pasta or thaw a roast?

Determined not to take the bait, she took another sip of beer and nodded. "I still have the box with all of mom's recipes."

The recipe box had been one of the few non essential personal items she'd squeezed into her suitcase ten years ago. She'd moved many times since that crazed, cross-country trek, and her mom's recipes had gone with her everywhere.

"So what do you say?" she prompted, daring to hope. *It's the whole olive tree, Pop. C'mon, take it.*

"Unfortunately I won't be there."

This was news! Even in his younger days, her dad had always considered vacations a waste of time and money. So far as he was concerned, the city had everything you could want or need. An afternoon in the stands at the old Yankee Stadium was as much of a getaway as he could stomach. Usually he'd preferred to watch the games parked in front of his TV with a cold six-pack and a can of Pringles.

A bad feeling settled into her stomach. Though she knew she would likely regret it, she asked, "Why not?"

He upended his glass, draining it of beer. "The landlord and I have a difference of opinion over the rent due." He set the stein down hard.

He was being evicted! "Let me help you out. I have money. I won't miss it." Whatever he owed would be a pittance to her.

He held up both hands. "Keep your money. I don't want a dime. From what I've heard about your movies, you've more than earned it."

In a weird way, he was right. She had earned her wealth by being savvy and smart, proactive and strategic, by taking ownership of her brand and eventually her films. Just about anyone could take off their clothes and fuck. Making people want to watch you do it for one hundred films raised the bar from porn to performance art.

Steeling herself not to lose her temper, not this time, she said, "I was going to save this for Sunday, but I guess I'll tell you now. I've retired. This latest . . . release is my last film."

He reached over and lifted her left hand. "What, no gold watch? And no gold ring, either."

Sarah snatched her hand away. "You haven't seen me in five years. Would it kill you to be a little bit pleasant? If not for me, then do it for mom."

His face hardened; his eyes bulged. He slammed his fist on the bar. The empty shot glass and bowl of peanuts jumped. "Don't you dare bring your mother up to me! She was a good Catholic woman, a good wife and mother. I'm glad she's in her grave, so she can't see the shame you've brought on yourself and me."

That did it! Sarah slid off the stool and onto her feet. "Yeah, well what about the shame you brought with your gambling and your women. Oh, yeah, you think I didn't know about the perfume on your uniforms, the lipstick on your shirt collars? You think I didn't hear mom crying late at night when she thought I was sleeping?"

"Shut your mouth and show respect. I'm your father."

"And I'm your daughter, your only child, and respect goes both ways. You want mine, then you can earn it starting by saying you're sorry."

"I'm supposed to be sorry! You're the—"

"I wasn't the one who came home drunk, or not at all, and made Mom cry. I wasn't the one who took what was supposed to be my tuition money for NYU and pissed it away at the track. You don't like what I've become, what I've done to survive, to *thrive*, fair enough. But before you throw any more stones, Pop, you take a good, long look at yourself in that dusty bar mirror." Shaking, she shoved a hand inside her purse and pulled out her wallet. She grabbed all the cash she had with her and slapped it down on the bar. "You can use this as a partial payment to your landlord so he doesn't toss your ass to the curb, or you can use it to get shitfaced. It's up to you. But from here on, I'm done with you making me feel guilty and ashamed about my life. Yes, I've made *one hundred* porn movies—" she deliberately pitched her voice just below a shout "—and I've also never stolen, I've never cheated, and above all I've never once treated another person with anything close to the contempt and cruelty you've spent the last decade dumping on me. So have a nice life, Pop. Here's three hundred dollars. Try not to drink it all in one day."

*** ***

Headquartered in midtown Manhattan, The Canning Foundation occupied a landmark Neo-Georgian townhouse, three stories of ponderous antiques, faded Persian carpets, and soaring plasterwork ceilings trimmed in crown molding. The air stank of must and old money, the legacy of more than a century of public service and private familial duty. Cole had always found the atmosphere oppressive but never more so than today.

Sitting behind his desk, a hideous, gilded Rococo monstrosity remaining from his mother's regime, he surveyed his surroundings. Interspersed among the shadowboxes and oil portraits of his frowning predecessors were framed photographs of smiling kids and their smooth-pated parents, the latter towing oxygen tanks and IV bags as they took part in various fantasy-come-true outings. Whether white-water rafting, zip lining, or taking in a theme park from the vantage point of a motorized scooter, the images' moralizing message was clear. Cancer can't keep a good parent down.

Other than his computer, the color photos were the sole connection to the twenty-first century. Everything else seemed stagnant, frozen circa 1940. Cole felt like a fixture himself, leaden and hollow, with little more animation than the marble philosophers' busts plopped upon pedestals, staring sightlessly back at him from sundry nooks and crannies.

Realizing he'd been reading the same paragraph for the past half hour, he shoved the report to the far edge of his leather-and-green baize desk blotter. A desk blotter, seriously! Who even used one anymore, not to mention a paperweight jade dragon reputed to have belonged to Winston Churchill? Cannings did, of course.

But he hadn't behaved as a Canning, not the previous Saturday.

The episode in the play park had rattled him badly. Liz and the kid and the dog owner all staring as though he'd just touched down from Mars. And then there was Sarah, regarding him with horrified eyes, eyes that for the first time saw how seriously fucked up he was, how *broken.* Too broken to consider seeing again? The prospect made him want to punch the wood paneling.

Good going, Canning, now she probably thinks you're a pussy.

Coming up was *Whipped and Creamed.* He'd thought to save the film as a sort of grand finale, but after the other day, he had something to prove.

No more procrastinating. He picked up his iPhone, brought up Sarah's number, and typed his text.

Tomorrow nite at 9. Ready to get . . . Whipped and Creamed.

He hit send. Almost immediately, relaxation rolled over him. Whether Sarah said yes or not, whether she gave him the chance to redeem himself or not, it was done. For the first time since walking away from her in the West Village, his tail dragging like that of the poor dog he'd frightened with his freak out, he felt hungry.

Leaning forward in his high-backed chair, he punched the intercom button for his assistant. "Karen, bring in the takeout menus. I'm ready to order lunch."

❋❋❋ ❋❋❋

"How was lunch with your dad?" Honey asked, when Sarah walked inside Liz's that night, feeling like she'd been whipped and not in a good way.

"We didn't exactly have lunch," Sarah answered, dropping her handbag on the carpet alongside an empty chair and collapsing atop the worn cushion. "We had beer and peanuts—and shots of whiskey. Actually I only had the beer."

Peter leaned over from his perch of the couch. "Oh, sweetie, I'm so sorry. I really thought making amends would help."

"You look like you could use these more than me." Honey pushed the box of Kleenex across the coffee table toward her, but Sarah shook her head. She'd already done her crying on her way back in the cab.

Ensconced in the center of the sofa with an afghan pulled over her crossed legs, Liz shook her scarf-wrapped head. "We were wrong to have pushed you. I've never met your dad, but after all the things I've heard about him over the years, I should have known better. I should have spoken up."

Sarah shook her head. She was a grown-up—even if she felt fairly little at the moment. "Thanks, guys, but you don't have squat to be sorry for. Peter, you meant well, and actually it ended up being really good advice. Even though things didn't go the way I'd hoped, I feel a lot better getting all the crap off my chest. My father will never change, but at least I can move on now."

Liz sent her a sympathetic smile. "Under the right circumstances, confrontation can be cathartic. In my hospital support group, the therapist is having us each write a letter to our cancer. Some of the letters are like olive branches, you know, making peace with the disease. In my case, I told cancer how I'm going to fucking kick its ass."

She darted a gaze to Jonathan's door, fortunately closed. Mrs. Ritter and her cats must be otherwise engaged.

Clapping and even one wolf whistle followed. Pounding her palms together, Sarah was grateful for the reminder that, while her personal life might be a wreck, it was at least a repairable wreck. Not everyone was so lucky.

Looking around the room, Liz gave her best imitation of what in their roomie days they'd jokingly referred to as the Royal Wave. "Yes, yes, I'm awesome, and don't I know it." Once everyone had quieted, she carried on. "Okay, does anyone have anything they want to bring up or announce before we wrap?"

Peter cleared his throat. "Well . . . I have kind of an announcement."

"Darling, do tell," Honey prompted in her best "Audrey" intonation.

Reaching for a cookie, her first food of the day, Sarah said, "It must be something really good. Look how he's smiling!" To Peter, she added, "I could do with hearing some good news."

Going beet red, he blurted out, "I told Pol the truth. He said he loved me, that what was past was past, and the next thing I knew I was down on one knee proposing. And he said yes! We're getting married!" He pounded the heels of his Mark Nason 'Strummer' loafers into the carpet.

Honey exclaimed, "How wonderful!"

Liz beamed. "Congratulations, you did it!"

"Congratulations," Brian echoed, hangdog expression lifting.

"I'm so happy for you," Sarah said sincerely. Ever since she could remember, she'd loved anything to do with weddings. From everything she'd heard from Liz and now Peter, his Irish boyfriend was his perfect match.

"I took a ton of pictures. Here, see." Beaming, he reached into his pocket and pulled out his Android. Photos of the bridegroom-to-be and the rings were passed around and duly admired.

Hovering over Honey, who held the phone, he explained, "We're getting matching bands from this cool custom jewelry shop. See, the engraving on the band? It's a Celtic cross."

"When's the big day?" Sarah asked, feeling the lump from earlier lodge again in her throat.

"We both really want a June wedding, which means I've got to pull this together fast."

Liz blinked. "June! But we're almost out of May."

"I know, I know, but I have to feel that if it's meant to be, we'll get into someplace."

The group disbanded. Only Peter hung around. Even after Liz excused herself to lie down, he stayed. Sarah had the weird sense that he was deliberately dawdling in order to get her alone. Her instinct proved to be on the mark.

Drying the last of the dishes, he said, "Sarah, I didn't want to ask this in front of the others, in case you might want an out."

"An out to what?" she asked, putting the leftover cookies back in their box.

"I know we've only known each other a short while, but I feel this incredible bond with you, like we're members of the same soul group or . . . something. Anyway, you've been so sweet and supportive, and . . . well, I was hoping . . . Is there any chance you might consider . . ." From across the small kitchen, he sent her a helpless look.

Laughing, Sarah said, "Peter, please just ask me whatever."

"Would you be my attendant? You know, my best . . . woman?"

Blown away, she blurted out, "Oh, Peter, I'm so honored you'd ask me. Of course I will. I'll even wear a tuxedo if you want."

He chuckled. "I'm sure you look amazing in tails, but a nice dress will be fine for City Hall."

"You're getting married downtown then?" A municipal wedding didn't quite seem to live up to the fairytale, but then Sarah supposed that their being able to legally marry was such a dream-come-true that the setting scarcely seemed to matter.

He nodded. "With Pol being Catholic, me being a lapsed Jew, and both of us being gay, a church wedding doesn't seem . . . realistic. But we want to make up for it with a reception somewhere fabulous."

"We'll put our heads together and come up with the perfect place," she promised, turning over the possibilities in her mind.

If she struck out, she could always ask Cole. He didn't like to trade on his family name, but he still had a lot of connections. She wasn't above bending his ear on behalf of her friend. If anyone could get them a booking on short notice, it would be him.

Her cell phone dinged, signaling a new text message. Curious, she excused herself to get her bag from the living room. Digging out the phone, she saw the text was from Cole and her heart leapt.

Tomorrow nite at 9. Ready to get . . . Whipped and Creamed.

In so many ways, that film represented the apex of her career. She'd won an AVA Best Actress Award for it. Not only had she starred in it, but she'd also produced it. And in twenty-four hours she'd get to revisit her breakout role as the insatiable sex therapist-cum-dominatrix with a real-life lover—Cole.

A throat being cleared had her looking up to Peter, who'd followed her over. "Judging from the expression on your face, that must be something really good—or should I say *someone?*" he added with a sly smile.

For the first time since the failed détente with her dad, Sarah found her smile. "It is," she admitted, dropping the phone back into her bag. "As I was starting to say, don't stress about finding a venue for the reception. If all else fails, I know a guy."

✻✻✻ ✻✻✻

Cole lay on his back in the center of Sarah's bed, sweat rolling down his sides. His arms were stretched high above his head, his wrists manacled in leather, the leashes leading away and securely fastened to the metal rungs of the headboard. The leather collar cinched securely around his neck, not tight enough to strangle but enough to make him acutely aware of every precious swallow. His shoulders, stomach, and outer thighs wore an expert cross stitch pattern of fine, red welts. The perspiring he was doing potentiated a subtly satisfying sting. The flogger, fashioned to resemble a riding crop, lay on the carpet, cast aside in favor of the vibrator Sarah now wielded. Following from the film, she would use the toy to pleasure herself while leaving her "patient" wanting and helpless, forced to watch until he finally succumbed to the onslaught of indirect stimulation. The "facial" she would give him with his spent seed would be the final humiliation. Sarah didn't yet know it, but Cole had a very different ending in mind.

Straddling him, she wore blood-red lipstick and the skimpy leather dominatrix outfit he'd bought for her the other week: vinyl zip-front corset, lace-up garter belt, and black silk stockings—and absolutely nothing underneath. Leaving her cunt uncovered was calculated to further fuck with his mind. Her pussy loomed, pink and pulsing, succulent and slick, forbidden fruit that, according to the film, he would be allowed no more than a nibble of.

Sweat slick and rock hard, he couldn't remember ever being quite this completely, painfully aroused. But then a woman of the world having her wicked way with him had long been a fantasy of his, even before he'd watched *Whipped and Creamed* for the first of probably a hundred times. The fetish had begun with *The Graduate*. If he'd been the dorky Dustin Hoffman character, he would have stayed with Mrs. Robinson and left her bland daughter behind.

New York had no shortage of women game for unleashing their inner bitch. Unfortunately it wasn't every woman who could sell it. Post-*Fifty Shades of Grey*, Manhattan socialites collected designer floggers as once they'd done vintage jewelry and couture evening clutches, but it didn't necessarily follow that they knew what to do with the equipment—or him. He'd experimented with Candace a few times. She'd gotten into the dressing up and talking dirty, but that was about it. After a few flicks of the flogger, she'd complained that her arm was getting tired, the game was boring, and couldn't they move on to the main event?

Sarah's striking arm hadn't tired, at least not that she'd let on. Small though she was, she was also impressively strong and splendidly skilled. She'd begun by teasing the suede tails over him—his shoulders, his belly, his cock. The tickling had segued to light lashing that had warmed his blood, heightening every sensation. Once she'd begun whipping him in earnest, she'd done so with an expert hand, steering clear of danger zones such as his face, heart, and kidneys. Knowing he was in such capable hands had enabled him to immerse himself without worry.

Far from appearing impatient or bored, she was totally into it, the role-play, the power exchange—him. Being on the receiving side of a professional porn star—okay, *former* porn star's—single-minded focus was heady stuff.

He lifted his head from the banked pillows. "You're pissed off about something, so use it. Use me."

This wasn't all acting. Something was eating at her. He'd picked up on it as soon as he'd arrived, asked her about it before they'd gotten anywhere near the bed. She'd shrugged off his concern, told him not to waste her time. "Do you want to get whipped and creamed or don't you?" she'd demanded sharply, and even though he'd come to think of them as friends, Cole hadn't had the willpower to resist.

"Shut up." She glared down at him.

"Make me," he taunted, knowing it was dangerous to dare her.

But then Cole lived for danger. At times such as this, he could almost believe it was the only thing keeping him alive, the only thing capable of convincing him that he wasn't the one left laying dead and dismembered on that makeshift minefield back in Iraq. Combining danger with sex intensified the rush, drove the high that much higher, catapulted the climax to the craziest crush.

Sarah's hand sang across his jaw, the strike a blur of slender fingers tipped in scarlet-painted nails. The sting made his eyes water. He blinked against the disorientation, a too-brief fix for all his inconvenient remembering.

"Again," he said, swallowing hard against the collar's cinching.

Her sexy, red mouth flattened at the edges. "Shut up."

He glanced downward to his cock, standing pole straight from his groin. The thought of all the ways she still might hurt him had him leaking.

She slapped him again—hard. The reverberation sent his senses seesawing, not just touch, pain, but all of it, every fucking thing. Her scent filled his nostrils—her perspiration, her perfume, her pussy heat. As boldly as she brandished the vibrator, Cole wasn't fooled. It was him she wanted, not some mechanical toy.

A moment's pause and then she decided. He saw it in her face first, the setting of her slender jaw, the hard glint of her slanted, cat-eyed gaze. His shoulder muscles bunched, his belly clenched, in part with excitement, in part with . . . fear. The adrenalin rush reminded him of approaching an active bomb, those first few seconds when you weren't entirely sure what you might have there. Sarah was like that now, an enigma, an entity he knew in pieces and parts, but for whom he was missing the composite picture. Not only wasn't he sure what she was going to do next, she wasn't sure. The latter made her absolutely lethal.

She was angry, so fucking gloriously furious. He'd always sensed it in her, this anger sizzling beneath the surface. He could only speculate as to the cause. Liz's illness was probably part of it, and then there was the father of whom she refused to speak. But Cole sensed that neither accounted for a complete explanation. Something bad had happened back in LA. A lost-little-girl look came over her whenever the City of Angels was even casually mentioned.

She didn't look lost now or anything close to a little girl. She slid up the length of him with utter confidence, not stopping until her sex reached the level of his mouth. He'd seen her wet, pink pussy plenty of times in close up—but not this close.

"This is all you deserve, dog." Her voice reminded him of jagged glass, cutting and cold. Dropping down, she ground her groin against his mouth. "Now eat me."

Cole buried his nose and mouth in her bush. He breathed her, his senses so overwhelmingly alert he felt as if the room must be spinning. The crispness of the damp curls brushing across his face, her vagina's velvety softness, the briny tang of her arousal. If she ended by suffocating him, well, he could think of worse ways to die.

"I said eat me out!" she commanded, grabbing hold of the head board to steady herself as she pushed harder into his face.

Salty slickness coated his lips. Plump, plum-colored lips brushed back and forth, spreading their juices. A swollen clit bobbed like a miniature cherry against his tongue. Cole suckled. He circled. A loud thump by the bed announced the vibrator's landing. In that moment, the power shifted. He might be the one of them tethered, but it was Sarah who was losing control. The power of what he could do to her, of what he was doing to her, was headier than any designer drug. Rushing on it, he licked and lapped, nipped and soothed. Sarah gyrated above him. Her thighs quivered. Her arms shook. On the cusp of coming, she let go of the metal bars and pulled back.

Cole stared up into her flushed face. Most of the red lipstick had been bitten off. Her eyes, rimmed by the heavy black liner, didn't look angry any longer but liquid and stricken.

He caught her gaze with his. "You can tease with all the toys you want, but we both know that nothing and no one is ever going to feel as good inside you as I do."

Sarah didn't speak. She didn't slap. She didn't make a move to retrieve the vibrator or the flogger. The script from *Whipped and Creamed* . . . they might as well have burned it. Suddenly it was only them, not film characters playacting but two flesh-and-blood people probing the boundaries of passion and trust.

Holding his gaze, Sarah glided downward. She took his penis in hand, positioned herself over him, and came down—hard.

"Fuck me, then," she said, sounding resigned.

Cole didn't need to be told twice. He lifted his torso and hips, driving as deep as he could go. If she hadn't been so drenched, he would have hurt her, but he was past caring about that and so, he knew, was she.

Sarah groaned and rocked against him. Her hands slammed into his shoulders, pushing him back to the mattress, her nails raking his already-scored skin. She pulled back and impaled herself yet again. Pinned beneath her, Cole moved the only part of his body he still could—his hips. He thrust upward, hard, sharp, deep. A lesser lover might have lost her seat but not Sarah. She rode him just as hard, pushing him to the edge of his physical endurance and emotional control.

"Hit me again," he said, and this time there was no mistaking it for anything other than a command.

Sarah lifted her right hand from where it was anchored to his shoulder. She hauled back and struck him—hard. Cole fell back against the pillow. His head swam. The inside of his mouth tasted of blood. He swallowed, throat muscles working against the slave collar. He hadn't felt anything close to this alive since Iraq. Only now pain and fear were paired with pleasure—so much pleasure. And Sarah—for the first time since their games had begun, he felt like she wasn't holding back. She was giving him all of her, or at least all of her shadow side. Surrendering to the gift, he stilled beneath her. Sarah slammed her pelvis into his. She advanced and retreated, again and again, harder and harder. He felt the exact moment when her orgasm hit. Her eyes dilated, her mouth opened, and her skin flared, so scalding he wondered she didn't melt the vinyl. Her fingers bit into his shoulders like hooks, anchors against her body's shuddering. Like a velvet fist, her pussy pumped him, the contractions rhythmic and powerful. Perspiration pouring, Cole finally gave in. He followed her into oblivion, coming harder than he ever had in his life, harder than he'd ever thought it was possible to come. Penis pumping, seed spraying, a single word, a name, broke free from his bruised lips.

Not "Sugar" but "Sarah!"

Chapter Nine

Sarah was dashing out the door to meet Peter for their first wedding-planning lunch when her cell phone sounded. Shit! Clipping the post onto the back of a pierced earring, she grabbed for the phone with her free hand. Double shit—it was Martin.

She hesitated and then picked up. "Martin, hi!" she said, hoping she sounded sufficiently enthusiastic.

"Hi yourself, beautiful. How's the Big Apple treating you?"

Even though she'd been deliberately ducking him, it was good to hear his voice. She might not miss LA; she didn't miss the city at all, but she did miss the few friends she'd left behind there, her manager among them.

Smiling into the receiver, she couldn't resist reminding him, "I grew up here, remember?" As someone involved exclusively with adult films, Martin saw LA as the epicenter of the universe.

"So that means I can't be concerned?" His testy tone was tinged with hurt.

"Of course you can. Sorry. Everything's fine, really good actually," she added, thinking back to the previous movie-night meet up.

"Really good" didn't begin to do it justice. She and Cole hadn't just veered off script. They'd rewritten the scene completely, taking *Whipped and Creamed* to a whole new level and rocketing her to a Big O the likes of which she'd never before experienced. Two days later, her body was still deliciously sore in all the best places.

Afterward, they'd shared a shower, a bottle of wine, and a carryout meal. Not only was he awesome in bed but he was also so easy and fun to be around. Being with him was like having your fantasy lover and your best friend rolled into one, and not in a creepy way but in a . . . *really good* way. Too bad he didn't seem to like dogs. Every time she'd tried bringing up what had happened in the play park, he changed the subject or tried making a joke of it.

Caught up in her thoughts, she suddenly realized that she wasn't the only one of them not talking. Silence and Martin didn't go together, not unless something was bothering him.

"Martin, what is it?"

His heavy breath blew in her ear as though they were in the same room instead of more than two thousand miles apart. "I don't know if I should tell you this, but I ran into Danny the other night at Villa. Actually he was in the line outside it."

Located in a former LA speakeasy, Villa catered to the scenester crowd with its library feel, splashy Golden Globe centerpiece, and insanely well-stocked marble-top bar. Hearing that Danny was hanging out there pretty much doused her hopes that he might have decided to get sober.

"Shit," she said. Then it struck her. "He was waiting to get in?" That was another bad sign.

"Yeah, and I'd say his chances of seeing the inside of that club without you on his arm were pretty slim. He looked . . . rough."

"I'm really sorry to hear that," she said sincerely.

Any romantic feelings she'd once felt toward her ex were long gone, but he was still a person, and one with whom she'd spent a substantial chunk of her life. Even if he had gone about trying to get her back the wrong way, by leaving scary stalker notes, she had to believe those actions were the booze and drugs at work, not the real him. Still . . .

"You didn't tell him where I was?"

"Of course not! If he finds out you're in New York, it won't be from me. Client or not, I've got your back, baby—always have, always will. You should know that by now."

The rebuke was deserved. She should know better than to have asked. Martin, of all people, knew what she'd gone through those last few months in LA. "You're right, of course I do. It was a stupid thing to say. I'm sorry."

"Don't worry about it, kid. You're safe, that's all that matters. Anyhow, along with checking up on you, I'm calling to let you know that *Camera Sutra* is doing killer, your biggest blockbuster yet. We made bank in the first week. I wouldn't be surprised if it doesn't score a slew of AVN awards, including best picture."

Loosely scripted along the lines of the *Kama Sutra*, her final film featured a sultry blond photographer (her) encountering a winsome young male model who she took on as her muse. The Pygmalion-themed script had originally cast the male actor as the photographer—of course!—and her as the ingénue—ridiculous!—but Sarah had insisted on a full revision. When she still wasn't one hundred percent happy with the result, she'd sat down and rewritten it herself. Such was the power of being one's own producer. Martin's news was a vindication that depicting powerful women in porn was long overdue.

"That's awesome," she said, pleased and yet not nearly as thrilled as she would have been even a year ago. The film was a solid, sex-positive, woman-positive piece of work, but it was still porn—and porn no longer defined her.

"So, keeping busy?" Martin finally got around to asking.

Eager to bring him up-to-date, she answered, "I've reconnected with an LA friend who moved back here. Liz Carter, you probably remember her as—"

"Spice Carter! Dark hair, dark eyes, and built like a brick shithouse. The tits on that girl could have suckled a small village."

Sarah hesitated. It had been a long time, if ever, that she'd thought of her friend in those terms. "Yes, well, she has a graphic design business and a kid now." She didn't mention Liz also had cancer. Other than Cole, Sarah hadn't shared that information with anyone.

"That's great. Give her my best."

"Okay, I will."

"Speaking of which, when am I seeing you again? Rested up and raring for number one hundred and one? I hope so because a great script just crossed my desk, and I think you're really going to dig the—"

"Martin, stop!"

"What? What is it?"

Holding the phone to her ear, she fought back guilt before answering, "Look, I've got to be honest. I've had more than two months to think about it, and retirement still feels like the right decision—completely. I know it's not what you were hoping to hear, and I hope we'll always stay friends, but I have to do what's right for me."

"And what, being a billionaire, award-winning, adult-film actress and producer isn't cutting it for you anymore?"

He was disappointed, she got that. Still, she wasn't the only one of them she'd made rich these last ten years. Martin had done very well for himself managing her. She was no longer the twenty-something ingénue looking to him for guidance. She'd grown up and moved on, and now it was time for him to do the same.

Firming her voice, she said, "I have other things I'm focusing on." She thought of the book, but in his current frame of mind he'd likely dash it down. Besides, what if it turned out not to be a book at all but simply a series of juicy-but-disjointed ramblings? Worse still, what if it sucked?

"Yeah, what's his name?"

Sarah bristled. How dare he treat her as if she was some brainless bimbo! As if taking off her clothes and fucking on camera was all she was capable of! But no, this was Martin, her Martin, a squishy, soft teddy bear beneath the façade of hardened Hollywood agent. He hadn't meant it that way, at least not totally. He was just upset.

Seizing on the chance to turn the topic, she admitted, "Among other things, I'm helping with a friend's wedding." She summed up Peter and Pol's marriage plans in progress. "Who knows, maybe I'll do event planning for awhile," she quipped. Working to make her new friend's dream wedding a reality was unexpectedly satisfying.

She'd expected him to continue to push to change her mind, but instead he said, "Look, I've gotta run to a meeting. We'll talk again soon."

"Martin, about that press release announcing my retire—"

"Ciao, baby."

He clicked off, or perhaps they'd lost the connection. Sarah set down the cell with a sigh, feeling as if her business in LA wasn't quite finished. If worse came to worse, she would write the damned press announcement herself and post it on her website. Whatever she decided, it would have to wait until after her lunch with Peter.

✳✳✳ ✳✳✳

Ordinarily Cole wasn't big on business lunches. He considered them to be a waste of money and time—especially his. Usually he had his assistant call in a carryout order to be delivered to his desk. But when an existing top-level donor such as Mrs. E. L. Elmhurst was considering making the Canning Foundation the beneficiary of her considerable estate, she had the right to expect some courting. Prior to ceding her position to him, his mother had conducted her fund-raising socializing exclusively at the nearby 21 Club. A devoted regular, she still received the Club's selective silk scarf at Christmastime, duly numbered and decorated with the insignia and signature Jockey logo. But the classic New York venue, with its unapologetically old-school menu of Creamy Chicken Hash and Mixed Grill of Game, was too blandly conservative for Cole's bolder palate. Union Square Café struck the respectful balance of elegant ambiance and fine food without coming off as decadent or flashy. It was one of his go-to venues for work-related wooing.

Moving along Union Square West at a slow stroll to accommodate Mrs. Elmhurst's advanced age and high heels, Cole battled back his impatience. Owing to the previous hot night with Sarah, he'd gotten a later-than-usual start to the day and no breakfast—at least not of the caloric kind. He only hoped the blue hair beside him was too deaf to catch his stomach's uncouth growling. His reservation was for one thirty, later than he would have liked but the best his assistant had been able to do at the last minute. Still, given the money he regularly unloaded, they'd better give him the requested window table, or he was going to be seriously pissed.

"Colvin, I'm so pleased you've come back to us in one piece," Mrs. Elmhurst remarked, not for the first time since they'd met up at his office.

Unlike so many of his buddies, he'd come home with his body intact, but his mind and soul were far from whole. Though he'd begun sleeping better since he'd started seeing Sarah, nightmares filled with spewing guts, flying limbs, and, above all, the terrible screaming still haunted him.

Fortunately Mrs. Elmhurst didn't seem to require a response, likely another reason she and his mother were friends and had been since dinosaurs roamed. "Your poor mother was beside herself those two years you were in Iraq. Remind me again what it was you did . . . over there."

"Explosive ordnance disposal." Taking her arm, he turned them onto Sixteenth Street.

She screwed up her face. "That sounds so very . . . risky."

"It was. It *is*," he added, thinking of those still fighting the War on Terror in Afghanistan and elsewhere.

Rich men made wars and then sent poor men to fight them. Enlisting during the Surge had been his contribution to evening the odds, or so he'd told himself at the time. Predictably, the move had galled his parents, but the youthful rebellion had boomeranged in his face.

"Well, it's not every day I lunch with a war hero," she simpered, her ring-covered hand squeezing his forearm.

The sobriquet set his teeth on edge, but if ever there was a time to grin and bear it, now was it. Six and a quarter million dollars would allow him to help a hell of a lot of kids dealing with stymied dreams and sick parents. Still, her inquisitiveness had him seriously craving a cigarette—and a cocktail. Since he'd started seeing Sarah, both vices had been substantially reduced.

Ahead, the restaurant door opened. A hot blonde wearing sunglasses and a broad-brimmed sunhat stepped out onto the sidewalk. A buff, well-dressed man with shoulder-length blond hair and a carefully clipped goatee followed her out. The woman seemed familiar. Curious, he checked her out. Laughing, she turned and reached up to straighten her date's tie. Cole blinked, wishing he'd remembered his sunglasses. The bright light must have been playing tricks on his eyes, because he could swear the hot blonde was Sarah. She *was* Sarah! She linked arms with the guy. Cole felt a growl building.

Seeing her and "Fabio" begin to backtrack toward Fourth, he sped up, ferrying Mrs. Elmsworth forward. "Sarah!" he exclaimed, planting them in her path.

She slipped her arm free from her companion's. "Uh, hi." Behind the screen of dark lenses, her gaze flickered from him to his companion.

"Sarah, aren't you going to introduce us?" her date inquired, his gaze stroking over Cole.

She looked between them. "Sorry, where are my manners? Peter, this is Cole Canning. Cole, meet my friend, Peter." She sent a significant glance over to Mrs. Elmhurst, still huffing and puffing.

Recovering from the lapse of etiquette, Cole turned to his lunch date. "Mrs. Elmhurst, I'd like you to meet—"

"Elaine Elmhurst though everyone calls me E. L." She offered a gnarled if perfectly manicured hand, shaking Sarah and . . . Peter's hands in turn. Her gaze settled on Sarah. "I don't believe I caught your surname."

Sarah swallowed hard. Cole tracked the ripple as it traveled the column of her slender throat, the same throat he'd planned to bless with bites and kisses when he next saw her. Even though he'd been the one to say he was too swamped to manage a second mid-week meet up, suddenly Friday felt too far away.

"Halliday," she answered, looking as though she wished the sidewalk might swallow her. Cole knew the feeling.

"Halliday," Mrs. Elmhurst intoned, appearing to consider. "Are you any relation to the Hallidays of Bridgehampton?"

"I er . . . don't believe so," Sarah said, casting Cole a look as if to say, *what the hell were you thinking?*

Ignoring it, he said, "We're about to have lunch at Union Square Cafe. I saw you just came from there. Any recommendations," he asked, as if he didn't know the menu by heart.

Peter answered instead. "Oh, it was all fabulous, but the duck breast is to die for."

Cole ignored him.

"I do love a good duck breast," Mrs. Elmhurst chimed in.

"Well, don't let us keep you from your lunch," Sarah said, grabbing her "friend's" arm and tugging him toward Fifth, the opposite direction from earlier. "It was a pleasure meeting you, E. L."

❊❊❊ ❊❊❊

"What the fuck was that about?" Sarah demanded when Cole showed up unannounced at her door later that night.

She wore a white terry-cloth robe, a bath towel wrapped around her head, and absolutely no makeup. Doing his best to ignore how good she looked and smelled—who knew fruit-scented bath gel could be so erotic—he shouldered his way inside.

Bypassing her, he set down the wine he'd brought, a 2001 pinot grigio that the clerk at Union Square Wines had sworn was worthy of its *Wine Spectator* high marks. Now that they were into June, it was getting too warm for reds.

"Where do you keep your opener?" he asked, stepping inside the kitchen.

Green gaze flaring, she followed him in, making him regret leaving the bottle, highly breakable and fairly expensive, within such easy throwing reach. "Fuck my corkscrew. Stopping me in Union Square of all places, what were you thinking?"

He hadn't been thinking at all. His brain had been too fogged for that, a cesspool of jealousy and other confusing, conflicting emotions.

Rifling through kitchen drawers and slamming them shut, he demanded, "Would you have rather I passed you by? Stared straight through you? Jesus, Sarah, what do you want from me?" When she didn't immediately answer, he raked a hand through his hair. "What were you doing there any way? It's not exactly the best place for flying under the radar." The area was a huge tourist hub as well as part of NYU's city campus.

She drew back, fiddling with her robe front, drawing it demurely closed. "That's . . . none of your business."

She was right. According to their no-strings rule, it wasn't. Only Cole was past caring what might or might not be his business. When it came to sex, they'd blown past just about every boundary he could come up with, but emotionally Sarah still held him at arm's length, throwing up walls left and right whenever he ventured too close for comfort—hers.

"This guy . . . Peter is he . . . someone you see regularly?"

He'd expected her to deny it. Instead she admitted, "He is . . . one of them, anyway, but usually just on Monday nights."

"One of them!" Cole scraped both hands through his hair, mostly to keep from reaching for the knives. That explained why she always had "plans" on Monday night. "Jesus, Sarah, how many are there?"

For a moment she looked confused, and then suddenly her eyes cleared, and a smile broke over her face. "Three . . . well, four counting Liz."

Three . . . four! She was fucking her friend, too! Jesus Christ, what kind of a sick bitch was she? "Should she even be doing . . . *that* in her condition?"

She burst out laughing.

"What's so goddamned funny?" he demanded, folding his arms over his chest as she doubled over.

Bracing her arms around her apparently splitting sides, she sputtered, "Y-you are. You're s-such a . . . jerk."

"And why is that? Because I'm not thrilled that you've exposed me to God knows what, maybe even HIV?"

Straightening, she dashed a hand across watery eyes, shaking her head. "I haven't exposed you to shit. We agreed on exclusivity for the duration of our arrangement, and I, at least, have kept my end of the bargain."

"Are you saying I haven't?"

She shrugged. "You tell me."

Somehow in the midst of his tirade, she'd managed to turn the tables on him. He swallowed a gulp of air and admitted, "I haven't so much as kissed anyone else since we met."

Sarah stared back at him, her expression unreadable. "Really?"

Holding her gaze, he nodded. "Really."

"Thank you for telling me."

"You're welcome, but what about Fabio?"

She grimaced at the comparison. "Peter is exactly what I introduced him as: a friend. We met in the group Liz hosts."

"You're in group?" he asked, wondering if whatever support she sought had something to do with why she'd left LA. Had he been so caught up in waging war against his own demons that he'd blinded himself to hers?

She hesitated. "It's a meet up for former adult entertainers, anyone from videographers to executive escorts to . . . me. We get together on Monday nights and talk about . . . whatever's on our minds."

"So it is a support group?" The one PTSD group he'd sat in on had seemed like a bunch of sad sacks sitting in a circle, but maybe he hadn't really given the experience a fair chance?

"I guess you could say that."

Curious he asked, "So what was Peter's . . . line of work?"

Her face became fierce. "That's none of your damned business."

Holding up his hands in surrender, he closed the last of the open drawers with his hip. "Sorry, you're right. I didn't mean to pry."

"The hell you didn't," she said, though her expression eased. "What I will say is he went back to school to finish his degree in interior design. He's spent the past year working for Ralph Lauren."

"No shit?"

Her gaze sharpened again. "Just because we've been in AE doesn't mean we don't have brains."

"Thanks for the clarification, but I'm aware." He reached out and made a show of brushing off her shoulder, partly to ease the tension but mainly because he just really wanted—needed—to touch her. "Don't mind me," he said by way of joking. "Just helping knock off that chip. For a minute there, it looked like it was back."

A furrow appeared above her eyes. "I don't expect you to understand."

Cole forced a shrug. "If that's true, then why not consider this as an opportunity to educate me?" When he put it that way, how could she resist?

She sighed. "Once you've been in AE, retired or not, the industry is always part of you. Moving into the mainstream isn't easy. The choices you've made aren't ones that most people can relate to. And there are soooo many misconceptions."

Curiosity piqued, he pressed, "Such as?"

She blew out a breath. "If you've acted in porn, you must be a sex addict."

"And that's not true? You certainly had me fooled." He softened the asshole remark with a smile.

She reached out to swat him. "You are such—"

Dodging her, he said, "An asshole, I hear you. But that time I was joking, so go on."

"Adult films are shot in very short time frames, anywhere from several days to just a few weeks. An average shoot is twelve hours, but I've been on set for as long as twenty. When you're filming as a lead, you work a lot—and don't roll your eyes at me. It is *work*. When the shoot wraps, you're tired, you're sore. Sex is the very last thing you want. I used to go straight home, wash my face, and then draw a bubble bath. Soaking in the tub and reading a romance novel were the only things that got me to unwind. Afterward, I'd sink into my California king—*alone*—and watch old movies until I fell asleep, which was usually in the first five minutes. Sorry if I'm busting any fantasies, but you did ask."

"No, go on, this is fascinating." It was.

"Having sex professionally makes you more discriminating in your private life, at least that's how it's always been for me. I've worked with all the leading adult actors in the business, guys who know every 'dick trick' in the book, as well as a few that aren't, who can stay on the edge for hours and then come on command—as in thirty or so seconds."

Thirty seconds, Jesus!

"After that, do you really think I'm going to go to bed with any gonzo that walks up to me in a club?"

Cole didn't like to think of Sarah going to bed with anyone else, "gonzo" or otherwise, not on screen and definitely not off. The thought of anyone else making love to her seriously messed with his mind. "I never thought about it that way before, but I see your point."

His concession earned her smile. "Thank you."

"You're welcome." He hesitated and then edged closer. "So how'd I get so lucky?"

She made a face. "What are you, fishing for compliments?"

"No, I'm asking . . . for the truth."

Sarah seemed to consider the question. "I liked your eyes."

"You brought me back home with you because you . . . liked my eyes?" This was a first so far as he knew.

She nodded. "That and you made me laugh."

He reached up and peeled the towel from her head. Honey-colored hair, still damp from the shower, spilled around her shoulders. "That's really interesting, because as I remember it, I was doing everything but back flips, and I could barely get you to crack a smile."

Smiling now, she quipped, "I do my laughing mostly on the inside."

"Is that so?" Setting the towel on the counter, he moved closer. "So if you just saw . . . Peter in group on Monday, why the lunch today? You guys miss each other that much?"

Sarah sighed. "Again, none of your business, but he proposed to his partner last week. They're getting married, and I'm the best woman, so to speak."

"That guy's gay?" If so, that was the best news he'd had all day.

She stiffened. "Yeah, why? Do you have a problem with homosexuality?"

"Me, no, I'm all for it." Her lips quirked, and he quickly clarified, "I mean I believe people should love and marry whomever they want."

Her approving nod took the pressure off—for now. "Actually I'm glad you brought it up, because I've been meaning to ask you something."

"Okay, shoot."

"They want a June wedding but given the short notice, we're having trouble finding a venue for the reception. I was wondering if you might have any leads. Someplace nice but not too extravagant that can accommodate up to forty people."

Cole thought for a moment. "I might." Alger House off Sixth Avenue and Bleecker Street might just fill the bill, assuming it was available. Until he knew for certain, though, he didn't want to get Sarah's hopes up. "Let me make some calls tomorrow, okay?"

"Okay, that'd be great. Thanks."

He reached out and tucked a damp lock of hair behind her ear. God, he loved her like this, no costumes, no cosmetics, just fresh, clean woman.

"Now that's settled, let's get you back to smiling."

He dragged his fingers along the line of the robe from the vee neckline to the belt at her waist. Parting the fabric, he slid his hand over the well of her belly and then lower, his palm cupping the thin strip of coarse curls. Cole smiled. It wasn't only her hair that was damp.

He slid two fingers inside her. Sarah's eyes flew open.

Working her pussy, Cole focused on her face, her eyes especially. "Are you smiling here? No, what about here?" He wiggled one finger.

Rocking ever so slightly toward him, Sarah bit her lip. "No."

"Hmm, I'll have to try harder then." He crooked his finger, then pressed the knuckle over what he was pretty sure was her G-spot. That time Sarah jumped. "Well, okay, maybe I am a little."

As apologies went, an orgasm was a hell of a lot more effective than flowers. Still, later as he lay in bed with Sarah half-asleep and snuggled up beside him, he couldn't dismiss the inconvenient truth. Sugar—Sarah—was seriously getting under his skin. Back in Iraq, her screen persona had captivated him, but that surface-level lust was nothing compared to the reactions—feelings—the flesh-and-blood lover evoked.

Moving forward, he'd have to approach their arrangement with greater caution. Sarah was a really great fuck and a really great person, but he couldn't afford to let himself feel more for her than lust and liking.

As much as he might want to, he just couldn't go there.

Chapter Ten

"*IED to the left!*"

"*Jesus, help us!*"

"*Exit the kill zone! Exit the kill zone! Get outta there!*"

The kill zone, the kill zone, the kill zone . . .

Engulfed by stinging smoke and blistering flame, spewing guts and flying nails, Cole opened his mouth, a scream scoring his throat. "Noooooooooooooooooooooooooo."

Slender arms banded about him, towing him out of the nightmare and back to consciousness. Floral-scented hair fell against his cheek. Hands, gentle and knowing, stroked back the hair from his sweating forehead. A voice, soft yet firm, reached out to him through the darkness.

"Cole it's all right. You're all right. You're not alone. I'm here—Sarah."

Sarah. Shuddering and lathered, Cole pulled himself upright. A wave of nausea rolled over him. He doubled over. Bandaging both trembling arms tight around his middle, he curled into himself, head tucked against tented knees.

Sarah sat up beside him. She wrapped her arms about his hunched shoulders, a futile effort to still his shaking. "Baby, you're okay. It was just a dream, a nightmare." She pressed a kiss atop his sweat-matted hair.

Despite how confident she sounded, she had it all wrong. Cole wasn't anything close to okay. And his nightmare wasn't any dream at all. It was an instant replay.

He lifted his head just enough to look at her. "Sarah," he said, the sound of her name on his lips anchoring him to the present—to sanity.

Her strained gaze met his in the semi-darkness. "Cole, what is it? What's wrong? Talk to me."

His throat was raw from screaming. When he finally spoke, his voice was quaking and gravelly. "Our convoy was headed on a reconnaissance mission. We'd been on the road for about ten minutes. I was the one to spot the IED. We cleared the area, and then pulled over so my team could stabilize it for removal. Compared to the stuff we usually came across, this bomb was a cakewalk. Most IEDs are constructed without metal or electronics, which makes them impossible to detect with standard monitoring equipment, but this one was old school."

He hadn't realized it at the time, but it was also a decoy, a distraction.

"Disposing of it was bread-and-butter stuff. I told my teammates, Sam and Joe, to hold back. I'll never forget saying, 'I've got this, guys.'"

"Because you were trying to protect them," she broke in, defending him.

Only Cole didn't deserve defending, and he knew it. He shook his head, sweat from his hair spattering the bed sheet. "I was arrogant, fucking full of myself. The guys in the unit had started calling me the Bomb Whisperer. I pretended not to like it, but I did. Too much."

Cinching her arm around him, Sarah whispered, "Go on."

"That's when . . . Kirby showed up."

"Kirby?" Sarah's question struck him like a bullet in the darkness. Cole braced himself to take it. "Our dog."

✳✳✳ ✳✳✳

"Possible enemy combatant at three o'clock."

"Shoot, it's just Kirby," someone, Sam maybe, had called out.

Shoulder weapons lowered. Strained faces broke into smiles. Relieved laugher made the rounds.

The medium-sized, brown dog crossing the road toward them was a welcome sight, their unofficial mascot for the last few months. Like so many abandoned animals in Iraq, Kirby had shown up at their base camp one day scrounging for scraps, his rack of ribs threatening to poke through his concave sides. Despite being emaciated and full of fleas, he was unflappably good-natured. Before long, rotating turns sneaking him scraps had become part of everyone's routine.

Some wiseass had suggested calling him Spot, but Cole had vetoed that and come up with Kirby. The name had just seemed to fit. Kirby's coat was brindled, not spotted, his flea-bitten fur a mosaic of various tans and darker browns, his once-white paws the rusty color of the unpaved roads. He had bright, alert eyes and a perpetually lolling pink tongue that made it seem like he was grinning. In a land with so little to smile about, a friendly face meant a lot.

Kirby trotted up to them, tail wagging. He'd gone missing a few days earlier, and Cole had begun to think he might not be coming back. Unlike the pampered pets he'd grown up with, companion animals in wartime Iraq lived short, harsh lives frequently ended by brutality. The roadsides were littered with carcasses, many of them dogs killed or cut open by the enemy and stuffed with improvised explosives.

Relieved that hadn't been Kirby's fate, Cole called over his shoulder, "I'll catch up later. For now, keep him back, okay?"

"Will do." Joe, the goofy, sweet kid from Tennessee who they all teased for dipping tobacco, was a sucker for anything with four legs and a tail. Pulling off his glove, he whistled through his fingers. "C'mon over here, boy."

Cole's other teammate, Sam, started walking over, his face wreathed in a wide grin. "How's it goin' buddy?" he said to the dog. "We thought you went AWOL."

Eager to be done, Cole focused back on the bomb, ignoring the nagging feeling that something wasn't right. The temperature had climbed to almost one hundred and twenty degrees Fahrenheit, and the advanced bomb suit he'd donned wasn't exactly lightweight. Basting inside it, he was setting himself up for a good case of heat stroke. It wasn't until he'd finished neutralizing the explosive that it struck him.

What was Kirby doing wearing a collar?

Cole whipped around. "IED on the dog! Exit the kill zone. Exit the kill zone! Go, go, *go!*"

On his knees petting Kirby, Joe swiveled toward Cole, eyes frozen and mouth agape. A few feet away, Sam stalled in mid-step.

Cole hauled up his heavily padded arms and flagged them back. "Exit the kill zone! Exit the kill zone! Get outta there!" he screamed, hoping to jar them into motion.

Ahead of him, the earth heaved. Blacktop ripped up like ribbon. The plume of smoke reminded him of a twister he'd once seen on *Storm Chasers*. Suddenly he was awash in a hailstorm from Hell, pelted by nails and rocks, dirt and debris, as well as some sticky resin that smelled like melted metal. Blood?

"Everybody's good, everybody's good," he screamed, hoping to calm whoever might be left alive to hear.

He raced through the shimmering wall of heat, into the smoke and flames as fast as the heavy armoring of his suit would let him. Even shielded inside it, he felt like his skin must be melting.

Voices, frantic and furious, shouted him back. *"Get back here, you crazy motherfucker!"*

"Canning, clear the kill zone. That's an order!"

"Jesus Christ, Cole! Cole!"

Ignoring them all, he combed through the rubble, tossing aside a tree limb as though it weighed no more than a toothpick, kicking at charred grass and melted machinery. He found Joe first. His head was blown off. So were his legs. The arms were still there, shorn off at the elbows. Cole stared at the trunk, unable to comprehend that it was his teammate and friend. Joe, the sweet, aw-shucks kid who'd been raised by his "granny," who'd enlisted hoping to do his war-veteran daddy and country proud. Joe, who'd once confessed in the dead of yet another sweltering night that his biggest fear was being captured and beheaded by the enemy.

"Shit, they don't waste time beheading grunts like us," Cole had assured him, stubbing out his cigarette in the sand. "Now get some sleep."

Cole's eyes poured, tearing with grit and grief. "Joe, Jesus Christ, no."

But it was Joe all right, or what was left of him. The dancing girl crowning the corpse's left bicep proved it beyond a doubt. The stupid tattoo was perfectly, pristinely intact—go figure.

Moaning brought him whipping around. It was Sam, his other teammate, or at least the upper half of him. Cole barreled over, squatted and scooped him up, bemused by his legless body's lightness.

"My legs!" Sam wailed as Cole rushed them toward waiting arms and clearer air.

Lungs burning, Cole swore, "Don't worry, buddy. I'll go back for them."

He handed Sam off and wheeled around, intending to make good on his word. Hands caught at him, arms gripped him, towing him back to safety.

"Hold, you crazy motherfucker."

"Shit, Canning, he's gone. He's *gone!*"

"Jesus, you have a death wish?"

Gasping, he struggled against them. "I have to go back. Joe's head . . . Sam's legs . . . I have to go back. Motherfucker, lemme go. I have to go back. I have to go back!"

✳✳✳ ✳✳✳

"They wouldn't let me go back in."

Swiping at his damp eyes, Cole finished his story. Only now did he notice that Sarah had flipped on the bedside lamp. The weak trickle of light wasn't much, but it was something. His sweating had stopped; the shaking subsided. He eased himself out of her arms. The T-shirt she'd thrown on to sleep stuck to her, damp not with her perspiration but with his.

He leaned back against the headboard and sank hard fingers into his hair. "The bastards put nails inside the bombs to make them more . . . lethal," he explained, his voice sounding detached, clinical, far away. "And bomb dogs . . . Well, using animals that way goes back to the Second World War, maybe the first."

Understandably horrified, Sarah shook her head. "A strange dog would have been horrible enough, but Kirby was your pet."

"Yeah, well, like they say, war is hell."

Christ, he couldn't believe he was telling her any of this, stuff so deadly dark, so soul-splitting he'd never so much as breathed it to another human being.

She exhaled a heavy breath, her face nearly matching the sheet for whiteness. "The lab that ran up to us in the park last week, that's why—"

"I grew up with dogs, but now, I'm not sure if I can ever . . . Well, I guess you get it."

Rather than respond, she followed him to the top of the bed, propping pillows and pulling the damp covers up around them both. Settling in beside him, she patted her shoulder. "Lay your head."

Cole hesitated. "Are you sure you don't want me to go . . . back to my place?" He'd almost said "home," but his empty apartment hardly felt that. These days the only place that felt anything close to a home was Sarah's.

"Positive. Why, do you want to go?"

Cole answered honestly and without reservation. "No."

All these weeks, he'd worried about breaking down in front of her, and now that he had, the world hadn't ended. Sure, he felt embarrassed to think how he'd balled in her arms, but mostly he felt . . . relieved. For the first time, it occurred to him that what went down in Iraq didn't have to define the rest of his life. Fuck the Canning name, maybe it was time to give talk therapy a chance.

"Then stop being a hero and lay your head."

Cole slid down and rested his head on Sarah's shoulder. Her arm went around him. She brushed her lips over his forehead. "Better?"

"Yes."

Tightening her hold, she asked, "Too much?"

He burrowed closer. "No, just right."

Cole closed his eyes. For the first time in more than two years, he felt just about right, or close to it.

✳✳✳ ✳✳✳

Cole fell asleep almost immediately, filling the room with uncharacteristic heavy snoring. The nightmare and its retelling had exhausted him. Not wanting to wake him, Sarah lay still, watching as the sky showing through her skylight lightened, early morning shadows creeping across the ceiling. As glad as she was that he'd finally confided in her, it was a lot to process. Stroking his big, shaking body and fighting back tears, she'd felt as if her heart might burst. She'd known what had happened to him in Iraq had been bad—the military didn't give out those medals for desk duty—but before now she hadn't realized the horror he'd been through. Having gotten a glimpse of it, she couldn't seem to hold him tightly enough—not that he seemed to mind.

She pressed a kiss atop the dark head pillowed on her shoulder. "Good night, baby."

Stretching out a hand to switch off the lamp, Sarah settled back down beside him.

✳✳✳ ✳✳✳

The knock on Sarah's apartment door three nights later was Cole. She was running about five minutes behind, he about five minutes early. It was the first time they were seeing each other since the nightmare. They'd had one short phone call between his meetings and a few text messages to firm up details, but that was it.

Wondering what his state-of-mind might be, she met him at the door, shower fresh and wearing her robe, a black silk one this time instead of her trusty white terry cloth.

"Sorry," she said, stepping back from his kiss, a nonthreatening peck on her lips that still sent her senses spinning, "I'm running behind, pun intended," she added with a nervous laugh.

Tonight's meet up would be a reenactment of *Kink Ass*. Despite all the discussions they'd had in preparation, she was nervous about doing anal. She hadn't lied about her previous bad experience. The actor, a buddy of hers, hadn't set out to hurt her. It was the director's fault for being an asshole and rushing the shoot, as well as hers for being a martyr and not speaking up. But she'd been new to the business, the film was her first lead, and she'd felt desperate to make a good impression. Despite the lube she'd slathered on, Joe had breached her badly. For a week afterward, sitting down hadn't been much fun. Neither had going to the bathroom.

Still, the other night Cole had trusted her, and she was inclined to do the same. She actually believed him when he swore he'd stop before hurting her. Not many men could muster that kind of self-control once they were that far gone, but from their previous times together Cole had shown he could and would. She more than felt it, she *believed*. Maybe she hadn't left behind as much of that starry-eyed girl from Brooklyn as she'd once supposed.

"I'm in no rush," he said with a shrug, his warm gaze running the length of her, his eyes clear and his clothes free of any cigarette scent. "Want a glass of wine?" He walked in and set the bottle of wine down on the counter.

Following him over, Sarah spared a glance for the label, a beautiful Chilean Sauvignon Blanc that would pair really well with the poached salmon she meant to serve later—assuming she could make it back down the stairs.

The thought landed a nervous flutter in the pit of her stomach. "Thanks, maybe later."

He turned to face her, settling warm hands on her shoulders. "If you're having second thoughts—"

"I'm not. Well, maybe a little. But not really second thoughts, more like jitters."

One black brow lifted. "Jitters?"

She shrugged. "Sorry, I spent several hours yesterday talking Peter down from the proverbial ledge. He used the word, and I guess it stuck in my mind."

Planning her friend's dream wedding, it was hard sometimes not to slip into dreaming herself. Only in her version she was the bride and Cole the handsome, tuxedo clad groom, waiting for her at the end of the processional aisle with a smile that promised a shared lifetime of Happily Ever After. If only . . .

"Everything coming along okay?" he asked, uncorking the wine. Owing to their previous impromptu meet up, he was familiar with the location of not only her wine cork but also the full array of her kitchen utensils and cutlery.

Warmed by his interest, Sarah nodded. "Yeah, it's going great. Just the usual snafus and last-minute details to smooth out, nothing I can't handle. I'm enjoying it—really," she added when he looked like he didn't quite believe her. "And Alger House is such a gem. I can't thank you enough."

He shrugged off her thanks, as though securing the elegant yet affordable venue was nothing. "You'll let me know if you need me to step in?"

She nodded. "I will, but really, you got us the venue. That's the main thing," she assured him.

Along with the anal, she'd been working up her nerve to ask Cole to be her date. Even if they were only fuck buddies, going with someone she knew and liked—a lot—was bound to make the day more fun and meaningful. Even though she'd be among friends, going solo would seriously suck.

He poured the wine and tasted it. "Not bad," he said. "Are you sure you don't want one. It might help you relax."

Sarah shook her head. "I'm good for now, thanks." She had so many butterflies in her stomach it would take something a lot stronger than wine to settle them. "Shall we?" she asked, looking toward the stairs.

Setting down his glass, he said, "Ready anytime you are."

The boner pressing against the crotch of his jeans confirmed it. Reminded of his length and breadth, Sarah swallowed—hard. His was a lot of cock to take anywhere but especially . . . *there.*

Anxious though she felt, she was excited, too, as well as prepared. She'd set her trusty vibrator out on the nightstand, fueled with fresh batteries, along with an untouched tube of the flavored lube they both liked and several condoms, the latter an absolute must. The bed-sheets were changed, the bathroom immaculate. She'd paid special attention to scrubbing out the tub, assuming that she at least would want a long, soaking bath later.

She drew a deep breath, channeling her movie character, a gamine-like girl about to be awakened to the kinkier pleasures. Though no longer an ingénue, the role felt like a better fit than it had eight years ago, when she'd first breathed life into "Evette." At thirty-four, she knew and respected her body, both for its possibilities and its limits. This time if something hurt, she wouldn't hesitate to speak up. Reaching for her confidence, she started up the stairs, shedding her robe on the way, as she'd done in the movie.

You can do this. You will do this. You want to do this.

Cole's heavier footsteps echoed hers. Without turning, she knew he would be shedding his shirt as well. Heart quickening, she reached the loft. He followed her inside the bedroom, his arms closing around her, an inescapably firm grip that pinned her arms and sent her pulse racing. Through his pants, his erection pushed into the small of her back and then lower, brushing her buttocks. Sarah shivered.

Holding her against him, he angled his hot mouth to her ear. "Let me take you someplace, someplace you've never been before," he said, repeating the lines of the actor in the film. "You know you want it; we both do."

Only this time her partner was no nervous junior actor jonesing to put on his best performance for the camera. This time her lover was Cole, and when she opened her mouth to deliver her scripted response, "You're right. I do want it—you," the husky, trembling words resonated with truth.

"Then get on the bed," he said, dropping his arms. "I want you to be ready for me." He ended the order with a playful push.

Limbs shaking, she made it onto the mattress. Facing toward the headboard, she got onto her knees. Behind her, she heard a belt being unbuckled, and then the jangle of metal as it struck the floor. Footsteps, heavy and measured, brought him over to the bed. The mattress dipped as he joined her. Bare legs, warm, muscular, and fuzzed with dark hair, spanned her. His cock teased along her thigh, stunning her with its heat and hardness. Sarah squeezed her eyes closed, girding herself, a habit from childhood she'd never been able to break. Most little kids were scared of the dark, but early on she'd convinced herself that if she couldn't see something, it must not really be there.

Cole was definitely there.

His arms slipped around her, turning her over onto her back. Sarah stared up to Cole bearing down on her. This wasn't in the script. If he meant to take her in a modified missionary position, all bets were off. The angle might be as good or better for her butt, but the semi-headstand would do a number on her neck and back.

"What are you doing?" she whispered, foolishness given they were alone.

A smile played about the corners of his mouth. "Trust me," he whispered back, sliding down the length of her.

Gentle hands pushed apart her thighs, his head disappearing between them. Firm fingers spread her. A hungry tongue laved her, starting at her slit.

"Hmm," she murmured, lifting her hips to meet his mouth. "I don't remember this being in the script." Cunnilingus wasn't part of the plan, not that she was complaining.

"Shut up and enjoy it." Lifting his head, he grinned up at her.

Sarah obeyed, giving herself over to the surprise pleasure. In the past, a man's surprises invariably had amounted to misfortune, whether it was her Dad's draining her college fund or Danny raiding her dresser for money for booze. But being with Cole was showing her that surprises could be good things, very good . . .

By now he knew her body as well as she did. He licked and kissed and stroked her in all the ways she especially liked, steering her steadily toward climax. Sarah let herself drop over the edge. Shudders racked her, leaving her fevered yet chilled, sated yet wanting.

Cole flipped her over so that she sprawled on her stomach, landing on liquid limbs. She'd always enjoyed making love doggie style. Being taken from behind appealed to her submissive side. Now that she'd agreed to give anal another try, knowing her partner would enter her there—*there*—amped up the turn on.

Over the past weeks, they'd experimented with butt plugs of various dimensions. By now he knew her limits, as well as what she liked and didn't. Even so, she tensed, bracing herself for an intrusion she remembered only as pain.

But instead of a director barking orders, she had Cole crooning words of praise and endearment. "You have a beautiful ass," he said, shaping her buttocks with his big, gentle hand, his voice not barking at all but low and sensual, his hot breath striking her most intimate places.

He ran a light finger along the cleft as he'd done that day in the kitchen. Sarah shivered. Inching up onto her knees, she took hold of the metal bedrails. As always, they'd discussed the details in advance. Unlike in *Kink Ass*, she wouldn't be bound. Pairing bondage with an act that bore bad memories would be too much, too terrifying.

"Not only beautiful but responsive," he said, circling the puckered flesh.

Sarah started, her ass twitching. The simple stroking felt amazing and not only because of the taboo aspect. Beyond any head gaming, being touched there felt really good.

Teasing fingertips traced the curve of her buttocks. Hands, firm but gentle, urged her legs apart. With a start, she realized it was no longer his finger tracing her but his tongue. Fluttering kisses firmed to deeper ones. Light licks and gentle lapping segued to rhythmic sucking. A tongue's tip probed her.

This was new. This was different. Sarah might be an international porn star of one hundred films, but never—never—had she felt anything quite like . . . this. She moaned, bucking back against him. Her hands fisted around the bed rails. Perspiration filmed the backs of her knees. Not only her ass but all the rest of her seemed engulfed by a beautiful, budding ache.

Cole drew back. He reached across to the night table for the lubricant and one of the condom packets. She heard the foil tear. Stealing a backwards glance, she saw him cover himself with the condom, then slather it with lube, especially the tip. He squeezed more lube onto his fingers. Raising his hand to his mouth, he blew several fast, warming breaths.

Sarah turned away, anchoring her gaze to the rail. Slippery fingers found her, retracing the circles earlier mapped with fingers and tongue. Sarah ground her fingers into her palms, loving the feel of him there. If they went no farther than this, she'd gladly let him inspect her for hours.

But the scene called for penetration, not play. He slid his finger inside her, the entry so smooth she scarcely felt it. Sarah shifted on her knees. Compared to the dildos with which she'd experimented, one lubricated finger was nothing. He sank into her again, the pressure sharper but in no way unpleasant.

"Oh, Cole," she breathed, pushing back against him as he worked in a second digit, forgetting to call him by his scripted name or at least forgetting to care.

"Do you like that, baby?" he asked, again not from the script, his buried fingers softly scissoring.

Sarah answered with a groan. Fuck the script, this felt too exciting, too good to sweat six-year-old lines.

He withdrew again. Another telltale squishing announced he was squeezing out more lube. This time when he entered her, Sarah knew it wouldn't be with fingers.

Cole fitted himself against her. Unlike the clumsy actor, he didn't tear into her. He didn't rush in any way. He teased his sheathed cockhead around her opening, and then slid along her crack, again and again, until Sarah was no longer bracing herself to be breached. She longed for it.

Sarah wiggled her bottom, feeling as though she'd grown a second clit. "Please," she whimpered, bucking back only to have him pull away yet again.

By the time he fitted himself to her again, she was so relaxed, so turned on, so insanely horny she would have gladly had him ram her. Only Cole didn't ram. What felt like the very tip of him pressed into her, raising not the renting pain she remembered but only a slight resistance.

A warm hand reached around, smoothing over her belly. "Okay?"
Sarah nodded. "Y-yes."

He pushed deeper, his torso molding to her back. Sarah tightened her hold on the bars. She pressed her damp forehead into her forearm and focused on expanding to accommodate his invasion.

Stilling inside her, he gently bit the back of her neck. "Being inside you feels even better than I imagined," he said. "How's my girl?" he added, the question yet another unscripted one.

"Good," she answered, warmed by the unexpected endearment, wishing she were his girl in truth and not only in play.

A sharper thrust brought them thigh to ass. A dull pain, a shadow of what she'd felt six years ago, struck. Impaled, Sarah could do little more than lay there, her invaded body curling over her knees. Cole stilled again. Reaching around her, he cupped her right breast. Deft fingers played with her nipple, pulling and pinching and rolling it between his thumb and forefinger exactly as she liked. Sarah let out a low moan as pain ebbed and new pleasure scratched its way to the surface. He slid his hand downward over her belly and lower, threading his fingers through her narrow bush, playing in her pussy. Glancing down, she realized she was wet. Even though she'd already come, she felt a fresh climax building. She relaxed back into him. A moment before, she'd felt too full to do much more than breathe but now she seemed to fit his big, broad cock easily. Cole began slowly moving, sliding back and forth. She couldn't imagine how she would feel later, but for the moment her ass felt not only full but warm and wet and . . . tingly. She experimented, clenching and unclenching her inner muscles as she'd long ago learned to do with her pelvis. Doing so felt good, really good, and not only to her. Cole's deep-throated groan reverberated throughout the small room. He quickened his pace, his thrusts still gentle but regular and rhythmic.

Oh. My. God. Was it possible to come simultaneously in two orifices? Despite all the double penetrations she'd watched other actresses undergo, until now she'd assumed any orgasm was an act. Feeling herself closing in on climax, Sarah was no longer so sure they'd all been faking it.

Dropping one hand from the bedpost, she reached for her vibrator. She flicked the switch with her thumb and brought the buzzing wand to her front. She was close, so close . . . Just another few thrusts from Cole and—

Cole ground against her. "God. Jesus. Fuck. Sarah!"

The sensation of his penis pumping inside her put to shame all the butt plugs and ass masters she'd tried. Clutching the bedrails like a drowning woman, Sarah surrendered, screaming her pleasure into the pillows.

✳✳✳ ✳✳✳

Lying in her bed with her bare backside molded against Cole's front, Sarah sighed into the pillow. This was nice, really nice. She wouldn't have figured him for a spooner. Ordinarily she wasn't one herself. Having a man hang on her post-sex had been one of her pet peeves. With Danny she'd popped out of bed as soon as she could without starting a fight, and then expended whatever post-coital energy boost she'd got on vacuuming or doing the laundry. But with Cole, she felt too deliciously languid to want to go anywhere or do much of anything beyond lazing about—especially as staying in bed often led to a bonus round.

"How are you doing?" He lifted his head and kissed the top of her shoulder. For a tough former soldier, he was a surprisingly affectionate man.

"I'm good." Sarah was glad he couldn't see the sappy smile she no doubt wore.

He trailed his fingers along the length of her bare arm. "I didn't hurt you, did I?"

She rolled over to face him. "I'm a little . . . sore, but not because you hurt me. Actually, it was . . . nice."

She'd used muscles and body parts she didn't ordinarily, at least not in that way. The soaking bath they'd taken together afterward had helped, as had cuddling.

"Just . . . nice?" He fell back, pantomiming stabbing himself in the heart.

Laughing, she tapped her forefinger atop his nose. "Okay, really nice."

Dark eyebrows lifted, creating that little forehead furrow she loved to kiss. "Nice enough to do again?"

"Well, I don't think I'll want to make it a regular thing, but once in a while, sure."

"You mean like for special occasions?" he said, grinning. "'Honey, I just got a raise, so bend over and give me your ass.'"

Sarah held onto her smile, although she felt her happiness slipping. His reference to a future they wouldn't ever have seemed anything but funny. It was, however, a reminder.

Grabbing hold of the sheet, Sarah sat up. "There's something I've been meaning to ask you." Suddenly it was junior prom all over again, only this time she wasn't wearing clothes or braces. Steeling herself for a letdown or worse, humiliation, Sarah bit her lip. "I don't suppose you'd want to come to Peter's wedding with me?"

Cole sat up beside her. "That depends. Are you asking?"

"I am," she said quickly, threading her fingers to cover any shaking. "I'd make it clear to everyone that we're not, you know, together." Was it her imagination, or did his face fall?

"Sure. It's the thirtieth, right?"

"Yes," she answered, amazed that he'd remembered. Then again, he had gotten them the venue, so that's maybe how he knew.

"Great, then it's a date." His casual tone sent Sarah's heart twisting.

Seizing on the possibility of more sex as a mood booster, she settled back against the headboard, deliberately letting the sheet slide. "Do you remember that scene in *Wet Dream* where the male lead eats me out until I squirt?"

In reality, she hadn't come at all, let alone squirted. A body double had had to be brought in for the pussy close-up, but Cole didn't need to know that.

He turned to her, his smile spreading. "Yeah, I do."

Holding his gaze, she asked, "Think you can make me squirt like that?"

"I don't think, I know. I *have*," he added, reminding her.

In one swift motion, he shifted to cover her with his body. He jerked free of the covers and glided downward. Lifting her hips, he brought her pelvis to meet his mouth.

Watching his grin disappear between her thighs, Sarah melted back against the banked pillows. So long as she remembered that none of it was real, that Cole wasn't hers for keeps, where was the harm in pretending?

Chapter Eleven

Unlike the Boathouse in Central Park or The Plaza Hotel, Alger House on Downing Street in the West Village wasn't on the general public's radar screen for weddings, but Cole had known a guy who'd known a guy who'd gotten them in. The private townhouse exuded a vibe that was at once stately and serene. Its loft garden room proved perfect for a smaller wedding such as Peter and Pol's. Booking close to the date had actually been a bonus so far as keeping costs down went, as had slating their celebration for a Saturday afternoon rather than evening. Afterward the newlyweds would spend their nuptial night at the nearby Washington Square Hotel. The splurge stay would serve as a holdover honeymoon until they could afford the trip to Ireland they were saving toward.

Wedding Saturday arrived with a sprinkling of showers that sent everyone into a panic—everyone but Sarah. To add further drama, Pol's best man called to say he was flattened with the flu. On standby to help Sarah manage the mayhem, Cole ushered both grooms to the waiting limo, handing them matching grey silk umbrellas she'd purchased "just in case."

Once arrived at Alger House, guests deposited sodden umbrellas and damp wraps at the entry-level coat check and then followed the silver calligraphy signage up to the great room. The latter was set up for the reception with several long buffet tables, a grand piano, and cloth-covered four tops festooned with vases of white tulips banded by silver ribbon. An open staircase led to the loft where the ceremony and cock-tail hour would take place. A harpist's soft strumming guided them to the garden room, an intimate space of white-painted brick walls, gently worn antique furnishings, and marbles and potted palms interspersed throughout. A few minutes before the ceremony was set to begin, the sun burst forth, beaming through the skylight to bathe the bridal party and guests in a mellow, midday glow.

No one glowed brighter than Sarah, or so it seemed to Cole. Having grown up in a household with a fashion diva mother and two sisters, he knew that her peach dress was "chiffon" and "tea length," her strappy high-heeled sandals most likely Manolos. She'd done something different with her hair. The blond locks were upswept and held in place not by the ubiquitous plastic clip but by a myriad of pins, invisible except for the seed pearls decorating the tips. A few soft curls had been left loose to frame her face. Pearl-and-diamond ear-rings winked from her lobes; otherwise she wore no jewelry. Switch out the color of her dress to white, and she could have easily been the bride—his bride.

Holy Shit . . . Where the fuck had that thought come from? But even as Cole bombarded himself with those questions, he acknowledged he already had the answer: straight from his heart.

Watching her sail through her best woman duties—making certain Peter carried both something borrowed and something blue; settling his elderly mother into a high-backed wing chair, one of the more com-fortable seats; checking in with the caterer to ensure that proper care was being taken of the cake—Cole was hard put to hold back express-ing his awe. Yes, Sarah was a past porn star and the hands down best fuck of his life, but she wasn't only those things. She was so very much more, not only to him but to everyone fortunate enough to have their lives touch hers, however briefly.

Coughing and fidgeting feet confirmed the guests were growing restless. Cole had seen Sarah disappear with Peter into a side room when they'd first arrived. He decided to follow them and make sure nothing was wrong.

He found them inside the antique bathroom. Outfitted with stained-glass windows and a fainting sofa, it also served as a changing room and lounge area for brides—or, in this case, grooms.

"Everything good in here?" he asked from the doorway.

Bent over the marbled sink, Peter answered with a groan and patted cool water onto his cheeks.

Sarah looked over her shoulder to Cole and mouthed, "Hope so."

Peter turned off the tap and straightened. Dividing his gaze between Sarah and Cole, he admitted, "I don't know what's wrong with me? I've been looking forward to this day for as long as I can remember." He jerked an elbow toward the door Cole had entered through. "That man waiting out there is the absolute love of my life, and look at me." He held out trembling hands. "I'm shaking like I've got the DTs again."

Cole joined them at the sinks. He'd never felt more ill-equipped to comfort someone, but still he tried. "Easy, buddy, it's just nerves. You'll get through it."

Sarah took Peter's hands in her steady ones. "Cole's right. Nothing's wrong with you. You're getting married. It's normal to be nervous." She punctuated the pep talk with an encouraging smile.

Releasing Sarah's hands, Peter blew out a big breath. "You're right. So distract me." He jerked his goateed chin toward Cole. "I thought you and Hunk-a-licious must have something going on that day we met up at Union Square, but you know me, I don't like to pry."

Yeah right, Cole thought, resisting rolling his eyes.

Peter tsked. "Bad girl, you've been holding out on us in group. Other than yummy, what's he like?" He made a show of checking Cole out, the "gay glance over" or so Sarah had teasingly called it. "You know what they say about big hands and big feet going with a big—"

"Christ, man, you're making me blush," Cole cut in, his face feeling suddenly sunburned.

Obviously feeling better, Peter divided his gaze between them. "So what's the deal with you two? Sarah insists you're just friends?"

Cole honestly wasn't sure what his and Sarah's "deal" was, not anymore. It would take another few months to cycle through the rest of her films, but once they reached the magic one hundred number, where would that leave them?

"Lucky for Sarah I'm taking myself off the market, otherwise you and I—"

Wedding or not, joking or not, Cole wasn't about to have this conversation standing in . . . a bathroom of all places.

Meeting Sarah's amused gaze, he said, "I'll see you both outside. Break a leg or . . . something," he added, giving the groom a light punch on the shoulder.

Mindful of his duties as usher and stand in best man, he herded the stragglers into the remaining seats and then took his place at the front of the room beside the second bridegroom.

Pol leaned in and whispered, "He's a ruddy wreck, isn't he?"

Staring down at the tops of his wingtips, Cole hesitated. "Noooo, not exactly . . . well, okay, maybe a little bit," he admitted, looking up.

To his surprise, Pol chuckled. "That's my Peter. The other night I predicted he'd be at sixes and sevens, but the dear, daft man wouldn't have it."

"You're not upset?"

A shrug of shoulders answered that. "Why would I be? He loves me dearly and I him. Mind you, he's a bit of a drama queen, but then that's the lad I fell in love with. He'll be out in his own good time and make a grand entrance into the bargain." He punctuated the prediction with a wink.

Talk about unconditional love. "Wow, okay, well, that's awesome," Cole said.

Folding his hands behind him, he looked over to where Sarah stood with Peter in the alcove. All at once, the room rose. An air of shivery expectation settled over the assembly, or so it seemed to Cole.

Sarah turned to Peter, and Cole thought he saw her mouth the word, "Ready?" She tucked her arm into his, and they started forward, their measured steps muffled by the Persian carpet. The flower-festooned mantel served in place of an altar. The grooms wore matching gray cutaway coats with a single button at the waist, ascots, and silver-striped trousers. Though Cole hadn't given much thought to it before, they really did make a handsome couple.

A beaming Pol stood perfectly still, watching as Peter and Sarah approached. Reaching them, she handed him off to his husband-to-be and stepped to the side.

The interfaith minister, a middle-aged motherly type with a priest collar and a gentle smile, gestured for the guests to resume their seats. "Dearly beloveds . . . "

As Cole knew from Sarah, both grooms had written their own vows, composed in private and as yet unshared with anyone, including one another. Peter pulled a folded square of paper from his breast pocket with a visibly trembling hand and began:

"Pol, a year ago you not only caught my eye. You captured my heart by being exactly who you are: the sweetest, most loving, compassionate, and sensitive person I have ever known. You've been not only my partner in passion but my best friend through the ups and downs, the good and the bad, and everything in between."

Cole's gaze went again to Sarah. Thinking of the tender way she'd held him in the aftermath of his nightmare, he felt a lump move into his throat. Weeks ago he'd made peace with her being not just his fuck buddy but his friend. Only now did he acknowledge an even scarier, if still secret, truth: she was his *best* friend.

"You've believed in me when no one else would, urging me to chase rainbows and build foundations beneath my dreams. More than anyone, you have loved me with compassion and patience, selfless understanding, and unconditional acceptance."

Unconditional acceptance—more than anyone, Sarah had seen Cole's warts, and yet she still chose to be with him.

"I promise to spend the rest of my days by your side, to laugh and cry with you, to believe in and support you as you do me, be we rich or poor, healthy or sick. Together we stand stronger and live bolder and better than we could ever hope to do alone. Waking up and falling asleep beside you are and will *always* be the best parts of my day. Today I pledge you my love, my trust, and my fidelity—forever."

Forever was . . . a really long time to dedicate your life to someone. Joining your life with another person's until death parted you—would Cole ever be able to make that kind of commitment? Until now, he hadn't given it much thought, hadn't imagined he'd ever want to, but glancing over to Sarah had him thinking that maybe not every marriage had to end up as empty as his parents' had.

Tears streaming, Pol followed suit, his vows a traditional Celtic wedding prayer, which he recited first in Gaelic and then again in English. "Peter, I pledge my love to you, and everything that I own. I promise you the first bite of my meat and the first sip from by cup. I pledge that your name will always be the name I cry aloud in the dead of night."

The other night when Cole had climaxed, the only word he could seem to form was "Sarah." Sugar was as good as a ghost to him now, a fantasy from his formerly hyper-charged imagination. Whether she wore black bondage wear or an oversized sleep shirt, Sarah was all he saw.

"I promise to honor you above all others. Our love is never ending, and we will remain, forevermore, equals in our marriage. This is my wedding vow to you."

By the time the rings were exchanged and the marriage pronounced, there wasn't a dry eye in the house, including Cole's. Jesus, when had he become such a pussy? Looking beyond the embracing couple, he caught Sarah watching him and returned her misty smile.

Afterward, flutes of champagne and sparkling cider were passed around. Sarah's friend, Honey, broke hands with her date, a dissipated thirtyish man in a seersucker suit who Cole didn't much like the look of.

Hurrying forward, she hugged and air-kissed each groom in turn. "I am so very happy for you both!" she declared in her distinctive voice, her accent sounding vaguely British but not quite. Though her broad-brimmed pink hat cast her face in shadow, Cole was reasonably certain the smudge topping one tear-damp cheek was a bruise she'd tried covering with makeup.

Blinking watery eyes, Liz echoed the sentiment. "I'm not usually big on weddings, but yours . . . Sarah, you've outdone yourself."

"Thanks, but I had a great team," she said. "Jonathan, you were an awesome ring bearer."

Jonathan's black button eyes shone. "I know, I really rocked it, didn't I?"

Guffaws greeted the declaration. Cole threw his arm about the boy. "You certainly did, buddy. If I ever need a ring bearer, you'll be the first kid I call on." As soon as the words were out, it struck him that he'd made a Freudian Slip of the worst kind.

Looking up, he caught Sarah's eyes on him, her expression wistful, even a little sad. "We wouldn't be here without Cole. He found the venue for us and managed to get us in with just a few weeks' notice."

Everyone but Cole raised their glass. Holding Sarah's gaze, he slowly shook his head. "I'm just the gopher. Sarah did all the heavy lifting, so if we're toasting anyone, it should be her."

"How about a dual toast?" Liz proposed, her gaze dancing between them. Lifting her cider, she said, "To Sarah and Cole, thank you for bringing us all together to celebrate our dear friends' special day in such grand style."

"To Sarah and Cole," everyone echoed, including Jonathan, who slugged down his Shirley Temple from a grown-up glass.

Sarah cleared her throat. Cole saw that she was doing her best not to cry. "If we're finished with our mutual admiration, the buffet is opening downstairs. There's a carving station, a raw bar, a French crepes station, and one for sushi." She looked over to Liz. "I asked the chef to be sure to include some vegetarian rolls."

Liz smiled. "I never doubted it." Setting her hands on Jonathan's shoulders, she said, "What do you say to some food to go with all that sugar you've been knocking back?"

"Okay," he said, relinquishing his drained drink.

"We'll see everyone in a bit," Liz said, steering him toward the stairs.

"I think I'll join you," Honey said, glancing across the room to her date, openly flirting with one of the female servers. She turned away and hurried off.

Left alone together, Cole turned back to Sarah. "Can you finally relax now?"

"Who says I'm not relaxed?" Sipping her champagne, she continued scanning the party like a vigilant hostess.

Helping himself to a miniature crab cake from the tray of a circulating server, he exhaled roughly. "It's like you're channeling Jennifer Lopez from *The Wedding Planner.*" Not even the gorgeous musician and actress could compare to Sarah. Whether outfitted in a party dress, bondage wear, or bundled up in a bathrobe, she did it for him like no other woman ever had—or would, he was coming to think.

"Life is like one never-ending movie marathon to you," she remarked irritably, a frown marring her pretty face.

Her snappishness had Cole wondering. Reenacting the scenes from her films had been his idea, but once they'd got going, she'd certainly matched him for enthusiasm. Had the game stopped being fun for her? What was he missing?

"I thought you liked movies."

She sent him an exasperated look. "Of course I do, it's just that I like to think that at least a few things are still sacred, weddings especially. Would you believe I used to play bride when I was little?"

Cole snorted. "You played *bride*? Is that even a real kid's game? Are you sure you don't mean doctor?"

She reached out and hit him—hard. "That's exactly what I mean. Everything's a joke to you."

Making a show of rubbing his shoulder, he shook his head. "Not everything," he said softly. Iraq wasn't a laughing matter in the least. The other night in her arms he'd told her things he'd never uttered to another living being.

She stared at him so hard he was amazed her eyes didn't cross. "Well, you can at least show some respect."

"Sorry," he said, wondering again why she was so bent out of shape.

A group cheer drew their attention over to the fireplace where Peter and Pol, faces wreathed in smiles and gloved hands holding flutes of sparkling cider, mugged for the wedding photographer.

Watching them, Sarah took a sip of champagne. "They make such a handsome couple."

His own champagne forgotten, Cole drank in the purity of her perfect profile. *I love you*, he felt like saying, but really where would that leave them? Instead, he settled for a safer admission. "You look beautiful, by the way."

Turning back to him, she answered, "Thanks, by the way."

They shared a smile. Opening up to her in the aftermath of the nightmare had been a game changer in more ways than one. Try as he might, he couldn't go back to thinking of her as just a fuck buddy even if he wanted to.

Cole didn't want to.

"I tried telling you earlier, but you were busy." Petulant as that probably sounded, he wasn't used to sharing her.

Her gaze softened. "Well, you've got my attention now. Is there anything else you'd like to tell me?"

She wasn't acting any role now. Sugar was totally out of the picture. The question came entirely from Sarah, *his* Sarah. Cole knew how to deal with Sugar. Sarah, however, remained a puzzle he wasn't anywhere close to solving. He hesitated, feeling as if bricks had dropped on his chest. Suddenly his tie felt too tight, his tuxedo too constricting.

She shook her head, looking at him as though he were a lost cause. "I should go check on the cake." She shifted to walk away.

Impulsively, he shot out his hand and grabbed her arm. The unexpected force sent champagne sloshing the rim of his glass. "Sarah, wait."

Startled, she swung around. "What's gotten into you today?" she demanded, shaking him off or trying to. "This isn't some movie scene we're reenacting. This is real life, my friend's wedding, so stop acting like everything's about you, because this once it's not."

Startled, he shook his head. Was that really how she saw him? "It's not about me. It's about you, I want to—"

A flash and pop cut Cole off, peppering his vision with black dots. His ingrained response was to tackle Sarah and hit the ground. Before he could, several young women scribbling on notepads and scruffy guys shouldering cameras crowded up to them.

"So Sugar, how long are you in New York?"

"Are you filming here?"

"What's the real reason you left LA?"

"How's your substance abuse recovery coming along?"

Cole stepped in front of Sarah, shielding her with his body. "Stop shooting—now!"

Looking back at Sarah, he saw that her startled face confirmed what, in his gut, he already knew.

Their days of flying under the radar were over.

❄❄❄ ❄❄❄

"I am so sorry, Ms. Halliday. They told me they were with the wedding photographer. I thought something might be off, but the cameras—"

"It's okay, Randall," Sarah assured the harried event coordinator, giving his shoulder a pat. "Once we get this glass cleaned up, it will be like they were never here."

If only that might be true! In the midst of hiring vendors for all aspects of the event, she hadn't once considered a firm to handle security. Thinking of the damage that couldn't be undone, she looked over to where the server was sweeping up bits of broken glass. Who knew one shattered camera could create such a mess?

When his order to stop shooting had gone unheeded, Cole had charged, tearing the camera off the nearest guy's shoulder and smashing it before everyone's startled eyes. The second camera guy hadn't required any convincing. Like spooked mice, the four had scurried toward the stairs, one shouting threats of suing and such, which sounded pretty empty to Sarah given they'd intruded on private property.

The camera was the only casualty. Having seen him in action pulverizing her purse snatcher, Sarah knew the crew had gotten off lightly. Now that she was aware of his PTSD, she marveled at his self-restraint.

Smashing the camera had made a powerful statement, but they hadn't escaped the range of smart phones. Imagining the pictures they'd gotten of her, open mouthed and cowering, she felt more vulnerable and exposed than she had on any porn film set.

Addressing the room, she said, "Sorry for the distraction, folks, but let's get back to celebrating the reason we're really here." She lifted her champagne flute, hoping the others would follow. "To Peter and Pol, we wish you a long life, much love, and of course, great sex."

Shouts of "huzzah" and "here, here" rumbled through the room. Satisfied that the event was back on track, she turned to Cole.

Having a big, virile man get physical to defend you, not once but twice, was every woman's fantasy. It was a major turn on, no doubt about it, but she was too shaken to even think of sneaking away with him for sex. If reporters had tracked her here, they could follow her elsewhere, too. Ten years in LA had taught her how intense these things could get. Would she find a posse waiting outside her building when she went home? Would they dog her on her walks to and back from Liz's? If they went knocking on her dad's door, someone well might end up shot.

Beyond the obvious leak, how had they found her? Liz was above suspicion, and she couldn't believe any of the other FATEs would reveal her. Had someone involved with the wedding, one of the vendors perhaps, recognized and reported her whereabouts? What was the going rate for ratting out a celebrity? Or was being in the know as to the whereabouts of the so-called rich and famous a sufficient high of its own? Maybe it was the bragging rights as much as the money that brought people so low.

"What, no lecture?" he asked, glancing down at his split knuckles.

Except for his tuxedo being gray rather than black, he looked almost exactly as he had on the night they'd met—slightly disheveled and primally sexy. Then she'd been willing to settle for a thrill ride of erotic moments. Now she wanted more. She wanted the Big White Wedding with all the trimmings, the Happily Ever After once the vows were exchanged. She didn't want to playact at being a bride. She wanted to be a bride—Cole's. But as his earlier reticence had so painfully confirmed, he wasn't interested in that kind of permanence, certainly not with her.

Heart in her throat, she shrugged. "So far as I'm concerned, that asshole got what he deserved . . . less actually."

Flexing swelling fingers, he grinned. "Would you believe that before I met you I was a peaceable man?"

She shook her head, wondering after today whether he would still want to see her. They'd just been outed. As disastrous as that felt for her, Cole had his own deal to protect. Pornography and kid-focused philanthropy weren't exactly compatible message points. He might be made to choose—and soon. Twitter would be exploding. For all she knew, the story might end up trending. The first round of blog posts would be up by that evening. Longer articles would make it into tomorrow's print papers.

"Sorry, I'm not buying. By the way, you make a great bouncer."

"Thanks, I do, don't I?" He shoved his hitting hand into a footed champagne bucket and pulled the bottle out.

Seeing him start for the stairs, Sarah said, "Hey, where are you going? I was kidding."

"Well, I'm not. I'll save you a dance," he called back. Another joke.

Sarah started after him, but Peter intercepted her. Hand on her elbow, he steered her away. "Sarah, sweetie, they're getting ready to bring out the cake, and you're the only one who knows where it goes."

✳✳✳ ✳✳✳

Cole and Sarah stayed beyond seeing the two grooms off. Waiting until the last guest was out the door, he walked up to her. Even though they'd gone on with the party as planned, he knew the paparazzi raid was uppermost in both their minds.

Laying his hands on her shoulders, he said, "It happened. It's over. You need to try and relax."

She exhaled heavily. "It's not over. It's just beginning." Expression exasperated, she held out her phone. "Would you believe I already have an email from a TMZ reporter requesting an interview exclusive and another from *Time Out New York*? And it's only been a few hours. Can you imagine what tomorrow will be like, and the day after that—and after that?"

Unfortunately she wasn't wrong. Taking the phone from her, Cole slipped it into his pocket. He wished he could do or say something to reassure her. He wished he'd done a better job of protecting her earlier. He wished he knew who the son of a bitch was who'd outed them, if only so he could put a face to the fantasy of wringing the life from his throat.

He tried telling himself it could have been worse. They'd been together at a private function, a wedding. They'd been caught on camera while talking—not fucking—as might have happened. For his part, it would be easy enough to claim they hadn't been on a date at all but had met by chance for the first time.

Whatever flack he caught from his family, the foundation donors, and board would be minimal compared to the media stalking Sarah now faced. And not only her but those close to her. Liz, Jonathan, and the other FATEs stood to come under scrutiny as "Sugar's" friends.

But they wouldn't stop there. Reporters might soon be staking out her place . . . if they weren't already. A wise man would break things off, but Cole made no claim to wisdom, not where Sarah was concerned. Even with his eyes wide open to all the risks, he wasn't prepared to stop seeing her.

Feeling protective toward her, he tightened his grip. "One day at a time, we'll deal with it. It's not like it's a matter of life and death."

For the space of several seconds, she stared at him strangely, making him wonder what he might have said. Giving up, he said, "I have an idea how to make you feel better."

At last, a smile! "Just one?"

His hands slid away from her shoulders. "Well, one at a time." Taking her arm, he led her up the stairs to the garden room and through it to the gilded bathroom.

Seeing where they were heading, she darted a nervous look around. "Here? What if someone walks in?"

Reaching for the door with his hurt hand, he shrugged. "There's an extra chair. I don't mind if they want to watch, so long as they don't touch," he teased, though the thought of anyone but him touching or even seeing Sarah was crazy-making.

As soon as the door closed, he pulled her into his arms. Lowering his head, he matched his mouth to hers, kissing her thoroughly and deeply. Drawing back, he admitted, "I've wanted to do that since before we left the house. You look amazing." *You are amazing*, he almost added, dragging his lips across the juncture of neck and shoulder.

She shivered and lifted her face to look up at him, the clouds in her eyes banished by the familiar light of desire. "You look pretty amazing yourself. I like you in tuxedos," she said, toying with his lapel. "That reminds me. Don't I still owe you a replacement?"

Cole laughed. His hands slipped to her waist. "I'll take it in barter." Turning with her in his arms, he lifted her onto the marble-topped vanity.

Her dress rode upward. Cole pushed it higher still. Her parted thighs provided a peak of open-crotched panties. Reaching down, he teased his fingertips along the lace edge.

"Sarah," he said, reveling in her wetness, her scent, her submission.

Laying a hand on either side of his face, she dragged him back down to her. Their mouths met. Their tongues sparred. She tasted of champagne and desire, sadness and regret. She drank him in as though she were thirsting, as though this was their last kiss and she was hell-bent to harvest all the memories she might.

She dragged her mouth away at last, her nimble fingers searching out his zipper. She tugged it down and freed him from his briefs. Her slender hand encircled, glided, squeezed. Teasing her thumb over the slit bisecting the sensitized head, she tested his wetness and his willpower.

Cole answered with a growl. Setting her hand aside, he focused on her perfect pussy. She was very wet and very pink, putting him in mind of a Georgia O'Keefe canvas he'd once come close to acquiring. He'd lost the painting to a higher bidder at a Sotheby's auction, but he didn't intend to likewise lose Sarah. Sex was the only way he knew to bind her to him, and he had every intention of using it now.

Spreading her folds, he positioned himself over her channel. One quick, clean thrust carried him inside her. The emotions of the day made restraint seem foolish. God only knew what tomorrow, or even the next hour, would bring. For the present, Cole's reality was reduced to Sarah. The slickness of the pussy he pounded, the pull of strong, slender fingers in his hair, the slightness of the nubile body straining to meet his, the little moans that sounded almost like weeping.

They came hard, fast, and together, their urgent breaths and unbridled cries filling the room. Gaze melding with Sarah's, Cole released himself inside her, willing his eyes to tell her all the things he might never find the words, or the courage, to say.

❋❋❋ ❋❋❋

Cole lifted his forehead from Sarah's. "I got you something."

He retrieved his jacket and passed her the square box he'd earlier tucked into his pocket.

"I didn't have time to get it wrapped," he apologized, passing the gift over. The blue bow stuck on top had been the best he'd been able to manage.

"That's so thoughtful, thank you," Sarah said, taking it and lifting the lid. "I can't think what it is," she added, opening the hinged jeweler's case.

Watching her, Cole tensed, belatedly wondering if his "gift" was such a good idea.

Sarah's head shot up. "You got me Ben Wa Balls!" Put like that, he couldn't tell if she was pleased, offended, or simply surprised.

He followed her gaze down. Two weighted, platinum orbs sat on a bed of midnight blue velvet, the pull cord and adjoining chain set with miniature sapphires and diamonds. "I had them engraved," he said, pointing to their paired initials etched into the platinum.

"They're beautiful," she said. "I didn't know Ben Wa Balls could be so . . . elaborate."

Wondering if he maybe should have gotten her something more conventional, a diamond tennis bracelet or earrings, he asked, "Will you try them?"

She hesitated. "Now?"

Originally he'd meant to wait until they got back to her place, but given how their day had gone, who knew what they might face when they got there. "Sure, why not?"

Her mouth firmed as if she'd decided. "All right, though I'm a Ben Wa Ball virgin. I may need some practice putting them in."

Cole shrugged. "I have some time."

He helped her down, and she slipped inside the stall with the box. Impatient, he walked back and forth before the mirrors, pausing every now and again to stare at the stall door. Other than her feet and a suggestion of motion, Sarah was hidden from him. Was insertion a . . . process? Should he offer to . . . help her? He'd never given such a gift to anyone, but when he'd come across a certain high-end and very discreet boutique in the Upper East Side, he hadn't been able to resist.

Eventually the stall opened. Smoothing her dress, Sarah stepped out. She came toward him, slender hips sexily swaying, her steps unrushed but in no way mincing.

"How do you feel?" Cole asked, scouring her face for a reaction. "They don't hurt, do they?" he added in sudden alarm. He'd assumed she knew to leave the bejeweled chain out for removal but maybe he should have made certain first.

Her mouth tilted in a smile. "No, they don't hurt, but I definitely feel . . . something."

Cole grinned. "Define *something*."

She licked her lips. "Every step, every movement I make brings on a sort of delicious feeling of . . . fullness. It's hard to describe, but suffice it to say, I hope you don't have other plans for tonight."

So the balls were doing what they were intended to do—heightening arousal. What better way to relax from the stress of the day? "Every step?"

She nodded. "Yes." Pitching her voice lower, she confided, "My panties are already soaked through, and we haven't even left the bathroom. We'd better catch a cab home."

Every step, every movement. Cole felt his grin broaden. "It's such a nice evening, I thought we'd walk."

Chapter Twelve

Monday morning Cole had scarcely settled into his office chair when the crackle of the intercom cut in. His assistant, Karen, called out, "Mr. Canning, your mother is here to see you. Shall I show her in?"

Cole hesitated in answering, girding himself for the confrontation that was certain to come. He didn't need a crystal ball to know the reason for his mother's unscheduled visit, or to predict that the fallout would be fierce. The infiltration of paparazzi on Saturday had borne the predictable result. Sarah was outed as Sugar, and he as her "blue-blooded billionaire boy toy." Their joined names were splashed across every major gossip column and blog, not only in New York but nationwide.

Reaching up, he straightened his tie. "Yes, thanks."

He'd barely gotten the words out when his office door opened. Dressed in Prada from head to foot, her blond, helmet hair freshly colored, and wearing the ubiquitous Mikimoto pearl earrings and choker, his mother marched inside. "She forgets this was my office for nearly thirty years."

Cole rose to greet her. "Mother, this is an unexpected . . . pleasure. What brings you to Midtown?"

He crossed to the front of the desk to pull out a chair for her, but she waived him off. "What I've come to say won't take long."

Clearly she was braced for battle. Cole felt himself doing the same, his stomach clenching as though he was still the truant boarding school student who'd been sent down for ditching class and smoking a joint. But he wasn't that sheltered brat, not any longer. In Iraq he'd once faced down a mob of militant sympathizers who'd blocked his jeep, not to mention risking capture, death, and disfigurement for two consecutive 365-day tours. His mother was pushing seventy, didn't own any weapons, and barely reached five-foot-two wearing heels. They'd butted heads since before he was old enough to shave. What was there to be cowed by?

"Very well, Mother, I'm all ears. What's on your mind?"

She drew back, nostrils flaring. "Don't toy with me, Colvin." He hated when she called him Colvin, an ancestral surname with which she'd seen fit to curse him. "I may have stepped down as head of this foundation, but I still read the papers."

She produced a rolled up *New York Post* and held it out as though disciplining a puppy that had broken its house-training and soiled. Instead of using it to rap him on the nose, she threw it down on his desk blotter.

He shrugged. "I went to a wedding on Saturday with a friend, big deal."

"You attended a *gay* marriage as the escort to a *pornographic* film star."

"Same-sex marriage is legal in New York State and Sarah is a *former* adult-film actress."

"Actress, huh! Don't play semantics with me. She's a slut."

Like water off a duck's back, his mother's insults tended to glide off him. But hearing her speak of Sarah so, Cole felt his calm slipping—and his temper rising. "That's enough. Sarah is my friend."

Her mouth pursed, drawing his attention to the lines puckering her lips. They were both too old for this, the fighting, the pointless lecturing. "Yes, I know all about your degenerate *friends,* and until now I've held my peace. But this time you've gone too far. You've jeopardized not only your already-tattered reputation but the standing of this foundation."

Cole took a deep breath. "If you feel I've violated the morality clause in my contract, you're free to make your case to the board. On second thought, screw the board. I'll be happy to step down." He wasn't bluffing.

"Oh yes, you'd like that, wouldn't you. Once a quitter, always a quitter, or so your father used to say, God rest his soul."

The depth of her hypocrisy never failed to amaze him. His parents had barely tolerated one another. Separate bedrooms and separate lives had been their domestic status quo for as long as he could remember. When his father had died suddenly of a heart attack in his mid-fifties, he'd done so in the arms of his mistress of many years.

"Running this foundation is the sole structure to your dilettante lifestyle. Without it, you'd be free to pursue your . . . perversions full time."

His perversions, seriously? "This may be news to you, Mother, but these days nearly everyone owns a flogger and a copy of *Fifty Shades of Grey.*"

Flushing, she held her ground, not that he'd expected any less. "I'm past caring what you do in private."

"Glad to hear it," Cole shot back, wondering if she'd had him followed. He wouldn't put it past her. Wartime Iraq didn't have much to recommend it—bad heat, bad food, and almost constant mortal danger—but at least he'd been beyond her reach.

"But under no circumstances are you to see that . . . *creature* in public again."

An ultimatum—she really should know better than to go there. "And if I do?"

Lips trembling, she gathered a deep breath. "You will leave me no choice but to cut you out of this family, including its fortune."

"I see. If that's all, Mother, I have work to do. I hope you'll forgive me for not walking you to the elevator." He gestured her toward the door.

"I hope *you* understand. I won't warn you again."

He stepped back behind the desk. "Have a good day, Mother."

Watching her huffy exit, he considered his next move. Her ultimatum hadn't really surprised him. It alarmed him even less. Soldiering in Iraq had shown him how very little in the way of material comforts he needed to get by. Untainted food and water, a change of clothes, and a few hours of sleep in an actual bed had risen to luxury status. Even if she made good on her threat to cut him off, he'd be fine. He had advanced explosives expertise that any number of government defense contracting firms would covet, and a modest personal savings. He knew a lot of people with a lot less going for them.

Slipping into his seat, he picked up the newspaper and studied the captioned photograph. One thing was certain. The camera loved Sarah. Even caught by surprise with glazed eyes and ajar mouth, she was a stunner.

More than his mother's ultimatum, it was his feelings for Sarah that had him shaken. At some point over the past weeks, he'd stopped thinking of her as a fuck buddy and started treating her like his girlfriend.

Going as her date to the wedding had been a mistake and not just because of the paparazzi showing up. Looking on as Peter and

Pol exchanged vows and rings, he'd been slammed with the sense that he and Sarah were the only two in the room. He was falling for her. Beyond the sex, he loved being with her. Making breakfast together, fighting over the water temperature in the shower, and zoning out side-by-side on the sofa watching *Doctor Who*—it was as if he experienced everything for the first, magical time.

But more than anything, his revelations about what had gone down in Iraq bound them. For two years he'd steadfastly refused to talk about the war to anyone, even other vets. But Sarah wasn't anyone. She touched a part of him that no other woman had ever come close to reaching, made him vulnerable in ways he'd never before been. As any soldier knew, vulnerability was weakness, and weakness led to danger—big danger. If he didn't fix his attitude and fast, he might fall the rest of the way in love with her.

Pushing back from the desk, he picked up his iPhone and brought up Candace's number. He hadn't seen her since the night he'd met Sarah, almost two months ago. Curious as to what kind of greeting he'd get, he hit Send.

She picked up on the second ring. "You've got to be kidding me."

"Hey, beautiful, how's the headache?"

"It disappeared two months ago, along with you."

"Yeah, I know—my bad. I should have called. I've been slammed with work." The bullshit excuse was the best he could do.

Fortunately for him, she was still sufficiently interested not to hang up, not yet anyway. That didn't mean she wasn't up for making him squirm. "I saw you in the paper with your *girlfriend*. Funny, I wouldn't have figured you for the wedding type."

He forced a shrug into his voice. "What can I say? It was a slow news cycle, so they had to come up with something. I was helping out a friend, that's all."

"So Sugar Halliday is what, your bestie?"

Skirting the question, he said, "I didn't call to talk about her, I called about you. The foundation's holding a cocktails-and-dinner thing at the Met tomorrow night. We're hoping to raise start-up funds for the new mentorship program, and I'd love to have you on my arm. This time I promise to make sure any pasta is gluten-free. C'mon, what do you say? It'll be fun."

"Is Sugar busy?"

Cole blew out a breath. "You're the first person I thought to call." That much at least was true, although if she gave him much more grief he'd close out the conversation and move on to the dozen or more prospects in his address book.

As if sensing he was reaching his limit, she softened her voice and said, "In that case, I guess I'll forgive you."

Wishing he felt more of . . . *anything*, Cole said, "Great, I'll pick you up at seven."

"Sounds perfect . . . And Cole?"

"Yes?"

"I'm glad you called. I've missed you."

"Yeah, me too." The glib lie rolled off his tongue as smoothly as before, only now it brought an unprecedented pang of conscience.

Cole clicked off the call. Beautiful, wealthy, and pedigreed, Candace would be the perfect antidote to the rumors that he and Sugar— Sarah—were an item. But more importantly, their "date" was almost certain to get back to Sarah. A picture was indeed worth a thousand words, and given the guest list of high-profile public figures, including the city's mayor, there would be plenty of paparazzi covering the event. He didn't want Sarah to get the wrong idea about them, especially since he'd gone off map the other day and let his emotions get the better of him. They had a good thing going—and another seventy plus films to power through. So long as they stuck to their sex-only agreement, there was no reason he couldn't continue seeing her. The situation was win-win for them both.

So why did he feel so shitty about it?

✳✳✳ ✳✳✳

Sarah was stepping out of the shower when Cole's text came in. *Need to cancel tomorrow nite. Something came up. Call you for rain check?*

Tamping down her misgivings, she reached for her robe. She slipped it on but not before glimpsing her newest bruise in the mirror, a yellowish discoloration on her buttock courtesy of the marble bathroom counter.

Once they'd got back to her apartment, Cole's "gift" had succeeded in taking her mind off her media worries, at least for the short-term. By the time they'd reached her building, she was in such a heightened state of arousal that she hadn't been able to think beyond fulfillment. Intercourse with Ben Wa Balls had been amazing for them both. She couldn't wait to try it again. Cole's text, though, had her wondering if she would have the chance.

It wasn't his rescheduling that bothered her. It was the *way* he'd gone about it, canceling via text message rather than calling. And it was weird that he'd waited until seven on a Monday night to text her. He knew she had her FATE meeting every Monday from six to eight PM. Only tonight she didn't. With Peter and Pol still in honeymoon mode and everyone having just seen one another at their Saturday wedding, they'd collectively consented to canceling that week's meeting.

Earlier in the day, there'd been an obvious reporter snooping around her building. Her email inbox was so full she was seriously considering hitting "Delete All" and closing the account. Her phone had rung a few times too, though none of the callers had left any message. Had

Saturday's paparazzi run-in caused Cole to wonder if seeing her wasn't maybe more trouble than it was worth? Picking up her phone, she sent him a quick text back. *Sure, NP.*

NP—no problem. If only she believed that was true.

*** ***

The fundraiser dinner had been a misery for Cole. Even as he went through the motions of hosting—the welcome speech, the silent auction, the shameless guilting you had to go through to get money out of people these days, even the rich ones—he was incapable of not thinking of Sarah. Like a sexy ghost, she'd haunted him throughout the evening. Crazy as it sounded—was—he hadn't been able to shake the feeling that he was cheating on her. Misguided guilt aside, he'd just really missed her. More than once, he'd caught himself wondering what she might say about something that took place, what funny crack she might make aloud or whisper in his ear.

Candace was well-connected, well-heeled, and, he knew from their previous encounters, a seriously solid fuck. Her frequent touches throughout the evening—her bare foot sliding up his pants leg, her hand squeezing his inner thigh beneath the table—made it clear she was willing to forgive and forget the past few months of neglect. If he went to bed with her, the makeup sex would be hot, he was sure of it, with her working double-time to woo him back. And yet he spent the Uber car ride back to her Upper West Side apartment coming up with excuses for gracefully getting rid of her.

At her pressuring, he got out and walked her up to her building entrance. Outside the glass doors, she lifted her face to his. "Coming up?" From her confident smile, he could tell the question was perfunctory.

Cole hesitated, planting his feet on the pavement. Forget fucking, the thought of kissing her goodnight suddenly felt unthinkable. Seeing Sarah had as good as gotten rid of his game with other women. She might as well have cut off his balls.

And the worst of it was he felt guilty—guilty!—as though he was doing something wrong, as though he was cheating. Was it even possible to cheat on a porn star? But who was he gaming now? Sarah had stopped being that to him weeks ago.

Watching her mother Liz's boy, Jonathan, moved him in ways he couldn't begin to express. Day by day, being with her broke down each and every stereotype he'd held onto. And then there were her FATE friends, all former adult entertainers. Liz was funny and gutsy and brave, a great mom to Jonathan in the midst of fighting for her life. Peter was a hoot with a heart of gold, clearly crazy in love with his new husband. Honey and Brian, while quieter, had seemed like really cool people, too.

Stepping back, he said, "Thanks, but I have an early morning."

A furrow appeared between her eyes. "That never stopped you before. C'mon, one drink." The invitation came slightly slurred.

"You've already had a lot to drink." She swayed toward him, a deliberate play, or so he suspected. "So have you, so what?"

Actually he'd had only a few glasses of wine. Like his smoking, his alcohol consumption had lowered significantly since meeting Sarah. Being with her felt so amazing the last thing he wanted was to blunt his senses in any way.

"All the more reason to call it a night."

She glared at him. "What's your problem?"

His problem was Sarah, but he could hardly say so. Aware of the doorman watching them through the glass, he said, "It's too late for this."

Her eyes narrowed. "Sure you don't need a shot of *Sugar*?"

Definitely in Sarah withdrawal, Cole felt as transparent as the glass doors at his back. "We're friends." He'd sworn something similar earlier to his mother. The lie didn't sound any more convincing this time.

She rolled her eyes. "Whatevs."

"Goodnight." He turned to go.

She caught at his arm. "If you want to call up your *friend* and have her come over, I could be . . . into that."

He'd had a few threesomes before. So long as swords weren't crossed, he'd been cool with sharing. But sharing Sarah with anyone, man or woman, wasn't something he could bring himself to consider—ever.

"Thanks, but I don't think so." He shook her off.

"Cole, come back. I didn't mean to be a bitch. I'm just buzzed. Aren't you at least going to kiss me goodnight?"

"No, Candace, I'm not." He turned away. "Goodnight. Take care of yourself."

Directing his steps toward the waiting car, he acknowledged he was really saying goodbye.

✳✳✳ ✳✳✳

Sipping coffee at her kitchen counter and skimming the paper's online Arts & Entertainment section, the photo of Cole with the beautiful redhead slammed Sarah like a sucker punch. So much for something coming up, the formal foundation fundraiser at the Met looked anything but unplanned or last minute. Of course he couldn't have taken her, she knew that, but why had he felt the need to lie? Couldn't he have . . . gone alone? Taken a . . . cousin or some-one similarly platonic? Regardless, being seen out with a prominent socialite so soon after Saturday should go a long way in diffusing the rumors that he was with "Sugar." So far as reputation management was concerned, it was a stunning strategy, unless of course the date had been real and not a ruse.

To be fair, Sarah had been as adamant as he about upholding their no-strings rule. She should know better than to want more now. She *did* know better. Even if she were an elementary school teacher rather than an adult film star, Cole was as unattainable as men came. And yet she couldn't fight her feelings. Watching him pushing Jonathan on the swings, seeing him with Liz and their other friends at the wedding, she'd found herself fantasizing about what it would be like to have him in her life permanently, for keeps and not only for sex.

Her phone rang. Her heart rate ratcheted. She fished the phone from her purse. Seeing Peter's name on her cell, she tamped down her disappointment and answered.

"Hi newlywed," she said with false cheer. Just because her love life was in the shitter didn't give her the right to crap on everyone else's.

"Hi yourself," he answered, sounding happier than she'd ever heard him. "Pol and I just got around to opening our wedding gifts, and oh my God, Sarah! You planned our entire wedding and now this. A two week all-inclusive trip to Ireland, I—we—don't know what to say."

This time Sarah smiled for real. "Don't say anything, just go and have an amazing time."

"I'd say we'd name our firstborn after you, but well, that'll probably mean a puppy."

"That's okay, I like puppies." With Cole likely out of the picture, she might as well move forward with getting a dog.

Clicking alerted her to another incoming call. A reporter probably. She hadn't been bugged as much as she'd expected, but she hadn't been left alone, either. Putting Peter on speaker, she looked down. The caller wasn't a reporter at all. It was Cole!

Breathe, Sarah, just breathe.

Impatient to be off, she said, "Pete, I've got to run, but give my love to Pol, and well, bring me back a sweater."

He chuckled. "You've got it, sweetie. Ta."

Ending the call with Peter, relief rushed her. Cole hadn't dumped her! Guys like Cole didn't call to tell you it was over. They just didn't call.

Still, she forced herself to count to five before answering. "Hello."

Cole's voice greeted her from the receiver. "Hi yourself. What's up?" He sounded pretty much as he always did, but Sarah sensed a slight strain to his voice.

Holding the phone to her ear, she focused on smoothing any tremor from her tone before answering. "You tell me."

A long pause and then, "About the other night—"

"I don't care about you canceling," she cut in, "but lying to me isn't cool. I deserve better than that."

"I didn't actually lie, I just—"

"Look, unless you missed the memo, seeing other people socially is fine."

Socially but not sexually. Glancing back to the computer screen to the image of Cole wrapped around the redhead, Sarah couldn't imagine he hadn't done both. Whoever and whatever Candace Bennett was to him, Sarah wanted to rip out her rival's red hair by the roots.

"You don't have to explain yourself to me, but you do have to respect my time."

"Agreed, and for what it's worth, I feel really badly about canceling on you at the last minute."

"Don't worry about it. I . . . made other plans." Her "other plans" had involved taking Jonathan to the park and then treating him to a Shake Shack cheeseburger, but Cole didn't need to know that.

"Let me make it up to you. Have dinner with me tonight. Fuck the media. We'll go anywhere you want."

"I don't think that's such a good idea. Besides, after last night, you're probably off the hook so far as any scandal."

He hesitated. "Maybe I don't want to be off the hook."

Sarah paused. She was offering him his out. Why didn't he just take it? "I promised to take dinner over to Liz's. She's feeling rough after this morning's treatment." Weakening, she added, "I'll be free after eight, only I don't feel like going out."

"No problem, I'll pick up dinner on my way. Chinese, sushi, pizza—"

"Whatever. I don't have any preference."

Fucking and feeding—the two F's, only tonight she doubted they'd be doing much of either.

"Great, I'll see you at eight then." She'd expected him to sign off; he wasn't ordinarily one for long phone conversations, but instead he held on. "We're good then?"

"Yeah, sure, we're fine." She'd never been less fine in her life, but she was an actress, after all. She'd faked multiple orgasms before an entire production team. Certainly she should be able to pull off a decent performance of nonchalance over the phone. "I've got to go. Bye." Sarah set down the cell.

He wanted to see her again. He'd even sort of apologized. They could pick up exactly where they'd left off. That should be enough for her only it wasn't, not nearly. She blamed herself, not him. She'd been just as adamant about their no-strings rule as he had. They'd started out with a level playing field: sex only, lots of it, and all in the spirit of consensual adult fun. She hadn't expected to develop . . . *feelings* for him.

Feelings, who was she kidding? She was in love with the son of a bitch.

Just like the Nazareth song said, love hurt. It really, really did.

Only an A-class idiot fell in love with her fuck buddy. The longer she stayed in their arrangement, the more hurt she'd be when it ended. There was only one "solution" so far as she could see.

She'd break things off with him tonight *before* any clothes came off.

✳✳✳ ✳✳✳

Sarah dropped off the groceries at Liz's and then stuck around to make a simple dinner of pasta tossed with olive oil and steamed veggies. Given Liz's nausea, Grandma Campanelli's spaghetti sauce was definitely ruled out. She'd been throwing up off and on all day. Even though she swore her stomach had settled, she only managed a few forkfuls.

Liz set her cutlery down on the plate's edge. "I'm sorry, Sarah. It really is delicious. I just . . . can't."

Feeling her heart drop, Sarah was determined not to show how worried she was. "Do you want me to make you something else, a poached egg maybe?"

Liz answered with a weary head shake. "I just can't stomach anything right now. I'm still so queasy. I don't understand it. Usually the anti-nausea meds kick in by now."

Concerned, Sarah admitted, "You don't look so good."

That Liz had dispensed with the habitual head scarf was a testimony to how bad she must be feeling. Pearls of perspiration gathered on her upper lip and smooth scalp. She leaned across the table and pressed the back of her hand to Liz's clammy forehead. It felt warm.

Liz chuckled. "That's because I have c-a-n-c-e-r."

Knowing how Liz hated being fussed over, Sarah dropped her hand and moved back. "Thanks, but I got the memo. Still I think we should call the doctor and check in."

Liz sighed. "You'll only get the answering service telling you to dial 911 if it's an emergency. This morning's appointment really took it out of me, but Dr. Gleason told me to expect to feel worse before I feel better. He was right."

"But—"

"Please, Sarah, just let it go." It was the closest Liz had come to snapping at her—ever.

Against her better judgment, Sarah relented. "Okay, but then let me stay with you tonight."

Canceling her "date" would mean delaying breaking things off with Cole, but another day or two wouldn't make any lasting difference. Beyond bed, their "relationship" wasn't going anywhere.

Liz's missing eyebrows lifted. "And miss out on another date with the Incredible Hunk? Nice try, but I think not."

"For the record, the other night he canceled on me."

Liz shrugged. "So don't let him get away with it. Tell him how you feel, what you want, and he can either choose to get on board or not."

"We have an agreement, remember? Rule Numero Uno: no strings, just sex."

"Agreements get renegotiated all the time, and as they say, rules are made to be broken."

"Not this one."

Liz cocked her head. "You know what I think? I think someone's scared, and I'm not talking about Cole."

"I am not . . . scared."

Liz looked at her askance. "You used to be a good actress, I'm just sayin'."

"Okay, so I don't want to end up as yet another woman he's ditched for trying to get too close, so sue me."

"For all you know, he feels the same way about you."

"Yeah, right, and that's why he asked another woman to his tight-assed charity event?"

"Didn't you tell him you were lying low, flying under Ye Olde Radar Screen, yada yada?"

Liz had her there. "Yeah, but—"

"No buts. So far you haven't even let him take you out to dinner, and suddenly you expect him to ask you to be his date for a black-tie function where scores of paparazzi are bound to be. Seriously, Sarah, you can't have it both ways. Behind-the-scenes fuck buddies or public couple, *decide*."

"He doesn't want a girlfriend."

"He said that what . . . eight weeks ago when he was drunk. Are you going to hold him to that single statement for what, the rest of your lives?"

"No, of course not, but—"

"No buts." She grabbed Sarah's hand, squeezing with surprising strength under the circumstances. "Look at me, Sarah. I mean *really* look at me. I am the absolute fucking poster child for 'Life is short.' Everything I thought I had handled, everything I thought I knew, is either bullshit or a big question mark. I used to hate how easily I put on weight, how top heavy I was, and now I'm under a hundred pounds and flat as a board, praying I survive the poisoning to get cured. I left LA to prove to myself I was done with porn, to raise my kid away from it, and yet all my closest friends here in New York are former adult entertainers, including you. Once I got here, I worked myself to the bone building up my graphic design business, worrying how I was going to afford to send Jonathan to college, and now I'm not even sure I'll live to see him graduate elementary school. Life's too short not to take a chance on being happy. Serious shots at happiness, and great guys like Cole, don't come around all that often. When they do, it's up to us to act, to make like the ancient Romans and *carpe diem*—seize the day. So seize the fucking day,

Sarah, seize it!" She collapsed back against the chair, her fingers slipping free of Sarah's.

Taken aback by her friend's fierceness, Sarah said, "You're right. I have been too cautious, too afraid of getting hurt again. But it takes two to tango. I can't force Cole to be in a relationship with me." She couldn't—not anymore than she could make him love her back.

Liz's expression softened. "I've seen you two together, the way he looks at you when he thinks you're not watching, the same way you look at him when you think no one will see. The way you guys were at the wedding . . . Face it, you both blew past the fuck-buddy stage weeks ago."

"You're right, I did, but I'm not so sure he did."

"You won't know that for sure unless you put yourself out there and ask him. Promise me you'll at least think about it."

"Okay, I promise," Sarah said, thinking of the coming night, not a "movie night" but a date, or so Cole had seemed to frame it.

Walking back to her building, gaze scanning the street for probable reporters, she thought over what Liz had said. The same speech coming from anyone else would be easy to dismiss, but Liz was her best friend, her person. They'd both had a parent who had in one way or another failed them. Although Liz had moved to LA a few years ahead of Sarah, they'd both gotten into porn for pragmatic reasons. Having cancer and fighting for her life seemed to have lent Liz an enhanced clarity that Sarah lacked, certainly where Cole was concerned.

He hadn't so much as mentioned what movie they might act out. Instead he'd asked her out to dinner as if they were having an actual date. Had she been too quick to shoot him down? An actual date with Cole, how might that go?

Thanks to the paparazzi crashing the wedding, they were already busted. So far the world hadn't ended. He'd called, wanting to see her again, in public, no less.

Maybe I don't want to be off the hook.

Was getting away from the sexually charged atmosphere of the apartment and going somewhere to talk worth a shot? Once she got back to her apartment, she'd call and tell him to forget takeout and make a restaurant reservation instead.

A note taped next to the mailboxes announced the elevator would be shut down for repairs starting tomorrow. Fucking great! While she certainly didn't miss driving in LA traffic, she suddenly found herself sighing for her two-car garage. Living in Manhattan, who needed spinning classes? These days she went to yoga purely to be polite.

Punching the up arrow, she figured she might as well enjoy this particular "amenity" while it was still functional. The elevator ascended with a cryptic creak and landed with a bone-rattling jolt. Grateful when the doors opened, Sarah stepped quickly out.

She stuck the key in her door and opened it. The apartment seemed crowded with scenes of her and Cole. Even the damned air was scented with his particular aftershave and musk. Pissed off about that, she crossed the threshold, thinking to open a window to air the place out. Her sandal crunched on something other than floorboards. She looked down and saw a cream-colored envelope bearing her footprint. Someone must have slipped it under her door during the day. That was weird. She'd paid the rent a few days ago. All her other mail came to the box below.

She stooped to retrieve it. Standing, she turned the letter face up . . . and froze. Calligraphy—bold, thick, and familiar—swam before her eyes. Panic plowed into her. Her blood froze. Her body shook, not just her hands but the whole of her. Her stalker had followed her to New York! He'd found her! He must have seen the photo of her and Cole at the wedding and hopped on a plane.

Hands shaking, she forced herself to break the seal.

Every bitch has her day. Yours is coming—soon—with a final photograph to send you on your way a la Camera Sutra.

So much for poetry. None of the previous notes had been so brief— or so angry. Her heart hammering, she fell back against the door. This was bad, really, really bad. She needed to get the hell away from here and fast. This time she'd go totally off grid, somewhere no one knew her. Her thoughts flew back to Liz as she'd just left her. Like it or not, she'd made promises, put down roots. She couldn't run, not anymore. She'd committed to staying for Liz and Jonathan and the group and . . . Cole? Fuck buddy or boyfriend, disappearing on him with no explanation, not even a goodbye, didn't feel fair. More than unfair, it felt . . . wrenching.

But she had to do something, starting with contacting the police. Whoever wrote that note needed serious professional help. If it was Danny and he'd followed her to New York, he was sicker than she'd supposed. Keeping the note to herself would be beyond stupid. Looking back, she couldn't believe she'd stayed silent about the others. The only person she'd confided in was Martin. Obviously the PI he'd hired hadn't panned out. She reached for her phone to call him, but then thought better of it. He might well try talking her out of going public, but beyond that, she didn't need him anymore. She could stand on her own two feet.

She was Googling the police non-emergency number when her cell sounded off. "S-arah!" Jonathan's voice, terrified, hysterical wailed into the receiver.

Sarah snapped to attention. "Jonathan, take a big breath and tell me what's happened."

"Mommy . . . she's on . . . on the bedroom floor . . . twitching."

Sounded like a seizure—shit. "Is she breathing?"

"I . . . I think so."

"Listen to me very carefully. I need you to be a big brave boy and hang up and call 911. That's 9-1-1. The operator will ask you for your name and address and some other information. Can you do that for me, baby?"

"I . . . th-think so." He repeated his address: 200 Mercer Street, Apt 4F.

"Great, now hang up and make the call. I'm on my way." Grabbing her bag and keys from the counter, Sarah raced out of the apartment.

Chapter Thirteen

The first time I set eyes on Sarah, Sugar, I nearly blew my load. Even before she had a clue about how to do her hair and makeup, how to dress, how to walk into a room and light it up, I saw how special she was, how amazing she could be.

All this time I've waited for her to see me, really see me. That's what I wanted then. It's what I've always wanted.

But to the Sugars of the world, men like me are putzes, stepping stones. My gifts and homage have gone ignored, and now my patience and my pilgrimage have come to an end.

Since I can't get Sarah to see me, I'll see her . . .

Dead.

Liz had suffered a bad reaction to the new antiemetic medication. Fortunately it didn't happen that often, but it did happen. It wasn't until Sarah was settled into the waiting room that she checked her phone and saw Cole's text.

Outside your building with soggy Chinese takeout & no key. Where ARE you?

Shit! In the cluster fuck of calling the doctor's after hours service, triaging Liz according to the emergency operator's instructions, and calling Honey to come over and sit with Jonathan, she'd forgotten their date. That was what her mother would have called poetic justice, but right now all she could think about was Liz.

She tapped out a short, just-the-facts reply.

With Liz in ER. Looks like bad reaction to chemo. Sorry about soggy Chinese. Maybe you can find a "friend?"

Seconds later he texted back: *Is she ok? What hospital? PS: Not looking for anymore "friends."*

Yeah, right, asshole! *Not sure, admitting her for observation. Sloan-Kettering, but we're ok. PPS: Leftover Chinese makes great breakfast.*

Makes great midnight snack too. On way.

Sarah paused, thumbs hovering over the iPhone screen. *Thanks, but not necessary.*

Sarah threw her phone in her bag and got up for another vending machine coffee, not because it was remotely drinkable but for something to do. Sitting alone waiting on the doctor's report was driving her crazy. Texting back and forth with her BFB—Best Fuck Buddy—wasn't helping, either.

A ding announced the landing of yet another text message. This time, Sarah left the phone inside her purse.

***** *****

Cole looked down at the two bags of Chinese carryout. He hadn't known what Sarah liked, so he'd ordered one of all the usual suspects on the menu. In true Canning fashion, when all else failed, he'd reached for his wallet and thrown money at the problem.

That worked with most other women but not with Sarah.

She hadn't answered his last text message. He had a pretty good hunch she wasn't going to. He didn't blame her. If their roles were reversed, he probably wouldn't reply either. That didn't mean he was happy about it.

For the first time in his life, he was the one left holding the bag—and the phone. Unbidden, he felt a surge of sympathy for Candace and the other women he'd dated since Iraq. Being on the wrong end of a silent phone seriously sucked.

Standing around doing nothing had never been his forte. No matter how hard he tried staying put, no matter how many times he tried telling himself that Sarah's sick friend and her sick friend's adorable kid weren't his problem, it was no use. Above all, Sarah was his problem. That she might need him but be too stubborn and independent and brave to admit it ripped at his heart. And the hell of it was that he wanted her to need him. He wanted to be the one she turned to, whether she was worried or scared, horny or pissed off. The need to see for himself that she was okay trumped all his rationalizing. He'd never wanted to shelter and protect someone so much in his life.

So why the hell was he still standing on her street corner? Shifting the food to one hand, he lifted the other to flag down a cab.

✳✳✳ ✳✳✳

Sarah sat alone in the ER waiting room. At home with Jonathan, Honey had started a phone tree for their group. The bulk of the concerned text messages and phone calls had hit about an hour ago. Predictably, everyone's first response was to want to run to the hospital, but Sarah had counseled them all to hold tight and stay put, at least until the morning. Liz wasn't yet allowed visitors. She was just now getting settled into her room. There was no point in flocking to the ER just to hang out with each other in the waiting room. Still, without company the hours crawled by.

She folded her arms about herself and closed her eyes, trying to nap, but the neon lighting and the intermittent intercom shout-outs made sleep of any kind pretty much impossible. Her brain was too wired to focus on any of the magazines she'd picked up, flipped through, and put back down again. Most of them were at least a month old anyway. She didn't have her iPad with her, so she couldn't read a book. That was probably for the best. The device was largely loaded with romance novels. Given her circumstances, those were the last materials she should be reading.

Looking for distraction, she dug the phone from her bag. Another text from Cole—Jesus, give it a break. She should ignore it like the last, but she could feel her willpower weakening, and not only because it was pushing toward 2 AM. Being worried, pissed off, and now bored made for a really bad combination.

I want to help. You don't have to deal with this alone.

Sarah gritted her teeth. *There's nothing you can do. And I'm fine.*

Bullshit, you're exhausted.

How the f*ck would you know that?

Look up.

Why?

Just do it.

Sarah looked up. Cole walked toward her, a carryout bag in either hand.

Rising on shaking legs, she managed a smile. "You really don't take no for an answer, do you?"

"Never." He dropped the food on the coffee table and opened his arms.

Sarah had no reserve to resist. She fell into them. Leaning into his strength and warmth, she pressed her face against the side of his neck, inhaling his tangy scent, wishing she might stay close to him like this forever. "I said I was fine."

She looked up in time to see him smile. "Yeah, you did. You used to be a better actress."

Thinking how earlier Liz had said the same thing, she found herself smiling back. "I've been hearing that a lot lately." She hugged him harder. "I can't believe you came. I can't believe you're here."

"Of course I came," he answered in a thick, scratchy, voice although she was pretty sure he'd cut way back on the cigarettes. "Did you think I wouldn't? That's what friends do. They cover each other's back."

Sarah stiffened. Cole was nothing if not a stand-up guy, but she mustn't mistake his kindness for more than it was.

Tensing, she eased away. "Right, about that—"

"Are you here for Liz Cunningham?"

Sarah swung around to the doctor. "Yes, I am. I'm her friend—and her medical power of attorney," she added quickly in case he was thinking about turning her away.

His expression eased into a smile. "Fortunately that shouldn't be needed tonight. Allergic reactions to antiemetics aren't common, but when they occur they can be serious. Your quick response in getting her here made a huge difference."

"It's her son who deserves the credit. He found her on the floor and called me. Fortunately, I live just a few blocks away."

"Well, he's a very smart young man, and you're a very good friend."

"Can I see her?"

He hesitated and then nodded. "Yes, but only for a few minutes. She's settled into her room and resting comfortably. She just woke up, but we're keeping her sedated."

"Great, I won't stay long." She glanced back to Cole. Despite what he'd said, she didn't expect him to hang out waiting. Now that he'd discharged his friendship duties, he'd want to head home. Letting him off the hook, she said, "Looks like I'm going to be taking a second rain check on dinner." Or breakfast or post-two AM snack, whatever it was.

He shrugged. "That carryout isn't going anywhere, and neither am I. We'll both keep until you get back."

✳✳✳ ✳✳✳

Once Sarah saw Liz looking so much better, her adrenalin bottomed. Returning to the waiting room where Cole sat watching reruns of *That '70s Show*, hunger warred with fatigue. Her stomach growled, and her legs felt weak. He was right. She really did need to eat something that didn't come out of a vending machine. He'd used the time she was away to clear the coffee table of magazines, set them aside in a neat stack, and unpack the food containers and chopsticks.

Taking it all in, Sarah shook her head. "You're going to make someone a wonderful wife someday, but I don't think you're actually allowed to bring in food."

He followed her gaze to the tented "No Food or Drink" sign on a lamp table. Smiling, he leaned over and flipped it facedown. "Don't you know by now, Sarah, it's better to ask for forgiveness than permission? Besides it's just us." He patted the couch cushion.

She hesitated and then dropped down beside him. "Geez, the restaurant owner must love you. What *don't* you have here?"

He looked almost embarrassed by the question. "I . . . wasn't sure what you liked." The admission came out almost as shyness.

"I like all the flavors, remember," she shot back, giving him her best "Sugar" smile, but she was too beat to channel the porn-diva mojo.

Instead she focused on feeding herself. As hungry as she was, it was an effort just to chew. At Cole's urging, she managed to scarf down a few spring rolls before giving in and curling up on the couch.

"Just going to . . . rest my . . . eyes."

✳✳✳ ✳✳✳

Cole settled Sarah's head more comfortably on his shoulder. He reached over and smoothed back the hair from her brow. She didn't stir beyond snuggling closer. Cole smiled and pressed a kiss onto her head. She was out like a proverbial light, which was no surprise to him. She'd obviously been running on fumes since before he'd got there. Now that Liz was out of immediate danger, she'd crashed. Cole had experienced a similar reaction in the aftermath of diffusing a particularly difficult explosive device.

The doctor had been right. Sarah was a good friend. As Cole well knew, she was a good person all around. Strike "good," she was great to and for them all—Liz, Jonathan, her FATE friends, and him—especially him. He was a better man for having met her and not only because his smoking and drinking were down and his sleeping up. Thanks to her, he'd learned to laugh again, to joke, and to be himself without any bullshit or posturing. In just two months, she'd become so much more to him than a fuck buddy. If he were honest, he'd admit that all the ways she was "more" frightened him half to death.

Three months ago he'd been high-fiving himself for having scored "Sugar" as his no-strings-attached lover. Looking down at Sarah's profile, peaceful in sleep, he couldn't imagine feeling that way now.

But like Jekyll and Hyde, Sarah and Sugar were a package deal. Accepting one meant accepting the other. And it wasn't like the "Sugar" aspect of the duality was in any way hard to take. He loved how down and dirty she could get, both in bed and out of it.

But he also loved the way she hogged the shower, her fussiness about cooking only organic food, how she reached for the hair clips when she was in a rush rather than obsessively primping as so many of his girlfriends had done. He loved *her*. The disastrous date with Candace had confirmed it.

Still, knowing that the world, or at least thousands of people on the planet, had seen your woman not only naked but fucking other guys wasn't something he'd ever considered before. It would take a strong man to cope with that and still be okay. Cole knew he was strong . . . but only to a point. The tours in Iraq had humbled him, too. He understood his limits, not only physical but psychological. He knew what it meant to live with something you couldn't go back and change. Regrets didn't help. They ate you alive.

He loved Sarah, he knew that now, but did he have what it took to live with her very public past?

✳✳✳ ✳✳✳

Sarah awakened to her head pillowed in Cole's lap, his slightly bleary eyes smiling down on her. Pushing upright, she asked, "How long have I been like this?"

"Coupla hours."

She swung her feet onto the linoleum floor. "You sat up all this time, didn't you?"

He shrugged. "Sometimes in Iraq we'd be on patrol and a sandstorm would come up, or it would be a hundred plus degrees in the shade. Sitting up for a few hours in the air conditioning is no big deal."

The macho routine was infuriating—and endearing. She stretched, stiff in places she couldn't name. "Well, you are like the best fuck buddy ever."

Was it her imagination or did he wince? "Thanks . . . I think."

Liz was switched to a new antiemetic and discharged with strict instructions to stay hydrated. Paperwork and waiting for sign offs from various physicians ate up several hours. By the time they were ready to leave, it was lunchtime. Even though there were plenty of cabs queuing up outside the hospital's main entrance, Cole insisted on calling for his car service to pick them up. Too tired to argue, Sarah let him handle the details. The curbside pickup was smooth; the hospital aide wheeled Liz out to the waiting town car.

Back at Liz's, Cole relieved Honey of her babysitting duties, ordered groceries from Fresh Direct, phoned in the new prescription for anti-nausea meds, and headed out with Jonathan to pick up pizza.

Occupied with settling Liz into the bedroom, Sarah couldn't resist pointing out, "They do deliver, you know."

"I like it hot," he replied. "Besides, Jonathan and I need some guy time, don't we buddy?" He reached down and ruffled Jonathan's hair, and Sarah's heart tugged.

Toeing the carpet, Jonathan shrugged. "Yeah, I guess so." Ordinarily he lit like a Christmas tree whenever Cole came around. Clearly the night had taken a toll on him, too.

"We'll be back in an hour," Cole said to Sarah.

"Okay, we'll be here."

He returned fifty minutes later with a smiling Jonathan. Along with the pills and pizza, he'd bought a magnum bottle of Chianti.

"Cole took me to the Apple Store, and we played around with all kinds of cool sh . . . stuff!" Jonathan announced, bounding into the bedroom to be with his mom.

Sarah ran her gaze over Cole. His stomach might be a rock-hard six-pack, but his heart was squishy soft where kids were concerned.

He set the pizza box and bags down on the counter and stepped inside the tiny kitchen. "Any idea where I might a find a corkscrew?" he asked, pulling open first one drawer and then another.

Following him in, she held back a chuckle. The corkscrew was in the first drawer he'd opened and in plain sight—talk about Man Goggles! Handing it to him, she glanced at the microwave clock. It was 3 PM. "It's kind of early for me."

Cole sloshed red wine into a water tumbler and handed it to her. "Like they say, it's five o'clock somewhere. Besides, you've had a hell of a night."

He was right, about that at least. "Thanks," she said, accepting the glass. "But so have you."

"And that's exactly why I'm joining you." Grinning, he took out a second glass and filled it halfway.

From the bedroom, Liz called out, "Someone have a glass for me. I'd drink the whole damned bottle if I could."

Sarah and Cole exchanged amused looks. Liz was definitely feeling better. "Hey, no complaints, you've got the good drugs," she called back.

Lowering his voice, Cole said, "Nothing wrong with her ears."

As if to prove it, Liz shouted back, "Hey, I heard that!"

Ordering Sarah to the sofa—"Do not even think of moving"— Cole saw that everyone was settled in with a soda and a slice and then joined them in the main room.

Flipping through the DVD stack of animated movies, he looked over to Jonathan. "So buddy, what's it going to be? *Wreck-It Ralph? 101 Dalmatians? Toy Story 2? Cinderella?*" He paused, lifting one eyebrow. "*Cinderella*, seriously?"

Mouth and chin covered in tomato sauce, Jonathan shrugged. "That one's my mom's. She got it when it came out on Blu-ray."

"Whew, good to know, you had me worried there. Anyway, partner, pick your poison."

"*Wreck-It Ralph*, I guess."

"Sounds like a solid choice." Cole popped in the movie, picked up his paper plate, and settled onto the floor beside Jonathan. He folded the huge slice in half and took a big bite. Chewing, he leaned back against the couch, his one shoulder resting against Sarah's leg.

Resisting the urge to reach down and stroke his mussed hair, Sarah said, "Don't you ever work?"

Mouth full, he managed a smile. "I do, but mostly I delegate."

Staring ahead at the TV, he reached up with one hand and took her foot, kneading the arch with his knuckles and thumb. The innocent pleasure was also bittersweet. Impromptu foot massages, yet another thing she stood to miss!

She hadn't expected to fall asleep again, but given how spent she was, the few sips of wine might as well have been Ambien. When she opened her eyes, the movie credits were rolling, and Jonathan was playing on Cole's iPad.

Blinking, she pulled herself upright. "Where's Cole?"

Eyes on the device, Jonathan jerked his chin toward the kitchen. "Cleaning up."

Pulling down the throw blanket that someone, Cole, had covered her with, she got up and tiptoed over to Liz's half-open door. Propped up on pillows, her friend was awake and alert and sipping a bottle of ginger ale.

Sarah poked her head inside. "Can I get you anything?" she asked, eyeing the water level in the plastic pitcher, a "souvenir" from the previous night's hospital stay.

"No, thanks, I'm good. But you can do me a favor and get yourself out of here and home. You look almost as bad as I do, and that's saying a lot."

"Thanks. I'm going to grab a few things from my place, but I'll be back."

"No you won't," Liz said firmly.

Sarah let out a long breath. Liz was stubborn, but then so was she. "You just got out of the hospital. You and Jonathan absolutely cannot stay here by yourselves tonight."

"I agree. That's why I had Cole call Peter. He and Pol are on their way over."

Wiping his hands on a dish towel, Cole came up behind her. "Actually they're here. I just buzzed them up."

Sarah looked back to Liz. "Why is it I have the feeling I'm being double-teamed?"

"Maybe because you are," Liz admitted with a smile.

"You snooze, you lose," Cole added, snapping the towel against Sarah's butt.

Outmatched and outnumbered, there was nothing for her to do but concede defeat. Privately, she admitted that the prospect of spending the night stretched out in her own bed held enormous appeal. "Okay, you both win but I'll be back bright and early tomorrow to see Jonathan to school."

"Great, thank you, now go, get outta here!" Lifting rail thin arms, one bearing a big, brownish bruise from the IV, Liz made a show of shooing her off.

"Okay, I'm going, but if anything happens, and I mean *anything*, you call me, got it?"

Liz crossed her heart. "Cross my heart and hope to . . . Well, let's leave it at cross my heart. And forget anymore needles."

By now used to Liz's black humor, Sarah crossed the room to the bed. "No one's dying, not on my watch." She bent down and kissed Liz's thin cheek.

She reentered the living room in time to open the door to Peter and Pol waiting out in the hallway. They bore flowers, a tray of Starbucks coffees, and tons of questions about how the night in the hospital had gone.

Sarah answered as best and as briefly as she could. "You call me if she needs anything, or . . . Just call me," she added, wagging a warning finger in their vicinity.

Expression earnest, Pol nodded profusely. "We will, we promise."

Peter's mouth kicked up. "Will you look at this one, from porn star to Jewish mother in less than one month, oy vey!"

Tired and stressed though Sarah was, their good-natured ribbing had her grinning.

Cole grabbed his jacket off the hook by the door. "Hold up, I'll walk you."

"Thanks, but I'm pretty sure I can find my way," she said, already starting toward the stairs. She'd postpone talking to him until she'd had some solid sleep and could count on being coherent—not cowardice or even procrastination but good common sense, right?

"Sarah!" He grabbed hold of her upper arm, stalling her in her steps.

She whirled. Glaring down at his gripping hand and then back up at him, she said "Okay, you can walk me. You don't have to act like some fucking prison guard."

He let go, his fingers falling away. Outside the apartment, he demanded, "What was that about?"

"What was what about?"

"You know what. I do something to piss you off?"

"No, why?"

"Forget it. Let's go before you fall asleep on your feet." He took hold of her arm.

They walked side-by-side in silence, pushing through the soupy summertime air, Cole with his hands stuffed into his jeans pockets. Coming up onto the Angelika Film Center, they turned the corner onto West Houston Street. From it, her place was a short six blocks— suddenly the longest six blocks of her life. Once, they inadvertently brushed shoulders, and Sarah shied away as though she'd been burned. In a way, she was about to be. They passed the bodega where they'd first met, and she found herself fighting sentimental tears. It had only been slightly more than two months, and yet in so many ways that night felt like a lifetime ago. Certainly it had been a turning point, the start to reclaiming sex as a private pleasure, not a commodity to be packaged and sold as entertainment.

She glanced over to Cole. Nothing in his rigidly set profile suggested he considered the mini market to have any sort of special significance. Then again, she supposed all New York convenience stores looked pretty much the same.

They turned left onto Elizabeth Street, their steps slowing. Cole might not yet know it, at least not for certain, but her street was their personal end of the line. Her building was almost within view. Between them and it lay an Asian food mart, several restaurants and wine bars, a vacant storefront with a "For Rent" sign defaced by graffiti, art galleries, and a smattering of chichi shops Sarah had been meaning to browse but hadn't yet bothered. Before now she'd considered herself too busy—with Liz and Jonathan, the book, and . . . Cole. The void he would leave in her life suddenly loomed as large and empty as the Grand Canyon.

Reaching the front steps to her brownstone, she turned to face him. "Thanks for everything you did back there."

It was paltry praise for all the help he'd given, not just for Liz and Jonathan, but for Peter and Pol, too. And her? The past months had seen her through a serious slump. In no small part due to him, she'd reclaimed New York as her home.

He shrugged. "I didn't do anything. I like pizza, I like wine, and I like hanging out with Jonathan. He's a cool kid."

"Still, it meant a lot. He's never had a father around. You spending time is a huge deal."

She turned toward the stairs. He started to follow her up, but she stopped him with a hand. "I'm not exactly feeling up to acting out any movies at the moment."

"That's okay, we can just sleep. You look beat." He reached out and brushed the pad of his thumb beneath her eye.

The tender gesture had her eyes filling.

His gaze widened, sucking her in. "Hey, what is it? What's wrong?" He made as if to hug her, but Sarah backed out of reach.

"Cole, I can't do this anymore." The withheld words tumbled out, inelegant but efficient.

He dropped his arms. "Okay, so maybe it was a little early to start drinking, but we only had one glass—okay mug." He tried for a laugh, his smile slipping when she didn't join in. "You're not talking about the wine, are you?"

She shook her head. "No, I'm not."

"Then what?"

"I can't see you anymore."

He shoved a hand through his mussed hair. "If this is about the other night, nothing happened between Candace and me—*nothing*."

"Thanks, but it's not just about that."

"Then what is it about?" A young mother pushing a stroller passed them. Sarah resisted the urge to shout, *I want that. That!* Instead she focused on Cole and tried to explain. "The whole no-strings-attached sex-only thing we've got going, I thought I could do it, that it would be enough, but I can't, and it isn't, not anymore." *Not with someone as special to me as you.*

He looked blown away, not that she blamed him. "But you said . . . I thought—"

"I know what I said; if it helps, you have every right to be confused and even pissed off. We had a deal, and now I'm breaking it, but I can't help the way I feel." Feelings, the f-word, there, she'd said it. "I want strings, tons of them, along with marriage and pets and kids and, fuck it all, a cottage with a white picket fence, or at least a brownstone in Park Slope with a back garden."

She'd lived the porn-film script for ten years now. It had been one incredible ride, but now she wanted a new script for a new story—a good old-fashioned fairytale.

He stared at her as though she'd tasered him. Silent, he stood down a step, his body language doing the talking for him.

Sarah filled in the silence for them both. "I know that wasn't our deal, and it's probably not even something you'd want, so I'm . . . letting you off the hook."

His gaze snagged hers. "How many times do I have to tell you I'm not asking you to let me off the hook? I just need some time to . . . process . . . everything."

More so than an honest, outright no, his stalling stung. She could have understood and respected him for walking away but she wasn't about to stand by and be strung along like he had Candace What's-Her-Face or any of the other women he kept in his back pocket.

"You take your time, the rest of your goddamned life if need be, but don't expect me to be waiting. As of now, I'm moving on."

"Sarah, I—"

She jerked away. "Go fuck yourself, Canning."

Fortunately her keys were in her jacket pocket. She ran up the remaining few steps, jammed her key into the outer door lock, and yanked back. In case he had second thoughts about following her inside, she pulled the automatically locking door closed behind her.

Steeling herself not to look back, she passed on checking her mail and shuffled over to the elevator. An out-of-order sign was taped across the doors. Fuck, she'd forgotten all about it. So much for holding out for an "elevator building;" her apartment would be a fifth-floor walkup for the foreseeable future.

Get hold of yourself, Halliday. He's just a guy. He doesn't have a magic dick.

Actually he kind of did, but it was his smile and all the rest of him that she would miss the most.

She opened the door to the stairwell and started up. Her eyes and nose had both begun running. She stopped and pulled a Kleenex from her purse before continuing on. Winded, she reached the fifth and final floor. Her apartment was at the end of the hall, one of three units. Other than the deaf old lady who lived across from her, her neighbors would be at work this time of day. Resolved to get her balling out of the way while no one was home to hear her, she stuck the door key into the lock. Without any turning, the door swung open.

It struck her. The broken elevator wasn't the only thing she'd forgotten from the other day. The note. Her stalker!

Oh my God!

Leaving the door ajar, she spun around, thinking she'd run down the stairs.

She never reached them.

A beefy arm wrapped around her waist, wrenching her inside.

"Get off—"

A gloved hand closed over her mouth, cutting her off her screams. She tried anyway, gagging on leather and the taste of her fear.

Still she fought, digging in her heels against the dragging. The door slamming closed sealed her fate—and her terror.

Chapter Fourteen

The scene with Sarah on her front steps had blown Cole away. How could he not have seen this coming? For someone who'd led countless reconnaissance missions, he was apparently pretty clueless when it came to stateside life.

The hell of it was he didn't disagree with anything Sarah had said, except for the last part where she'd cut him loose just because he hadn't greeted her news with an on-the-spot epiphany. He told himself that was only the hurt talking, at least he hoped so. Family, kids, permanence—he wanted all those things too, or at least he used to. Could he really have them with Sarah? Could he be with her knowing that more than half his friends and a major chunk of the western world had watched her fuck? What would they do when their future kid came home from school beaten up by bullies who'd gotten wind of Mom's movie career? It was *a lot* to think about. And yet . . .

A montage of memories hit him. Sarah dissolving into fits of laughter when he'd imitated David Tennant's *Doctor Who*. Sarah, her slender arms steadying him from shaking, coaxing him to unburden himself about Iraq. Sarah, face aglow, glancing over at him as her friends spoke their vows, making him think what a beautiful bride she'd be.

He was almost to the subway stop when it hit him. None of it mattered, not the potential public embarrassment, not his fusty family, not any of the countless other complications involved in joining his life with that of a former porn personality. None of it mattered, because, fuck it, he loved her! He loved Sarah.

He froze in his tracks, swung around, and began retracing his steps to Sarah's building, his strides becoming faster and longer until he skirted on sprinting. With every step that struck the sidewalk, he seemed to echo her name, her *real* name.

Sarah, Sarah, Sarah . . .

Talk about an idiot. Everything he'd ever wanted she'd laid at his feet, and he'd turned his back on her purely because of her past. As if he didn't have his own past, his own baggage. Having a seriously combat stressed boyfriend-cum-husband wouldn't always be a walk in the park either, particularly one that came with a pain-in-the-butt family, but up until a few minutes ago, she'd been willing to risk it. Hopefully she was still.

He passed the bodega where they'd first met. Despite his hurry, he couldn't resist stopping in. The dozen red roses would likely only last the day, but that wasn't the point. Holding the cellophane-bundled bouquet, he still felt like something was missing. The ice cream freezer caught his eye, and, heedless of the clerk and other customers, he threw back his head and laughed.

All the flavors! That's exactly what life with Sarah promised to be, not only in bed but out of it.

Cole grabbed a shopping basket and began loading up.

✳✳✳ ✳✳✳

A backward jab with her elbow won Sarah temporary freedom. She got in a few good kicks, but her struggling only delayed the inevitable.

She was going to die. Her attacker was going to kill her. But before that happened, he was going to hurt her. A lot.

Grabbing painful hold of her hair, he caught her mid dash to the door. Wrenched around to face him, she found herself looking into the pitiless, dark gaze glittering through the eyeholes in the mask. Buttons sprayed as he ripped open the front of her blouse. Her bra's front clasp likewise gave way to his grasping. Gloved hands pawed at her breasts. A vicious tug to her nipple had her howling. Her jeans' zipper was yanked down, the metal tab snapping off. A hard hand took possession of her pubis, the raking fingers curling into a fist.

She screamed and clawed at his masked face, gouging at his eyes. A punch to her jaw sent blood and saliva swooshing. Knocked backward, she crashed into the wall, her head hitting the plasterwork hard. Opening her eyes sent the room seesawing. Pain seared through her. The left side of her face felt both numb and enormous. The taste of metal coated the inside of her mouth. Everything hurt, but most of all her skull, which seemed to have simultaneously split in two and been filled with wet cement. Like the rest of her, it felt so heavy. She couldn't seem to hold it or herself up, not for long. Gravity's pull was too great to resist. Giving in, she floated to the floor. From her vantage point on her knees, her apartment looked like the set of a low-budget movie— bad lighting, minimal props. The overturned lamp, the smear of blood on the hardwood, even the Timberland hiking boots thudding toward her struck her as too campy to be real.

But it was real, all of it, no movie set but an honest-to-goodness crime scene—and her swan song, her final role was that of homicide victim.

Like one of her films, her life rolled before her mind's eye. She didn't have many regrets, but the few she had were hulking. Topping the list, she hadn't said "I love you" to Cole. Not outright, anyway. Ironic how in the midst of issuing her ultimatum she hadn't thought to add those three simple but all-important words. And now she was going to die with the sentiment unsaid. This script seriously sucked, the dialogue especially.

Her assailant dropped down before her. Grabbing hold of her elbows, he hauled her to him.

Anger renewed her strength. "Before you kill me, at least show me your face, you fucking coward." Her hands shot forward and pulled off his mask.

Martin's sweating face bore down on her. "You bitch!"

Her stalker was *Martin*! For several seconds, Sarah stared in disbelief.

A switchblade materialized in his hand. The hatred and lust blazing from his eyes frightened her as much as the blade. "You thought you could leave me, you ungrateful bitch. Who the fuck do you think you are? I *made* you!"

All this time she'd assumed her stalker was either a deranged fan or Danny. But confronted with the reality, it made sudden, sickening sense. The cream-colored stationery, the calligraphy, the stilted verbiage—none of it was Danny's style. Wasted as he always was, keeping up such an elaborate scheme would be far too much effort. Not so for Martin. He'd had all the time, all the access, and all the trust—hers—to pull it off. No wonder he'd been so adamant that she not report the incidents.

Holding the knife to her neck, he forced her onto her back. Kneeing her legs apart, he settled himself atop her. He reeked of scotch and sweat and lust. Perspiration beaded on his upper lip and plastered his bangs to his forehead. His hard-on pushed against her lower abdomen: only a semi, though the glint in his eye told her he'd get there.

Sucking his teeth, he teased the switchblade slowly down. "I always thought snuff films were disgusting, but now I see their appeal."

If she'd held on to any hope that she might talk him into letting her live, the reference to snuff—porn films that ended with the actor's actual death—killed it. "You're disgusting." Knowing she had nothing to lose, she lifted her head and spat, catching him in the eye.

A backhanded blow landed her back on the floor, her head knocking wood. Tears stung her eyes, slid back into her hairline. Looking down as he played the knifepoint around her nipple, she tasted bile bubbling up into her throat. Aspirating vomit would be an inelegant ending, but compared to what he had planned, it would be a mercy.

Across the room, the door crashed open, slamming into the wall with splintering force. "Sarah!"

Cole rushed inside, petals and ice cream cups flying. Reaching them, he grabbed Martin and hauled him off her. Sarah rolled onto her side. Spitting blood, she pulled herself up onto her knees. The room dipped. Fighting wooziness, she forced herself to focus. The two men were in a deadlock at the foot of the loft stairs. Although Cole had the advantage of superior size and youth, Martin was in better shape than she would have thought. He was also the only one of them armed. He not only had the knife, but clearly he knew how to use it. A steady stream of long slashes and short hacking jabs had Cole backed into a corner. The glistening red gash on his forearm showed that at least one of those blows had met its mark.

As if feeling it for the first time, he glanced down. Taking advantage of his distraction, Martin brought the knife back, and—

"Cole, look out!"

Cole dodged to the side. The blade sliced through air instead of skin. Committed to the attack, Martin momentarily lost his balance. Seizing his chance, Cole swung, his fist plowing into the older man's face. Martin fell back, blood spurting. Cole lunged, taking them to the ground. They rolled. The knife skittered across the floorboards. Dodging flailing feet and pummeling fists, Sarah clawed her way toward it. Hand curving about the handle, she snatched it up and retracted the blade.

Think, Sarah, think.

Her purse lay inside the door. It must have fallen off her shoulder when Martin first grabbed her. Praying she wouldn't pass out, she pocketed the knife and crawled toward it. Snagging the strap, she dragged it the rest of the way over. She spilled the contents and rooted through, finally finding her phone. The battery was down to five percent, shit! Her charger was in the bedroom upstairs. To get it, first she'd have to find a way around Cole and Martin. The apartment was tiny. Their struggle consumed most of the downstairs. A man's groan galvanized her. Cole's or Martin's, she couldn't say.

I love you, Cole!

She held her shaking hand over the keypad display and guided her forefinger to 9-1-1.

"911, what's your emergency?" the operator asked.

Thank God! "My name is Sarah Halliday. I'm at 204 Elizabeth Street. Yes, that's in Soho. Cross is West Houston. An intruder with a knife has broken into my apartment . . . "

❋❋❋ ❋❋❋

By the time the police arrived, Martin was a bloodied, blathering mess. Piecing together his disjointed declarations, Sarah was shocked to learn that he'd harbored a secret obsession for her from the first. Deluded enough to believe she'd come to him as a lover, he'd tried expediting the process by staging a stalking. Instead the ruse had spurred her decision to leave LA and the industry. Still, he hadn't expected her to stay away so long, let alone permanently. The wedding she'd confided she was planning had provided an ideal opportunity to leak her whereabouts to the press. He'd felt certain that being so dramatically outed would push her to come back to LA—and him. Only the desperate move backfired. When several days had passed and he still hadn't heard from her, he'd finally accepted the reality: she wasn't ever coming back, not to the industry and not to him. Coming across the press photos of her with Cole had pushed him over the edge—and onto a redeye flight to JFK.

Fortunately Cole had reached them in time. Despite being black-and-blue, Sarah felt ridiculously lucky. Her jaw was swollen but probably not broken, at least according to the paramedic. A split lip and minor cuts and bruises hurt like hell, but she'd always been a fast healer. It could have been so much worse! After answering the police's questions, she and Cole were taken to the hospital ER to be examined and X-rayed.

"We have to stop meeting like this," Cole said, hours later, shuffling into her curtained exam area, wearing a hospital gown and footies.

Sitting on the side of the table, Sarah laughed—and was instantly sorry. Being on the receiving end of a man's punch seriously sucked.

Cole, whatever his failings, wasn't a hitter. Even in the midst of their heaviest role-play, she'd always felt one hundred percent safe with him. An alpha male with a tender side—once he got his emotional shit together, he was going to make someone an incredible husband and future father. Candace What's-Her-Face or whomever he settled down with stood to be a lucky lady indeed.

"How's the arm?" she asked.

He held it out, showing off a line of neat black stitches. "The doctor who stitched me up offered to call in someone from plastics so it wouldn't scar, but I told her to go ahead. The whole time I was in Iraq, all seven hundred and thirty days, I never sustained so much as a scratch. I figure I'm overdue. Anyone asks I'm going to say it's a war wound." He grinned, but his eyes looked sad.

She tried for a smile. "Sounds like a solid plan."

"How's the head."

She pantomimed thumping her crown. "Still solid as a rock. The CT scan ruled out any trauma or concussion, so they're releasing me soon."

"Sarah, that's great!" He looked sincerely relieved.

She let out a laugh. "I know, right? I finally leave porn, and now I'm rendered brain dead—how much would that suck?"

His smile flattened. "That's not funny."

"Oh, c'mon, it is a little."

Meeting her gaze, he shook his head. "For what it's worth, I'm so sorry . . . about . . . everything."

Genuinely taken aback, she asked, "Sorry for what, saving my life?"

"No, of course not, but I am sorry for walking away in the first place, and then for taking so fucking long to come to my senses and turn back. If I hadn't stopped for those flowers—"

"You brought me flowers?" Vaguely, she recalled scattered petals and a strong, sweet scent when he'd broken down her door, but she hadn't given it much, any, thought until now.

He nodded. "Roses and ice cream from the bodega where we met. They were running low on stock, but I . . . I bought every flavor they had, even Chunky Monkey, which I know has bananas in it and you hate bananas but—"

"I love bananas." *I love you.*

Cole said, "You should come stay at my place."

She tilted her head, eying him. "You mean the Canning sanctum? Can this really be an invitation?"

He scowled. "Knock it off, and yes, it's an invitation."

"Thanks, but I have an apartment."

"Yeah, and it's now a crime scene."

He had a point. Even after the police tape was cleared, Sarah seriously doubted she'd ever be able to sleep there again.

"Then I'll stay at Liz's."

"On the couch? Really? After the night you've had."

"So, I'll buy an air mattress. Or maybe I'll check myself into the hotel—the Waldorf or, better yet, The Plaza. That Eloise-themed suite sounds like a kick."

It wasn't a bluff. She had money enough to rent every room in either hotel and never have it be missed. But she didn't really want to go to Liz's or a hotel, no matter how high-end. She wasn't fit to be someone's caretaker at the moment, nor did staying by herself hold much appeal. She wanted to be cuddled and cared for. As great as Liz and her other New York friends were, she didn't want just a friend right now. She wanted—needed—Cole.

Cole's voice broke into her reverie. "You can't avoid me forever, Sarah."

She rolled her eyes. "Obviously, not even my ER stall is sacrosanct."

"I mean . . . we should talk."

She folded her arms across her chest. "Thank you for saving my life. There, we've talked."

But as much as she hated to admit it, he was right. There was unfinished business still between them. She'd never got around to telling him she loved him. Going forward, whatever did or didn't happen between them, that box needed to be checked.

"Okay, you win. I'll stay at your place . . . for tonight."

✳✳✳ ✳✳✳

"You live at The Majestic!" Turning to face the Seventy-Second Street entrance to Central Park, bustling with rickshaws, runners, and food carts, Sarah's bruised face lit.

The iconic Art Deco property was one of a half dozen Upper West Side apartment buildings that boasted unimpeachable Old New York prestige and unobstructed views of the park.

Vaguely embarrassed, Cole nodded. "I've had the place for less than a year. My sister keeps nagging me to decorate. I still don't have much furniture," he added, though that might not be a concern for much longer. Assuming his mother carried out her threat, he'd be putting the pricey apartment on the market and moving above 96th Street sooner rather than later.

She regarded the arched entrance manned by a liveried doorman and then looked over at him. "Are you sure there isn't a service entrance you'd like me to use?"

The sarcasm wasn't lost on him, nor was the hurt it hid. Had it really taken a psychopath nearly killing her for him to open his door? The ride up to his eleventh floor co-op was the longest of his life.

Entering his northeastern unit, Sarah walked over to one of several large windows overlooking the park. "Oh my God, these views are a-ma-zing! And you have a terrace, too!"

"And a fireplace, a real one, not fake." Despite a long, cold winter, he hadn't yet popped the cherry on the wood-burning fireplace. But, if he had someone to make a home with, he had a feeling that would change.

She glanced back at him. "How can you bring yourself to ever leave?"

He shrugged. "I basically come here to shower and sleep, or at least to shower," he amended, thinking of his insomnia.

He wasn't cured, he might never be, but since Sarah had come into his life, stress symptoms such as sleeplessness no longer ruled him. Fuck the Canning "take it on the chin" approach to life, he'd even decided to work with a therapist who specialized in PTSD.

"A beautiful apartment like this should be lived in, enjoyed."

Walking over to her, he admitted, "You're right, it should."

She shoved her hands in her back jeans' pockets. "So do I get the tour?"

Assuming he didn't screw things up again, there'd be plenty of time for that later—beginning and ending with his bedroom. "Sure, but first . . ." He took her in his arms, fuck asking for permission or looking for some sort of sign from her that touching was okay again. "Yesterday you took me by surprise. That's not an excuse, but it is a fact."

She slanted him a look. Even shadowed with pain and weariness, her eyes were luminous, emerald orbs that beckoned him to strive for his better self, not settle for the ghost who'd slipped into his skin since Iraq. "Sorry, I guess I forgot I was supposed to stick to the script."

More sarcasm, but this time Cole was ready for it—ready for her. He'd hurt her; he got that. He deserved whatever shit she threw at him. He wished she'd tear into him, let loose and hit him even. Instead she remained cucumber cool, her gaze watchful, her body language noncommittal.

He rested light hands on the tops of her shoulders, forcing himself to hold her at arm's length. Assuming he didn't screw up again, they'd have the rest of their lives to go crazy on each other in bed. "This time it's my turn to do the talking and yours to do the listening, got it?"

Until now, he'd always chosen action over words; the latter he'd considered a waste. Enlisting in the army as a noncom and then training for a specialty in ordnance disposal had felt like the closest thing to a complete break with his passionless WASP family that he could make, short of swapping out his DNA. But lately he'd begun to wonder if he wasn't just an adrenalin junkie hiding behind higher ideals to score his fix.

But the other day on Sarah's steps, not sticking around to hash things out had been a huge mistake, one that had nearly cost her life.

"Okay."

Cole took his time. He hadn't realized it before now, but he'd been building toward this moment since the first time he'd set eyes on Sarah. He wasn't about to rush and risk fucking it up. Not now. Not after everything they'd been through.

Gently tracing her swollen jaw and bruised cheek, he looked deeply into her eyes. "I've been an ass."

"Yes, you have."

"Shhh, I'm the only one with lines, remember?"

"Right, sorry."

"I want all the same things you do—the house, the dog, the kids—and I want them all with you."

She sent him a trembling smile. "Thanks, that means a lot, but how do you plan to cope with the fallout from your family?"

He shrugged, wincing at the stiffness. "My family may disinherit me—let them. I've always been the black sheep, and if spending the rest of my life making love with a porn star is my punishment, well then I guess I'll just have to man up and take it."

"And the media?"

"The reporters will have a field day for a week, maybe two, and then Lindsey Lohan will crash her car or Kim Kardashian will get knocked up with somebody else's baby, and we'll be old news, back-page history."

"And your friends, including your army buddies who watched my movies along with you?"

Of all his inner obstacles, that was his biggest stumbling block. Smart of her to save it for last; only this time Cole was prepared. "Honestly, I'll handle it the only way I can—one step and one day at a time, with you right there beside me."

"You're sure about this?"

"I am, Sarah. Whatever comes our way, we'll deal with it—together."

Together. By the looks of her, she liked that word—a lot.

Eyes shining, Sarah reached up and took his face between her trembling hands. "I love you, Cole A. Canning. I forgot to say that yesterday."

"I love you, too, Sarah 'Sugar' Halliday. And if you'll have me, I plan on spending the rest of my life showing you just how much I love you, both in bed and out of it."

Sarah asked, "Should we start now? I'm pretty wired, and we do have at least another seventy films to get through."

Cole grinned. "Right now what I have in mind is more of an original screenplay, just you and me, no props, no script, the two of us on our own. Think you can handle ad libbing?"

Sarah smiled, wincing when the motion pulled at her cut mouth. "Well, I was trained as a method actress, and I've always believed in supporting indie films."

"Great, we can come up with a title for our project later—a lot later. For now, I can't think beyond taking you to bed. And heads-up, plan on getting comfortable, because I'm going to keep you there a long, *long* time."

She tilted her head to the side. "Is that so?"

Heedless of his stitches, Cole tugged her into his arms. "You bet it is."

She wound her arms around his neck. Even with their injuries, her breasts brushing across his chest was still the very best of feelings. "Are you sure you're not taking me to your dungeon?"

In answer, Cole reached around her, carefully lifting her into his arms. Carrying her through the living room, he couldn't keep from grinning. "Right now I'm taking you to my bedroom—*our* bedroom. I promise to build you as many dungeon rooms as your kinky little heart desires—just as soon as we get you moved in."

Epilogue

Barnes & Noble Booksellers, Union Square, One Year Later

"Ms. Halliday, when does your next book come out? I'm such a Fan Girl, I can't wait!"

"What's it like to write fiction?"

"What was your reaction when you first heard you'd hit the *New York Times* bestseller list?"

"Any regrets about retirement?"

"Sarah, baby, hold up the book and give me a smile."

The latter shout-out came from Cole. Standing below the bookstore's event stage, he positioned his Nikon to snap yet another series of photos for Twitter, Facebook, her website—who knew? Even before there'd been any inkling that her memoir, *Sugar*, would make *The New York Times* and *USA Today* bestseller lists, he'd boasted to anyone who'd listen that his girl's book was bound to be a blockbuster.

Flanked by her editor and in-house publicist, Sarah slid a book off the dwindling stack and held it up, smiling down at him as he clicked away. Earlier she'd given a reading, her first, to a standing-room-only audience. A lively Q&A period had followed. Twenty minutes into the autographing, the queue of customers still waiting to have books signed stretched all the way from the back of the store to the stage steps.

Beneath the cloth-draped event table, Sarah pinched herself, the only way she knew to prove she really was awake and not dreaming. What a difference a year could make. Not only was she a newly minted *New York Times* bestselling author, but she was also a soon-to-be bride!

Her and Cole's wedding would take place the following week, a low-key celebration for close friends and immediate family. Afterward, they planned to honeymoon in Paris, staying at her pied-à-terre in Saint-Germain-des-Prés. It would be her first time visiting the City of Lights with her beloved beside her. As thrilling as the past whirlwind weeks had been, she could hardly wait to get away with Cole. Beyond the three-book deal she'd just signed for an erotic romance trilogy—it seemed all those years of reading romances between takes had paid off!—she had even bigger news to share.

They were having a baby!

Smiling to herself, she bent her head to sign yet another hardcover copy from the dwindling stock, her Art Deco era diamond engagement ring flashing fire as the felt-tip pen moved over the first page.

"May your future be as sweet as . . . Sugar," she wrote and then signed beneath, not as Sugar but with her real initials, SLH—Sarah Lorraine Halliday.

"Thank you so much for coming. I hope you enjoy it," Sarah said, closing the book and handing it back to yet another excited-to-meet-her reader.

Flexing her stiffening hand, she looked down to the rows of folding chairs, picking out her friends' faces—Peter and Pol, Brian and Honey, and Liz. Even her father had turned out for this, her first public appearance as an author. Neither of them would ever forget the past, but his coming to the bookstore and then out to dinner with them all afterward was a big step toward building a happier, freer future.

Catching Liz's eye, she mouthed, "Five more minutes?" Holding up one hand, she smiled.

Her personalized, pre-signed book balanced on her knees, Liz smiled back. "No rush," she said, or so Sarah surmised.

In full remission, Liz had finished her final reconstructive surgery the previous month. With her short cap of glossy black curls, grown-in eyebrows, and sparkling dark eyes, she looked more like herself every day. After the wedding, she and Jonathan would celebrate by taking off for an all-expense paid, week-long vacation to Disney World, courtesy of the Canning Foundation.

Somewhat to Cole's chagrin, his mother had declined to make good on her threat to disinherit him. Apparently his engagement to a notorious porn star, while galling, had proven to be a big fund-raising boon for the foundation, drawing out other infamous celebrities to donate their time as spokespersons.

Bypassing the line, Cole bounded up the side steps and onto the stage, the yoked camera bouncing against his chest as he made his way over to her. As always, her heart beat picked up pace as he closed in. The combination of anti-anxiety medication and talk therapy had made a huge difference in their lives. Smiling and clear-eyed, he insisted he'd never thought he'd feel this good again. The PTSD was still with him, but these days it was more of an infrequent visitor than a permanent houseguest. He wasn't quite ready for a dog, so they'd compromised and gotten a rescue cat instead, a loveable marmalade tabby they'd agreed should be called Kirby.

Casting an apologetic look to those still waiting, Cole slipped behind Sarah's chair. Brushing his mouth over her ear, he whispered, "The text message just came in from my fund-raising director. You're never going to believe this, but an anonymous donor just gifted us two *million* dollars. And the best part—the money's earmarked for my new mentor program."

Like surprises, secrets weren't always bad, Sarah thought. Schooling her eyes to innocence, she shifted to smile up at him. "That's wonderful, baby. I know how much that program means to you. Now you can launch the pilot as soon as we're back from Paris."

Ocean-blue eyes scoured her face. "Why do I suddenly have the feeling this isn't exactly news to you?"

Biting her lip, Sarah hesitated. Now that he was sleeping through the night, he was impossible to get anything over on—almost. "Maybe you've been watching too many movies?" she suggested weakly.

His searching look eased into a smile, which grew into a grin. Heedless of the shuffling feet and fuming looks directed his way, he leaned down and planted a smacking kiss on her startled mouth.

Titters sounded from the line and the other side of the table. "What was that for?" she asked, feeling the familiar pull of desire despite their being in a public place and surrounded. Then again, doing very private things in very public places was sort of their forte.

Stepping back and dropping his voice several decibels, he said, "For making my real life a hundred times sexier and happier than any movie, no matter the rating." His solemn eyes, focused on hers, left no doubt that he meant every word.

"Does that mean no more movie nights?" she asked, pulling a pretend pout. Now that they'd gone through all her films, they still regularly repeated scenes from their favorites.

"Hell no," he said with a hearty shake of his head, forgetting to lower his voice, though at that point it didn't much matter. "If I have anything to say about it, and I'm pretty sure I do, *Mrs. Canning*, you and I will be doing movie night—with *all* the flavors—until our bodies are too brittle to bend."

—THE END—

Look for Jenna and Hope's next steamy
installment of their FATE series:
Honey

Chapter One

*E*mergency Room, *NYU Hospital, Present Day*

"Let's go through this again, shall we . . . ?"

Dr. Marcus Sandler surveyed the female patient perched on the edge of his exam table, a standout in an ER otherwise flooded with victims of the flu. Honey Gladwell, if that was even her real name, which he seriously doubted, didn't have so much as a sniffle. What she had was a whole lot harder to fix.

Someone, an intimate someone, most likely a man, had battered her. Even coming up on the end of a twelve-hour shift, not the eight-hour rotation standard for third-year residents, there was no mistaking a textbook case of domestic violence such as this.

The X-rays and MRI results were in. Ms. Gladwell had been lucky—this time. A fractured wrist, a chipped front tooth, a broken nose, and a blow to the left eye so severe she was lucky the orbit hadn't fractured were the worst of her injuries, the physical ones anyway. Assessing the psychological trauma of being used as a punching bag wasn't his bailiwick, but it couldn't be good. Whoever had done this to her was one sick son of a bitch.

Beneath the patchwork of cuts and bruises, she was probably pretty, though her face was too swollen for him to say for certain. What he could tell with certainty was that she was small, 5'2" without the ridiculous pencil-thin heels she'd hobbled in on and one hundred and five pounds, according to her triage vitals. The one-size-fits-all hospital gown swam on her. They might as well have given her a tent to wear. And she was young—twenty-six as of last week based on the birth date she'd given. Without a driver's license or photo ID of any kind, he was left with having to take her word on it.

Looking up from the chart he held, he tried again. "Can you walk me through how you got hurt?"

She lifted her chin, a classic symbol of defiance, even if, like her loyalty, the ballsy attitude was badly misdirected. "I told the nurse already. I fell. Down some stairs," she added as if an afterthought.

Falling down the stairs, talk about your clichéd cover up. Marc would have laughed if he wasn't so fucking sick of the same old story playing out yet again. Growing up in Harlem, he'd dealt with domestic violence victims aplenty, including his own mother. Why couldn't these women see that covering for their abusers was as good as giving the sick sons of bitches a license to kill—*them*?

"Where?" he asked, his fingers tensing on the clipboard.

Twirling a hank of brown hair that had escaped the once-elaborate upsweep, she bit her bruised bottom lip. "At home."

He looked from her ringless left hand back to her chart. Forty-one Park Avenue, one of those overpriced Midtown high rises that invariably announced itself with a water feature in the lobby and boasted a crap load of amenities that hardly anyone ever used. Her apartment was likewise easy to picture: a featureless one bedroom or junior efficiency with nine-foot ceilings and a private terrace with a partial view. It was the sort of building where a man who could afford it put up his mistress. The wife, if there was one, would be ensconced in a "classic six" in one of the esteemed pre-war buildings above Sixty-First but below Ninety-Sixth Streets. Go even a block higher and you were in Upper Manhattan, which included the once-dreaded Washington Heights neighborhood where Marcus still lived. Real estate really was all about location. Nowhere was that truer than Manhattan.

"Forty-one Park, huh? Sounds like an elevator building to me. Standards must be seriously slipping." He softened the sarcasm by shooting her a wink.

No dice. She glared at him. Her eyes weren't plain brown as he'd first thought but brown shot with amber—at least the one not swollen shut. The gold flecks crowding the iris told him she was angry—and that for now it was easier and infinitely safer to focus that emotion on him.

"The elevator is being replaced . . . I mean, repaired. We . . . I had to take the stairwell. It's a whole . . . thing."

Whatever else she was, she was a terrible liar. His God-fearing, church-going, Bible-quoting Aunt Edna could spin a better yarn than that without so much as blinking. In contrast, this poor kid was all but unraveling.

"Hmm, I'll bet. You should demand the management company return your monthly maintenance fee."

No response. She pressed her lips together, and he had a fleeting wish to know what they looked like when they weren't cut and puffy, raw and red. Right now her mouth looked almost as if it was turned upside down, the top lip fuller and wider than its bottom mate. Intriguing.

Not yet ready to give up, Marcus asked, "Do you live with a . . . roommate, someone who can help you out for the next few days?"

She stopped playing with her hair and shook her head. "No, I don't have . . . It's just me."

The best lies were half-truths. He'd bet his precious vacation leave she was a kept woman, a mistress, her rent and other living expenses picked up by a man who breezed in and out of her life on a whim—his—and who apparently got off on hitting women.

"Who did you say brought you in?"

His question prompted more glaring. "I didn't say."

He couldn't help but smile. She hadn't given an inch or shed so much as a single tear since he'd started treating her. She was totally brave and mind-numbingly stubborn. He couldn't help admiring both, even if they were summoned for all the wrong reasons.

"I'm just trying to make sure you get home safely," he said gently.

Her slender shoulders slumped as though she were finally succumbing to the exhaustion. "My . . . boyfriend, but he . . . had to go."

"He left you . . . in this condition!" Whatever slim benefit of the doubt he might have been prepared to tender the son of a bitch evaporated in that instant.

She shrugged, wincing as if the minor movement hurt her, which he was sure it did. "He has a very important job . . . in finance," she added with obvious pride.

So the culprit was some single-malt swilling hedgie or Wall Street trader, a suit who vented his frustrations with the recession economy by pummeling little girls. Ms. "Gladwell" wouldn't be the first woman to bear the brunt of a money man's high-stakes, high-stress lifestyle.

"I can take care of myself," she said suddenly, her shoulders straightening.

Obviously that was not the case, but as his attending was forever reminding him, he was a doctor, not a social worker and most definitely not a cop. Rather than refute her, he focused on her chart. The head wound would justify a full admission if he chose to go there. Who knew, maybe the down time would give her the space she needed to rethink her story—and her life choices.

Pulling the ballpoint from behind his ear, he said, "You sustained a nasty head wound. I'd like to keep you overnight for observation."

"I have to stay here overnight!" The way she said it made it sound like he'd sentenced her to Sing Sing.

"A twenty-three-hour observational period," he corrected. "That way the hospital won't charge you for an overnight stay." Despite the couture clothes she'd come in wearing, she hadn't listed having any insurance.

Her good eye shuttered. "That would be okay, I guess."

A nurse pulled back the curtain and poked her head inside. "Dr. Sandler, dispatch just called in a notification: nineteen-year-old male, GSW to the chest, intubated in the field, hemodynamically stable but might have a developing pneumo from a cracked rib."

Marc sighed. A gunshot wound—yep, typical Friday night. And he still had an ER packed with puking patients. As much as he might like to linger, he had to move on.

"Okay, I'll be there in a minute." He waited for the curtain to close again before glancing back at the girl. "So, we're set then. We'll get you into a room as soon as possible. It's a little intense right now with all the flu sufferers, so hang tight and try to rest."

"Rest? In this madhouse?" She rolled her eyes, the unhurt one conveying amusement.

She had a point. Neon lighting, nonstop scuttling back and forth from the various medical staffers, and callouts from the ubiquitous intercom hardly made it a napping zone—unless, of course, you were an exhausted intern. Back then, Marcus could have slept standing. Once or twice, he had.

For the first time that night, he felt a smile tugging at the corners of his flat-lined mouth. "Right, I know. Do your best."

The next several hours whizzed by. The gunshot victim from Spanish Harlem with the gang tats was joined by a NYU student goaded by his buddies into sticking a lightbulb up his butt, and a fast food worker burned by boiling cooking oil when the deep fryer malfunctioned.

By the time Marcus took a breather, it was nearly 1 AM. Hoping Ms. Gladwell might have had a change of heart—and story—he grabbed her chart and went to check on her.

Only she was gone. Shit! Marching over to the nurse's station, he demanded, "Who discharged this patient—*my* patient—without my knowledge?"

The nurse behind the desk looked up from the computer screen and shrugged. "She AMA-ed."

Left against medical advice, fuck! Incredulous, Marcus revved up to rip into her. "And nobody came to find me?"

"It's okay, I signed off." Dr. Denison, his attending, walked up. "Let it go, Marcus." Dropping his voice, he wrapped a fatherly arm about Marc's shoulders and steered him away from the station. "You're an excellent clinician, Marc, one of the most gifted trauma interns I've had in some time, but if you don't monitor your intensity you're going to burn out."

"Yes, but, sir—"

"To make it in medicine, emergency medicine especially, you need to accept that you can't save everyone. The sooner you make peace with that, the greater an asset you'll be to me, this hospital, and above all, your patients."

Knowing he was beat, Marcus backed off with a nod. "Duly noted, sir. Thank you for the feedback."

Thank you for the feedback—Jesus, what a brownnoser he'd become. He'd been attracted to trauma as the area of medicine where he could do the most immediate good, help the most people, but the past several months had punctured all kinds of holes in his dream bubble.

"You're welcome." Denison dropped his arm, muscular and dusted with white hairs, and stepped away. "Now do yourself and everybody else here a favor and go home and get some sleep. You'll need it. You've got to be back here in nine hours."

Marc nodded. "I will. Thanks."

Watching Denison turn away, he raked a hard hand through his hair. He couldn't save or even help everyone; he got that. But he might have helped her, Honey Gladwell or whatever her name was, if only he'd had more time.

Then again, maybe he did. Forty-one Park Avenue wasn't more than a few short blocks from the hospital. And he had, if not all the time in the world, the next nine hours.

Note from the Publisher

PTSD, or Post-Traumatic Stress Disorder, is an anxiety problem that some people develop in the aftermath of an extremely traumatic event, such as a crime, an accident or natural disaster or combat. Persistent intrusive memories, flashbacks and nightmares, avoidance of situations that may trigger flashbacks of the trauma, and intense anxious feelings are some of the symptoms of PTSD, according to the American Psychological Association.

But there's no need to continue to suffer. Help is available through support groups, therapy with a mental health professional who specializes in treating PTSD, and FDA-approved pharmaceutical interventions.

If you believe that you or a loved one may suffer from PTSD, visit the resource links below as a first step toward reclaiming mental health—and life—today.

American Psychological Association (APA):
www.apa.org/topics/ptsd
National Institute for Mental Health (NIMH):
www.nimh.nih.gov/health/topics/post-traumatic-stress-disorder-ptsd/index.shtml
PTSD Meetup Groups:
http://ptsd.meetup.com
United States Department of Veterans Affairs, National Center for PTSD:
www.ptsd.va.gov